NAZI GOLD

NAZI GOLD

RICHARD NISBET

Copyright © 2013 Richard Nisbet

The moral right of the author has been asserted.

Apart from any fair dealing for the purposes of research or private study, or criticism or review, as permitted under the Copyright, Designs and Patents Act 1988, this publication may only be reproduced, stored or transmitted, in any form or by any means, with the prior permission in writing of the publishers, or in the case of reprographic reproduction in accordance with the terms of licences issued by the Copyright Licensing Agency. Enquiries concerning reproduction outside those terms should be sent to the publishers.

Matador
9 Priory Business Park
Kibworth Beauchamp
Leicestershire LE8 0RX, UK
Tel: (+44) 116 279 2299
Fax: (+44) 116 279 2277
Email: books@troubador.co.uk
Web: www.troubador.co.uk/matador

ISBN 9781780885056

British Library Cataloguing in Publication Data.
A catalogue record for this book is available from the British Library.

Typeset in Minion Pro by Troubador Publishing Ltd

Matador is an imprint of Troubador Publishing Ltd

After finding a treasure in Libya with the help of some of my friends who, like me, were all ex Special Forces, I, like them, went home. I started visiting the Canary Islands, enjoyed it so much I bought a small villa in Lanzarote, but then I visited Fuerteventura, I liked it so much I sold the villa. In the next two years I went there eight or nine times. I started to get to know several people, some of them in businesses there; I would often call in on them when I visited the Island. The truth about why I went back there, I feel I should explain.

I was sitting at home in the back lounge of my cottage when the word 'gold' caught my ear, there was this programme on TV. about a group of men who were searching for missing gold, gold that the Nazi's had looted from across Europe. They had all the best equipment for the search, it said that this wasn't the first time a search had been mounted in the mountains. I listened on to hear they never found the gold after an extensive search by not one, but three different groups, nothing had been found. This reminded me of something else I had heard years before, how tons of gold had been taken up the mountains and buried, this really got me thinking. If tons of gold were indeed buried up in the mountains, then surely with all the modern equipment it would be found. Well, I thought, tons of gold would be pretty hard to hide…anywhere. If it had been found the whole world would know about it, but after all the years that have gone by, that gold is still unaccounted for, so where is it?

This intrigued me so much so, it started taking up most of my time. There was something niggling me about this, something I just couldn't connect with at this moment of time.

It was not until I got back on the Island, that something else drew my attention.

I was sitting in Rob's bar having a beer. I picked up the local magazine when something caught my eye, there was a story about a villa called Villa Winter. I read on and learnt that this villa was built in 1937 by a man named Gustav Winter, he was a top German Engineer and was also a Colonel in the Nazi's Party. He came here to grow crops and so on, bringing with him his wife. It stated that when he died his wife insisted that was the reason he moved here, for agricultural reason. However I listened to some locals who said this is stupid, no one could farm those lands.

I had a talk with Bob, he owns the bar, so he might know more about this Villa Winter. He came over to my table, which was outside with a large parasol above it, the warm sun blazing down on parts of my legs. He carried over two beers and sat down beside me.

"Well Eddie, you have something to ask me."

"Yes, this thing in this magazine about Villa Winter, what do you know about it?"

"Well for a start, it lies on the other seaboard down south, it's a dodgy drive down there along the side of the mountain range, with the sea the Atlantic on the left as you drive long the route to the villa. It's been taken over in part by a local farmer who is caretaker of the place. He has sheep, goats, hens and grows some crops inside the villa's courtyard as well as a garden at the front. There are several rooms in the place and a tower that looks out towards the sea. I don't know for sure who owns it, it could be the Council. It's a rough track all the way in, with some hairy spots where the land just drops away on the seaboard side, it can be dangerous should another car come along from the opposite side."

"So you are saying no one owns this place."

"As I said, could be the Council, that's the only ones I can think of. All other parties are well dead."

"Any chance we could go down there, for a look see?"

"Hey, yeh! I suppose so, when do you have in mind?"

"Whenever it suits you Rob."

"How about Wednesday."

"Great Bob…I mean Rob. I always do that, so never be confused if I say Bob or Rob, it's the same guy."

Rob was always at his bar, he did have other staff, so it was easy for him to take some time off, he also was into property and was looking for a place for me. I liked Rob, he served with 5Para, in fact there was a few ex Servicemen here, they all played golf and always gathered at Rob's bar after each game. I have been there when they got settled down and after a few drinks it gets hot, I mean they do singing, shouting and a little fist te cuffs, but nothing serious.

I wanted to make sure I took a camera with me for this trip down south. Another point of fact is this, the area we are going to is exactly the same shape as the whole Island…

Before I even made a move to go and see this villa, I already knew that several top Nazi's had visited the villa and indeed their families. It was also rumoured that Hitler and Eva Braun went to the villa then on to Argentina. Many U-boats patrolled these waters during the last war, many too, were attacked and sunk. Getting my hands on just how many U-boats there were could be found at the Archives in London, but that had to wait. Butter and toast some scrambled eggs and a nice cup of tea were going down great, until Rob almost smashed the door down in the apartment I was hiring.

"Come on," he said, "it's a long drive to get to this place, we need to get moving."

"OK, ok Rob, give me a minute." I quickly grabbed the items I was taking, which I had laid out the night before, they included two cameras, one a video camera.

Rob thankfully had a Landrover and a pretty good one at that. Going with what he told me, and the pictures in that magazine it was a rough ride to get to the villa.

"Have you got everything?" asked Rob.

I sat down in the front passenger's seat, looked into my bag then said, "yes I have, even some water."

"I forgot about that," said Rob.

We drove down the southern coastline from Caleta de Fuste, it was nice and cool at this time in the morning. Being just after seven o'clock the roads were quiet, so we made quick progress towards Cofete.

The Jandia is the highest point on the Island of Fuerteventura, from the pass you can view Casa Winter and the bay at Blaya de Barlovento. Getting down this track is no easy drive, you need to be alert and focused because there is no space to even park in places. It is one narrow track with the ground falling away down hundreds of feet, one wrong turn on the wheel could be our last. As we moved on I took photos of the journey inward, then Rob pointed out where there was a cemetery. So we moved down to it and got out of the vehicle, the wind was getting strong as I spotted a list posted on the outside. It said, these were fishermen that died, lost their lives at sea. I thought that's very odd, why bury these people here? I looked carefully at the list, and another odd thing was there were women on the list. I turned to Rob and said,

"Did women go out fishing?"

Rob shook his head then said, "I don't think so, they would be home with kids and getting the fishermen's meals ready."

"Have a good look at the photos then ask yourself, why would any family bury their loved ones in this desolate and forbidden place?"

I carefully looked at the names and counted at least twenty-five men and fourteen women, well I am saying, "that's going by the names." Yet the more I thought this over, it seemed very odd indeed that these people buried here were really not fishermen at all.

I put it to Rob who said, "Well Eddie, there have been many fishermen lost at sea, but nowhere on this Island is there a cemetery like this one."

"Well Rob, someone went to a lot of trouble to build this cemetery here, I have my doubts about it."

"Well Eddie, if you look away in the distance you just might be able to see Villa Winter."

"What… Where?" Rob pointed his finger to the area. I couldn't see anything except a light coloured patch of soil.

Once my eye got onto that, Rob said, "Move forward a little…"

"Oh yes I can see it, I see it." Way in the distance stood the Villa (see photo seven). Follow the sandy beach up to the mountain ridge, you see the light coloured sandy patch, right in front of it stands the Villa Winter. (Photo eight) it can be seen even better. I took photos all the time as we got closer and closer to the Villa. I asked Rob to stop, as I wanted to take a good shot of the Villa just where the track turns in an S shape up to the south side of the Villa Winter.

Something else caught my eye, the lack of any dwelling places all the way in towards this Villa. I didn't see one piece of stone structure that may have been a house. There was a bar cum eating house that more than likely was built to catch the tourist trade, because the Villa had become a place to visit.

As you see, the photos give you a very good look at the type of soil in this whole area, there is very little growing anywhere. Rob pointed to a mountain peak, so I got out the camera and took a photo, it showed a rocky and desert like landscape. It was like this all the way to Villa Winter, a barren wasteland that for me, you could grow weeds in the soil here.

The Villa must have looked out of place in its heyday, on our approach the tower loomed up on its left. This Villa had been clearly positioned, with a ridge of mountains to its rear, and to the Atlantic Ocean to its front. The road, or should I say the dirt track, snaked its way up the hill to where stone dikes had been built along part of the track and around the whole Villa. I took photos all the way up towards the Villa, as Rob drove slowly along the side of the stone dike. We stopped again and out came the camera.

Richard Nisbet

In the approach, the photos show a long stretch of sandy beach, the broad stretch of sand lies straight down from the Villa.

You get a great view of the peaks of the mountains, and we had to drive along some parts that was pretty dangerous. The view we had of the sea on our left, and the mountain ridge on our right was spectacular and forbidding.

We drove along well built brick or stone walls, where I took a 'shot' of the sea, then turned the camera up towards the mountains and there it was…the Villa Winter. It was a very desolate place looking all around it. There was a tower on the north West Side of the Villa, I'm sure this was once a very beautiful place. Some of the photos show how close the mountains area at the rear of the Villa. The arches lead out onto a veranda, the room inside is large with a big fireplace at one end. Going upstairs was dodgy, the stairs going up and broken away and you had to be very careful where you put your feet. In the tower I noticed many wires coming out of the wall, they certainly did not appear to be for lights, maybe searchlights and machines. Having paid the caretaker five bucks, we had gone straight to where the tower was, missing out other rooms. It was the tower for the moment that interested me. The view was spectacular, there was a full panoramic view of the Atlantic Ocean. Inside the tower it was obvious that they had stripped out everything, leaving just bare wires everywhere.

Rob and I backtracked back down into the courtyard, it had fruit trees growing there, with a few water melons and bananas. We moved into a room that had been sectioned off, as if there may have been bunk beds there at sometime in the past. Two other rooms led on from this one, they didn't have much headroom, and I got the feeling this may have been where the soldiers slept. Down in the cellar, it looked more like an operating room, with slabs, large sinks and an incinerator. It was a funny old set-up, at first we thought it was a kitchen, but then once we looked over other rooms it was obvious that the cellar was used for other things. Why was there an incinerator on the wall with a metal door covering it? There also was a dumbwaiter just inside the doorway, next to it was two storage cupboards. Although it was a cellar it had a high ceiling, there was just one small window at the rear of the cellar.

We went back up to the courtyard and into the front room, this was spacious with beautiful wooden beams across the ceiling. A big fireplace with a lovely surround stood on the right as we entered the room. It had large double doors that opened out onto a veranda, where the view of the sea was fantastic. We looked down on what used to be a garden; it now had a few bushes with hens and goats sheltering from the sun underneath each bush. There was little else not even weeds.

We tried to enter the south wing of the Villa, but the caretaker stopped us, mainly because he and his family had moved in. I had noticed how the wall at the south side didn't seem to run true, as if there was some hidden room or passageway behind it. I pointed this out to Rob, he agreed with me that there might be something hidden behind the wall. The reason I say this was the passageway out on the yard seemed to narrow as it travels towards the large room west wing where the veranda is. It was in fact, too small to have a room behind it, but there was enough space for a secret passageway.

Of course there wasn't much that could be done to check it out, with the caretaker always about watching where, and what we were doing. We couldn't look in places I so much wanted to, I was trying to tie up loose ends to what I was thinking. You know what it is like when you try to piece things together, well that's what I was trying to do. Was it possible that this Villa, the U-boats and the missing gold were some how connected?

I planned to find out, hopefully with the help of Rob. It was early days, I had a lot to look into, I was dying to get back to this place under darkness, so I could find out if there was indeed, a secret passageway. At some time I had to check out about the U-boats, and find out just how many were numbered also the three that made visits to Argentina. That would take me back to England and the Archives.

Behind the Villa was a huge area that had light coloured earth scattered over it, I suppose it never took anyone's notice, after all this Colonel Winter was working on the land. But I was now thinking was it underground he was working and all that soil and rock came from a tunnel?

The dirrent soil and rock is so noticeable from a long distance away, as is other areas. If a tunnel was built, then the proceeds would have to be brought up and dumped.

We couldn't get into most of the south wing of the Villa, I had seen enough to make me more interested in this place. All the time many people thought this hid a U-boat base, but that was never ever proved.

It was entirely now up to me to follow through what I felt about this Villa, the Gold and tunnels, and a sunken U-boat. All this was swimming through my head as we walked down the track to the Landrover. There was such a beautiful view with the blue Atlantic Ocean racing up golden sands that stretched as far as the eye could see.

I took a good look at the Villa as we got into the Landrover to slowly head back to a proper roadway. No question about it this whole area was carefully picked by the Nazi's, it could have been built as a holiday place for top brass Nazi's, then later used as a stepping stone to Argentina. One thing for sure, I was going to find out if there was any hidden tunnels or rooms in the place.

On our way back to Calete de Fuste, Rob had spoken to me several times, I was so deep in thought, I didn't hear him. He was asking me when was I going back down to the Villa.

Rob drove well along the narrow and dangerous parts of the track. In some places there was barely two feet to spare and we could crash over two hundred yards down into rocks. In these dangerous areas there was nowhere to pass another car.

Rob got me back safe to Calete de Fuste, dropping me off at the place I was staying. Then later that night I called in at Rob's Bar. I ordered a drink and sat down outside, the staff knew me and always checked if I was ready for another beer. Rob wasn't there until later. I lit my favourite cigar, which is laced with brandy, I also get meam in red wine tasted whisky, and dark rum. That is all I smoked in my stint in Vietnam. I had tried all the other shit, but that was not for me.

Rob turned up after 2300 hours. He joined me as we talked about our covert mission to the Villa Winter. Rob didn't smoke, when he smelt the aroma coming from my cigar, he asked to try one, I lit one up for him.

"Hey, this is good, this is really good!"

"Yes, they're pretty good alright Rob, but don't get into this dirty habit, save your lungs."

"I will Eddie."

Rob left me for a few moments to help serve at the bar as it was getting busy. I looked over the notes I had taken earlier. All those names outside that cemetery we counted, adds up to what number of men would be on a U-boat. Now that was indeed very interesting, but surely they all didn't die at sea? Could they all have been shot to keep the secret of the gold in tack? If that was the case, then surely there were those at the Villa Winter awaiting its arrival.

"Hey are you dreaming? Here's another beer."

"Sorry Rob, I was thinking."

"Pretty strong stuff, I called you three times."

"Oh, I was just thinking about all those names at that cemetery, funny how it tallies with the men than man a U-boat."

"So what if there's no U-boats around here, or have been since the last war?"

Rob gave me a funny look then said, "Eddie, are you saying there's a U-boat hidden on this Island."

"There could be Rob, of course it's early days. I have to get back down there, check out my theories, if they are right then I will go to London and visit the Archives."

"When do we go back down there, Wednesday or what?"

"Definitely Wednesday night. This caretaker, how old do you think he is?"

"I'd say he is over seventy at least."

"He wouldn't be German would he Rob?"

"It's possible but he looks Spanish, I'd say he is Spanish."

"Yeh, I'd say he is too."

I rubbed my chin, then took out another cigar and lit it, I lifted both feet and rested them on another metal seat.

The bar was really busy and it was late for me, so I said to Rob I'd see him about 2000 hours Wednesday night. Then I walked back to the place I was renting.

Wednesday night Rob and I went back down to the Villa Winter, we pulled up about two miles away from it along the far side of the Mountain ridge. We had to watch every step as the terrain was rough, the moon gave us some light, still we tripped up a few times. It was hard slog to get to the other side of the ridge, we came out way to the north west, so we made for the sea and an easier route down to the Villa. We walked along the beach for at least a mile, then we moved in towards the mountain to get a better advantage point where we could lie and observe the Villa and surrounding area. When we came the last time, it was so easy, this was more like getting behind the 'lines'. We sat there on the rocks above the Villa just to the left, as you would look at it from the sea up towards the mountains. Nothing moved, so we stealthily moved in.

We made for the veranda, that's when we found out there was no stairway up, so we had to climb up about twelve feet or so. Two areas had to be checked out, if indeed there was a hidden passageway down at the bottom of the tower. Then moving over to the south wing, we would have to get outside and stay very quiet, because right above was the caretaker and his wife. We walked slowly and very carefully across the rough ground, we picked a spot to make the climb up onto the veranda. We managed to get up there then Rob touched my shoulder, he pointed at a dog standing less than ten feet away. It just stood there looking at us. Now I am pretty good with animals, so too, was Rob, he acted before me. Calling the dog over to him by clapping his hands on his knees. The dog came to him, so he slapped it, it was friendly enough. The dog stayed quiet and just followed us.

In photo number sixteen, you see the south wing with the caretaker's buggy on the track, just behind it is the main entrance into the Villa, over to the right is where the animals are kept.

Those three windows, this is where the caretaker and his wife live, at the moment Rob and I are at the other side of the Villa, so we don't expect to disturb them…unless the dog barks.

Looking at photo number twenty-four, you see the tower, we are just to the right of the tower, it was in there I noticed the false wall. Our torches skimmed along the passageway to where the wall thickened, this thickening was actually joined to the tower construction. About head high the wall looked very smooth, Rob managed to touch it.

"There's something here Eddie, this is no wall, more like a trap-door."

We needed something so we could stand higher up, looking around we found a wooden crate out on the veranda. Rob got up and tried to see how to get the door opened, it just seemed impossible.

It must open inwards, otherwise you'd never get out once inside the door.

"Look for a lever, could be hidden close by, down each of the wall." We both felt our way down the wall and then I found the lever behind the brickwork, I pulled on the lever while Rob got the door open. It was positioned in a very odd way, if it did lead to anything. Rob entered first, having to crawl inside as the trap-door was not very big.

"Come on Eddie, I'll move in a little, close that door behind you." The place was pitch black, you couldn't see your hand held out in front of you, luckily we had the torches. We found ourselves on steps heading downwards.

"Count the steps we take Rob, we can then work out how deep we are going."

In all we walked down twenty-five steps, then there was a full side door in front of us. I tried it but it wouldn't open, Rob tried, and it cracked open like a piece of wood being split open.

The door then opened freely, we stood there looking inside, the first thing we saw was a big double bed with side lockers each side of it.

The whole place was decked out with the very best in furnishings. Wardrobes, soft chairs, large dressing table with a big mirror, a large table with a silk cover on it, sets of drawers, in fact there was two of everything in this room. It had others mirrors real odd ones, that we later found out why they had been placed where they were. Up in the centre of the ceiling was a glass dome, we uncovered it and to our surprise there was light coming in from the moon outside. This helped give some light to the room, we started looking around, and there was a toilet and shower unit just off this room. There was a wardrope cut into the rock, Rob went to look at it while I opened the drawers and wardrobes. There were loads of new clothes for a man and a woman. I go a quiet call from Rob,

"Eddie, come over here look at this."

I walked over to join him, inside this wardrobe was a safe. Rob got busy trying to get it open, while I walked around looking for any other way out. This room was quite fresh, for the long time it had been here, there was in fact ventilation going up from the ceiling. With the clothes was a sort of uniform with a swastika on the arm of it. At first I took little notice of the pictures on the bedside lockers. I just couldn't believe it. There was Hitler and Eva Braun, looking younger than they really should have been. Rob gave me another call. He had managed to get the safe opened up. Inside Rob brought out a wallet, there was two passports, one for Hitler the other for Eve Braun. There was a hundred and thirty thousand dollars in the wallet too they were Argentina. A buff piece of paper had a drawing, a map that showed a place in Argentine, a village with the name Eichman and others on a list. On another piece of paper confirmed what I had thought, there was gold sent up the Bavarian Alps as a decoy, the rest lay in a U-boat that was sunk. There were other photos of Hitler and Eva Braun with Eichman and several others. I thought there was nothing else in the wallet, but then I found another buff coloured letter, it told me where that gold was.

I quickly folded it up and stuck it in my pocket. Then Rob said, "Why did you do that Eddie?"

"Do what?"

"Why did you hide that letter?"

"Because this is something you might not be too keen to take part in."

"I came here didn't I, what the hell is it?"

"Rob, this could be dangerous."

"So what, I've faced danger before, don't forget I was in the Falklands, and that was no picnic."

I thought about it, then decided to let Rob know what the letter was. I took the letter out and handed it to him. He took it then said,

"This is in German, I don't know any German."

"Rob, I am after lost Nazi Gold, that letter tells me where it is."

"You're joking, I thought that had been found years ago."

"No Ron, it has not been found, there is tons of this Gold. I want to know now Rob, are you with me all the way on this?"

"Yeh of course I am Eddie, you can trust me."

"OK, what we have to find is an entrance to the tunnels, so let's look carefully around here first."

We took a wall each checking every inch of the walls and floor there had to be a way out of the room. We searched everywhere but found no way out except the way we came in.

"Come on Rob, we've been in here too long already, we can come back some other time."

"The best time, if we get here earlier is Thursday, the caretaker goes drinking in the village, he takes his buggy with him, so we can see he's out if that buggy is at the café."

Rob handed me the wallet as we made our way out of the trap-door, the dog had gone but there was light in the sky now as the sun would soon be up. Just as we were about to climb down off the veranda, the caretaker walked out of the far side of the veranda.

We both froze we didn't move an inch. We were still in the shadow it looked like he was looking straight at us. He was actually relieving himself, peeing into a tube that ran down into the garden. He finished and walked back inside. We got out of there pretty quickly and made for the beach, when there we ran back to the point that we came in. The sun was up and it was much easier to walk up the mountain and over the other side to the Landrover. Once we knew the route it didn't take too long to get back to Calete de Fuste. Rob dropped me off.

"I'll see you in a few days Rob, I want to go back home, maybe visit the Archives to get some facts right."

"OK Eddie, call me when you get back, I'll pick you up at the airport."

"Thanks Rob."

When I got back to the U.K. I made a point of visiting Julian Channer, whom I had served with in Special Forces, in fact he was one of the men who helped me find the treasure in Libya. My wife and his were good friends, Gloria was into all the women's clubs just like my wife. Julian and his namesake James had built up a chain of shops and were doing well. Their offices was in Kingston-upon-Thames. I parked my car near these offices and walked towards them, passing a man with a beard who was sorting boxes in a station wagon. I rang the doorbell twice, then I heard the man with the beard say,

"No one's in there at the moment, can I help you?"

I turned around and looked at the man. My God I thought, it is Julian.

"Is that you Julian?"

"Eddie, goodness me, what a surprise, how are you?"

I grabbed his hand and shook it warmly, "I just didn't know you with that beard."

"What are you up to these days Eddie?"

"Nothing much Julian, looking for gold."

"Aren't we all?"

"So you are doing well then Julian, you and James, by the way where is he?"

"James is out touring our shops, checking up, making sure all is kept up to standard."

"Well I am glad to hear you and James are doing so well, did you ever hear about the others or that Soccer Team?"

"All the men are doing well Eddie, as for that Soccer Team, they are still going strong."

"What about young Johnston and Jackie Turner, what ever happened to them?"

"They got married Eddie, both work with Squiresmills Soccer Charity. Why are you here Eddie?"

"I'm going to visit the Archives, there's a couple of things I want to clear up."

"You're on another mission, well if it's not too dangerous, I'm here if you need me."

"Oh thanks Julian, but it's early days nothing concrete yet."

"You did say something about Gold two years ago, after we found the treasure. What gold is that Eddie?"

"Nazi Gold Julian, tons of the stuff."

"I thought they found that years ago, was it in the Bavarian Mountains?"

"Oh yes they found gold up there, but that was peanuts, a clear decoy, fooling everyone. Their real haul is, well I hope it is, lying inside a U-boat off the coast of Fuerteventura. That's why I'm over here, checking out a couple of things."

"Well Eddie as I said, if you need me it's OK for me to join you. James has a good business head on his shoulders; he took well to all this, in fact I couldn't have done it without him."

"I'll keep in touch Julian tell Gloria I sent her best regards."

I left Julian as he went into the offices and headed in towards London.

When you get inside the Archives security is all over the place, with cameras and guards, once cleared to enter you must wait until the data you require is given to you, then you are escorted into a computer room where there are rows upon rows of computers. I slipped in the disc and watched the screen as U-boats came up. Kriegsmarine's U-boats, the V11 C had a range of 12600 miles it had a diesel engine, twin propellers and two full sets of torpedo tubes. The men slept in the torpedo rooms and at the forward section, above them were four escape hatches Balast lined the bottom in different sections of the U-boat.

Hitler was going to scrap these U-boats, but four were kept they moved in the south Atlantic, and indeed three visited Argentina, but there was one U-boat that was never accounted for. Now that's what I wanted to read. The last U-boat that surrendered in Argentina near Mar Del Plata was U-997. However there was three more with no number, used on other missions. I stuck in the disc, which gave full details regarding the Nazi gold. It said that some gold was indeed found in the Bavarian Mountains, coins, some small bars of gold but very few big bars of gold were ever found. There was still 2.265 tons still missing.

Right that's it I thought, I will get back to the Island and search until I find those tunnels, I felt certain they were there somewhere. Having seen all the tunnelling done by the Nazi's in Europe, it would be easy for them to do the same thing at or near, Villa Winter.

When I arrived back at our cottage in Devon, my wife, well she was used to me going off on some well, goose chase, as she would call them. Now I had the proof, it was as quick as I could to get back on the Island, I phoned Rob to meet me at the airport.

It was just great feeling that hot sun on my body as I came off the plane. I walked right through and out the front door where Rob was standing waiting for me, we shook hands and I got into the Landrover.

"Well Eddie, how did it go?"

"Just great Rob, I got what I was looking for and it more or less confirms what I have been thinking. That lost Nazi Gold is near that Villa somewhere."

"So what's next?"

"Rob, we must find the way into the tunnel, there has to be one coming from that Villa out to the sea."

"So I'm thinking you must think there is a sunken U-boat out there."

"Spot on Rob, and if I am right, there should be over 2.26 tons of it inside. We'll have a big job on our hands, if we need help I have a man I can trust who will be only too happy to help us out, his name is Julian Channer, he served with me."

"That's good enough for me Eddie, when are we going back down there?"

"Make it tomorrow night, same time."

The sun was blazing down as I reached my rented apartment, Rob pulled up to let me off, when someone he knew spoke to him. I just went indoors.

As soon as I got indoors, I got onto my laptop and began looking at any connected to the Villa, the U-boats or the gold. There wasn't much more to learn all but little bits and pieces. There are times when you get frustrated, but keeping a positive mind helps you do what you have to do. I was determined to get to that Villa and search until I found a tunnel.

I didn't sleep that night.

Nighttime is always the best time for illegal entry that is what we would be doing, as Rob kept telling me. No one seemed to know who owned this Villa, but one thing was certain, if no individual owned it, then the Government did.

For a change I took the wheel of the Landrover as we moved out of Caleta de Fuste and headed more west than south. There was no moon to help us as we made the long walk over the mountain and down towards the seaboard.

We took well over an hour and a half to get on the beach from where I parked the Landrover. This time we wasted no time at all in getting inside, a careful look around and we were back in through the small hidden trap-door and into the hidden room. We shone our torches around the room talking to each other in a whisper.

"I'll check under the bed Rob."

"OK Eddie, I'll work my way along this wall."

"I just thought of something Eddie."

I was lying down half under the large bed when he said that. I checked it first before pulling myself out from under it.

"What was that Rob?"

"Well if anyone was using this room, surely there would be a toilet?"

"You're right, why didn't I think of that, but you're right Rob. Where the hell is it? Must be another secret doorway in here."

We searched every inch of the room, but had no luck. We stood there looking at each other and wondering how would we make a hidden entrance to a toilet?

"Eddie, this wall over here comes out about two feet, then joins that one where the bed and lockers are, let's try there. Shining our torches on this part of the wall, we carefully inched along it, upwards, and side to side, but still no sign of an entrance.

"Let's try this," I said, as I walked over to the bed and lay down on it.

"Now, I'm getting up and need the loo, where do I head for?" I looked over at Rob standing with his back to the wall. I pointed straight at him.

"I would walk right over to where you are now standing."

"Yeh and do what? Pee on the wall!"

"We are looking for a door that opens out, but what if this door opens inwards, it could be already covered by the wall. Let's try putting our weight against this two foot corner."

Within seconds, the whole section opened up revealing a doorway.

"Eddie this is it, must be."

"Open it Rob."

"No you open it." I opened the door and there was a lovely bathroom with shower units, two of them. Hand towels, and big bath towels hung over a wall heater, there was even bars of soap in different colours wrapped in see through foil, hand clothes and shampoos sat in rows on a shelf that had silver bars along them to stop anything falling off. Both torches searched the room the beams passing each other in the darkness.

"Watch the time Eddie," said Rob as he walked into one of the shower units. I checked out the other one, then we both met in the middle of the bathroom. It was quite big, with a soft carpet running down the middle. There were silver coloured rings that had towels hanging from them, both units had a stool inside.

"Can you see anything Rob, another door or even a hatchway?"

"Nothing Eddie, these tiles over here look out of place with the others, they're not in line."

I walked over to take a look, sure enough, they were out of line. "I bet that's another hidden trap-door."

Before I had finished what I was saying Rob had it lifted up. "You're right again Eddie, there it is, looks like a stairway heading straight down into the blackness."

"Be careful Rob, might not be too solid, check it out before you go down any further."

Coming behind Rob, I shone my torch onto where his feet were, moving with every step, as we slowly descended stair by stair. I felt a shiver go through me as the cold hit me, Rob made a comment about the cold too as we stepped closer and closer to the bottom. We had gone down twenty-eight steps, and now we were at least fifty or sixty feet below ground level. Rob stopped, turned to me and said,

"Well we're at the bottom," he stepped aside, and we shone both torches quickly around.

It was a large cave cut out of solid rock, there were two sliding doors with a sort of wardrobe behind it, then something caught our eyes. Two airtight doors, one of which had a circular wheel to open it, there was none on the other one, it was most probably on the other side. We both stood there looking at them, Rob moved closer, trying to get the door, he put his hands on. I moved in closer and said,

"Wait Rob, don't open it just yet, let's think this over, there could be water on the other side."

"Yeh you're right Eddie, what in hells name would there be two airtight doors doing down here?"

"If my theory is correct, behind those doors lies a tunnel network leading out to sea."

"Are you serious Eddie, running out to sea…for what?"

"For a U-boat, and if I am right, that Nazi Gold is on it."

"Let's look in that cupboard," said Rob, moving away fast.

"Whoooa, what have we here?" said Rob, as he slid open the door, inside this cupboard or storage room were several things. The first thing I saw was a small generator, then some weapons hanging up on hooks, five divers' suits with oxygen tanks and way in the corner an old type safe. I looked at my watch and decided we better make for the surface.

We had no trouble with the hidden entrance, it locked cleanly as we slipped out of the Villa and made our way to the beach.

"Well Eddie, that's another good night, I believe what you said about that gold."

"Good, but tell no one not even your wife."

"Don't worry about that, I have no intentions of telling anyone."

Once back at the Landrover, I was dying for a cigar, so I lit one up just as the moon came out from behind some clouds, lighting up the rugged shape of the mountains behind us. I sat there smoking while Rob did most of the talking.

"You must have a great mind Eddie, you seemed to bring all these snippets together from the past, then slowly but surely string them together and Bingo, you hit the jackpot."

"No Rob, if I'm correct WE hit the jackpot."

"That would be my pension money."

"I would say it should be a lot more than any pension Rob."

"Why don't you call in later tonight to my Bar. Those Germans sometimes call in."

"I might just do that Rob."

Rob left me and I didn't feel tired so I just felt like a hot brandy, sat out on the veranda and lit a cigar. The sun was popping up over the hill, I could actually feel the heat build up on my legs. Aaah! It was a nice feeling after being down in those hidden caves. We went up the hill where homes and apartments were, all with a fantastic view. It surprised me to see so many people up and about so early in the morning. From where I was I could see the black rocks along the beach mostly lava, there was however, a lovely beach a sandy beach up near the harbour. By nine o'clock I felt tired so just fell on top of the bed, must have been sleeping very quickly.

I didn't budge until five thirty that afternoon. I made some coffee, then went to a restaurant I have often used here, always find the food first class. Had a few drinks then walked all the way down to Rob's Bar. Some staff knew me well and called me by my first name, as I did them. I normally sat outside with a beer and seldom drank spirits until late on, as it did help me to sleep. We were not going to the Villa tonight, so I made the best of it.

Rob came in after me and as usual gave me a "Hi", then checked out at the bar with his staff before returning to me with a big, cold beer.

"Are you here long?"

"Maybe an hour or so, you're pretty busy tonight."

"Women's golf today, they always call in. And I see the two Germans sitting over there."

Rob pointed them out. There was an old guy and a younger fellow both drinking. The older man had what looked like a brandy, while the younger man was drinking a pint of beer.

"Hey Eddie, when does that friend of yours arrive?"

"Julian and his wife Gloria arrive Friday morning, I will pick them up. What about the Germans, anything interesting?"

"No, not really, they have a few fashion shops on the Island, in Lanzarote too."

I noticed they went up and sang they danced all the time I was there, they seemed to enjoy themselves.

Rob and I sat well back from the others in the bar so we could talk without being overheard.

"Rob, if we wanted to check on Germans living here, where is the place to go?"

"I suppose the main library at Peurte del Rosario the Capital, that's the best place to get that sort of information."

"Those diving suits, will they be any good, and what about those oxygen bottles they any good?"

"Well the oxygen is no good, the suits could be deteriorated over the years. If we plan to go under water then I've a place to get all that gear, but it has to be returned on the same day."

"But that means we have to do this in daylight."

"We can do it. I have a boat I can get if we need it."

"I hope we don't have to get them from a German owned shop."

"No fear Eddie, this man is a friend never asks questions."

"Well that's good to know, we may need a lot more gear than just diving gear."

"Another beer Eddie?"

"Yeh, go ahead…thanks."

Surprise surprise, a young girl asked me for a dance, so I went up.

The strong German accent was clear coming from the older German who was up dancing and like me with a young girl. I enjoyed the dance it made me feel more relaxed.

Rob saw me looking at him and saying nothing after I returned to our table after the dance.

"What?" he said.

"Oh I was just thinking, that older German, would you think he might know about the gold?"

"Eddie, there's no way he knows and that goes for anyone else. If it's down there then those who did know are long gone."

"Hey I suppose you're right Rob."

I don't sing much, unlike my old buddy Sammy, he came with me into Libya to search for the Nazi treasure, which we found. Now here I was late on mind you and after a couple of brandies, doing my Nat King Cole. It went down very well, so I was pleased at that. Sitting back at the table, I was surprised when the older German said well done, to me for my singing, as he and the younger man went home. I felt it was time for me to go too.

Rob called in on me the next day, he had been to see the people who were renting out the diving gear. Of course it was early days, we still had to get through one of the those airtight doors.

Walking into the kitchen I said, "Want a coffee Rob, it's just been made."

"Yeh OK, I'll have a cup."

I sat two cups of coffee down on the table and then asked, "How about those diving suits and all the gear?"

"We are OK, I can get the lot but there might be a problem."

"And what's that?"

"We have to have the gear back on the same day we take it out."

"That could be a problem Rob, we may have to dive during the daylight hours, so how are we going to manage that?"

"I know you wanted this all done at night, but they are strict about diving gear, it must be returned before dusk."

"How about the gear down there, we could use it, we are not going down too far, what do you think Rob?"

"Yeh, I suppose so, we only need the bottles of oxygen."

"Can we return them at anytime?"

"Yes we can, in fact I can get all we need, no questions asked."

"Good, maybe it's better we just get the oxygen, then we can work away night or day, but we need Julian with us, if we dive."

"When did you say he's coming?"

"Early Friday, with his wife Gloria, she's an old friend of my wife, they will help move into the villa you found for me."

"Oh yeh Eddie, here's a list of all the Germans on this Island, all are in some sort of business."

I looked at the list, these names were on it, Hegel, Von Hister, Hessant, Korffhausen, Braun and Borman.

"You collect what oxygen we will need, get a good few Rob, we may need it when we get into the tunnels."

Fuerteventura is the largest of the Canary Island, so the locals say, it has a lovely climate, very warm in summer and quite warm even in winter. All the Canaries are volcanic, rocks push up out of the sea, that's why there is such a barren look about the lands. The landscape is changeable, with rugged areas of coastline with the odd oases here and there, most holidaymakers who come here have everything laid on for them, and only the few get out into the wild countryside.

All the hotels and apartments are near the sea, there is even manmade sandy beaches, and they are very nice. My first stay here was down near the sea in Caleta de Fuste, the beach at that area was just rocks and no sand, they had ground squirrels running about them, you often saw people feeding them. There is a lot to do around the Island, Golfing, fishing, caving, and there's the Zoo and wild Safari Park, camel rides, it goes on and on.

Well, so much for what's going on, I am up at five in the morning to collect Julian and Gloria from the airport, it's only half an hour away.

I mentioned about the Villa Rob found for me and my wife, well we moved in, but there is still a lot to get done, so my wife invited Gloria over for a holiday and of course, Julian came too. So things worked out better than I had ever hoped for, because while we were doing the search, the two wives would be happy getting on with giving a woman's touch to the villa.

There was a lovely swimming pool and many bushes going around the garden, they were at the rear, there was a double garage at the front with a red stoned driveway that held at least six cars.

There are rose bushes and small firs that line the lawn, which travels around the villa to the pool. I was so glad that Gloria was here to stay, I meant less hassle from my wife, being out all night, and now probably all day too.

I went to collect Julian and Gloria, still half-asleep, as I drove my new car into the car park. I was yawning entering the front doors, I saw Julian and Gloria, they were walking away from where I stood, it wasn't at all busy, in fact it was very quiet. I shouted out and it was Gloria who heard me, then hugs and some kisses, then Julian said,

"Look at you, you're well tanned and fitter looking than the last time we met."

"It's the hot weather, you don't feel like eating too much, come on give me a case, my wife can't wait to see you Gloria."

"Me too Eddie," said Gloria.

When I arrived at what was now my home, my wife was standing in the driveway, she ran out and the two women hugged each other. There were tears and excitement and a lot of fast talk as we went inside to show them around.

Once our guests had settled in, we had breakfast, then went out to sit by the pool, the sun was well up and warming the air around us, we settled down and taking in the sun, there was a delivery, a surprise delivery.

I have to explain this. While I went back to England, I must tell you I had a lovely collie dog called 'CY' he was ten years old, I had taken him for a walk down our usual route, near the river. He ran on like he sometimes did, but would always return to me, he had just passed the big rock and was out of sight, when I heard a shot. I raced down the path and as I came around the rock, there was 'CY' lying dead. This man shot him thinking it was a rabbit, I was in tears as I picked him up, I won't tell you what I said to the man, but it's not printable. Well, this special delivery came in, and Gloria and Julian got up and walked to collect it.

They told me to close my eyes, I did, and then I felt this furry thing land on my lap. It was a puppy, a collie with the same colours that 'CY' had. I was over the moon, I cannot remember if I ever thanked Gloria and Julian, I'm sure I did. The puppy followed me everywhere I went, even to the loo. What a wonderful surprise! That's what good friends do for you…wonderful stuff. I didn't even have to make a kennel or bed they all came together.

Once I calmed down, we sat chatting away, as the two girls went indoors. Julian then asked me,

"What's all this about?"

"Gold Julian, Nazi Gold and I believe I now know where it is."

"Where?"

"It lies just off the coast down near a village called Cfete, near the Villa Winter. Rob, he helped me, ex Para, has a Bar down in the village here. We found secret rooms and what I hope, is the entrance to tunnels that lead out to the sea. We still have to get into these tunnels. But so far, we have found the airtight doors, one with a circular bar that I'm sure will open it. Rob has been getting diving gear oxygen, there are suits down there."

"Hold on a minute Eddie, I'm not diving anywhere."

"No of course not. Rob and I will, we need you up on the boat, but it's early days, we still have to check out if there is indeed, tunnels down there."

"Is there anything you ought to tell me Eddie?"

"There's a caretaker down there at the Villa, but we can slip in and out, without any problem."

"Does your wife know about this?"

"Hell no Julian, you know what she's like about these Missions we go on."

"I thought as much, so it's hush hush then."

"Yes, too much is involved here, if this gets about we don't want others getting too interested."

"I know what you mean, someone like Eric Von Ludendorff."

"My God! Don't even mention his name."

This was a German who caused us a great deal of trouble on our last mission in Libya.

"I don't think we'll see him again Eddie."

"I wouldn't bank on it, he has spies everywhere, that's why this job stays dead quiet, we never draw attention to ourselves."

"Well I'll keep that in mind…this place you have it's just beautiful, you couldn't get anything better that this."

"Correct Julian, that's why I paid a lot of money for it, all custom built."

"There's a car pulling up the driveway."

"Must be Rob, come on Julian, I'll introduce you."

Rob jumped out of his Landrover and gave the thumbs up. So I knew he got what we needed.

I introduced the two and I was pleased that Rob took well to Julian, rank meant nothing now, but I did tell him Julian was a Captain in the SAS, one of my two 'bosses'. Respect was the order of the day for all of us, including those not present.

Rob had managed to get six oxygen bottles, so that was enough to keep us going. It was time for us to head down to Villa Winter. The two girls were happy enough, as we climbed on board Rob's Landrover. They were used to us going off on one mission or another.

On the way down, I filled in Julian on exactly how far we had got to…

We parked at the same spot as before, about two miles from the Villa, now knowing the best route to take over the mountaintop, it didn't take us as long this time. When we arrived at the Villa we lay low and observed for some time before moving in. The three of us moved swiftly and were inside the Villa in just a few moments. As we stood there in the darkness I whispered,

"Keep your voices down, it's OK once we get under ground. The hidden door is here."

I pulled it open and we slipped inside quickly, I then had to make sure I shut the door securely before heading down the stairway. Once at the bottom of the stairway Julian said,

"It's bloody cold down here."

"Yeh, it's cold, gets colder further down, but once into the secret room it gets warmer.

As we entered the room, Rob used the wheel to remove the covering that allowed light to fill up the room from the moon's beam, it was great when there was no cloud around it. Julian just stood there, he couldn't believe what he was seeing.

"My God, that's Hitler and Eva Braun, they must surely have stayed in this room."

"That's right Julian, and they both went to Argentina with a lot more Germans, before the war was over."

We gave Julian time to have a look around this very secret cave room, then we moved down further to where the diving gear and other stuff were. As soon as Julian saw the doors, he said,

"They're airlocks, there surely must be tunnels behind them?"

"That's what we hope to find out."

"Well, sometimes these types of airlocks need to be turned half a turn anti clockwise first before you try to open them."

"I didn't know that," said Rob.

I added, "Me too."

Rob looked over the diving suits, studied them closely.

"They're OK really, look as new, I think because they were locked in that cupboard, albeit a rock cupboard, it helped to preserve them."

Rob stripped down to his underpants, and I helped him on with the diving suit. Once on he said, "Well, how does it look? Check all over it."

Julian and I carefully looked at every inch of the suit it looked just grand.

"Well Rob, we have diving suits, what about that oxygen you got? How long will a bottle, like the ones you got, last?"

"You'll get about forty minutes, but you're better using just thirty, if we have to go down in that sea, timing is of the utmost importance, both of us must watch the time. If Julian is on the boat above us, we can put a line on each of us, then he can warn us when we are getting low on oxygen."

I then said, "Let's see what's behind those doors."

"Do what I say, turn anti clockwise then clockwise but do it very, very slowly, just barely move it, should there be any water behind the door, it will slowly show up, if nothing comes, then get it opened up."

Rob grabbed the wheel on the door and slowly moved it as Julian had said. While he was doing this Julian explained why there were two tunnels.

"The reason there are two tunnels here, is for airflow that a small generator can not only power lights down here, but can also be used to blow air down the intake tunnel, that's this one Rob is trying to open."

Rob stopped to have a rest and he said, "If there is tunnels here going out to the sea, it must have taken years to cut through all that rock."

Julian added, "The Nazi's could do that quite easily, in Germany they had whole factories cut out of rock underground in countries they had taken over. Doing this was pretty straight forward for them."

Rob gave a grunt and the wheel moved freely. "That's it, should open up now."

Julian and I moved in to help Rob get the big door open.

It wasn't easy, but slowly it opened up. There right in front of us was indeed a tunnel, with what we could see it was well made and had plenty of headroom. Rob stood back, turned and looked at the stairway we had just come down, and this I might add, is the second one.

Rob said, "I think I know why this place is set up like this. Let's assume there is a submarine (U-boat) lying out there in the sea, it must lie in a trough or depression on the seafloor, natural or manmade. If that is so, then this place floods over either going out to it or coming back, it may well have been used for the Top Brass in the Nazi's Party even Hitler and Braun, they could come and go as they pleased."

"You may well be right Rob," said Julian as he shone his torch into the tunnel. It showed a small railtrack right down the centre, so something was coming and going down here.

"I would suggest we check fully what's in that storage cupboard over there, before we go any further," said Julian.

"Rob, give me a hand to close over this door."

While we did that, Julian had pulled out the small safe, he managed to lift it up the smashed it onto a rock, it burst open throwing out its contents. There was a small, leather wallet holding gold bars, sixteen of them. A bunch of keys, letters and a plastic envelope containing thousands of American Dollars. There were also photos of high ranking Nazi officers and their wives, and one of Hitler and Eva Braun all were smiling. We all were looking at the photos and looking at the letters.

"What's that one on the top of this letter?" asked Rob as he handed it to Julian.

"That sign is the VRIL Society, scholars have been trying to find proof that this secret Society existed. This proves it does or it did, at one time. They believed that they had the power to rule the world."

Rob butted in, "They bloody well nearly did!"

I was looking at the gold bars, and thinking we might need the money from these to help set up this whole operation. "Who'd take these bars Rob?"

"There's an Arab in Lanzarote, he deals with stuff like that."

"Well, we have to pay him a visit. How much cash is there?"

"Just a minute," said Rob. "Over a hundred and thirty thousand dollars American."

"Right, let's get out of here, we'll be back to get right into those tunnels tomorrow night, come on."

In all that was a good night's work, we now had more than enough funds to cover anything we required to get the job done. We now had to visit Lanzarote and see this Arab gentleman.

Without further ado, we were off to Lanzarote that very morning tired, but raring to go. We drove at the Corralejo to get the Ferry over to Lanzarote. Well, I can tell you the place was packed with holidaymakers, young and old.

Rob knew more about this man than we both did, so I let him do the talking once we got there.

I parked my new four by four near the docks, as we walked to a bar to get a drink and waste some time because we were too early to call on the man. Julian treated us to a drink, so we sat out in the shade and I lit a cigar. It was nice just sitting there watching all the holidaymakers walk by. Funny, when you have been well trained you can actually tell where people come from, their shoes, boots, their clothes, even in some cases, the way they walk. Well there were so many of them walking past us, thank goodness we were in the shade, the sun was boiling hot, the cold beer helped cool us down.

It was time to return to the vehicle, as we had to move down to the old town. Just before you come to the old town there is a road going past the hotel on the right heading up the hill, that's where I once stayed at a Villa. Anyway, we just managed to get a place to park, then Rob took 'point' as he knew where to go. Up a back street passing some old houses he stopped outside a wine coloured, thick wooden door. Rob knocked on it and we waited.

An old man came to the door and Rob quickly explained who we were.

"Come in please," the old man took a look outside, then closed the door and walked past us. "Just follow me please."

We walked through a shop full of odds and ends, there was clocks, vases, statuettes, carpets, spears, daggers and some beautiful boxes all sizes, standing neatly on antiques that would be at home in some Palaces across the world. We stopped at a secured area, it had steel bars, the old man opened this metal cage and in we went. Rob put the gold on the table, while the man took out one of the bars, he weighed the bar then took it to a bench and did a test on the gold, he came back to the table we all stood at, then said,

"This is very good gold, the best. Do you want cash or a cheque?"

I said, "We would like cash please."

"Aah, well that is a lot of money, if you come back in an hour, I will have money for you."

"How much money?" asked Rob.

"180 thousand Euros…that's a good price, for no questions asked."

Rob turned looking at me and Julian, his mouth wide open.

"Did you hear that," I answered him.

"Yes I heard him, it's worth more than that, but beggars can't be choosers."

I looked at the old man and said, "OK, we'll come back later." Turning to Rob… "Grab that gold."

Rob picked up the leather wallet and we walked back out into the blazing heat. We had time to kill so we went back to the same bar we stopped at earlier.

There wasn't a cloud in the sky and once we returned to that bar and sat down, you soon felt the heat tinkle your skin. Even so it was just nice sitting there with a cold beer and looking out at the blue ocean. Just up from where we were was a Casino, I remember winning some money in there just a couple of years ago. We only had a couple of beers each, then we headed back to the old town. The old Arab opened the door, as we walked inside we saw other men.

"Good evening gentlemen, I would like to ask you some questions."

"Who's asking?" said Julian.

The man then introduced himself as the Chief of Police for Lanzarote.

"What is it you would like to know Sir?" said Julian speaking in his best Officer's voice.

"The Gold Señor, where did it come from?"

We looked at each other, because we didn't expect this. I said quite quickly, "we have broken no laws, so why the question?"

"Aah you see this amount of gold must be recorded. Where did this gold come from Señor?"

I had to think very quickly, and the only thing that came to mind was the fact we had a boat lined up to go diving, so I told him we caught the gold in our fishing nets.

The two men with the Chief kept looking at the bars of gold, they probably had never seen one before.

"That is OK Señor, but I would like you to accompany me to the Police station so we can record this."

He took the wallet containing the gold and we followed him to the door. We followed their car to the Police station and they were very polite and gave us coffee while we waited. I was given a form to fill in. Julian and I studied it with Rob looking over our shoulders to see what was on the form.

Quietly Julian said, "Answer it truthfully."

I filled up the form and gave it back to the officer who had given it to me. He handed it on to the Chief.

"Thank you Señor, we shall deal with this as quickly as we can, have some more coffee while you wait."

Half an hour later one of the policemen returned and handed the Chief a large buff envelope.

"Here you are Señor, your gold is worth 240,000 sterling."

We all looked at each other barely able to believe what he had said. I thought that in sterling it is well over a quarter of a million. I counted out ten thousand, handed it to the Chief and said,
"This is for the Police Fund."

The Chief was more than helpful, as he would forward the rest of the money to my account in Fuerteventura. We all shook hands and we soon cleared out of there heading straight to the docks and the ferry.

It was a quiet crossing and it gave me some time to think. I had ordered some special gear we might need. So I had to call in at the airport, I went to the information desk to ask where I could pick up my crate.

"Hi, I am Edward Blake, I've come to pick up this." I handed over the docket, and she asked me to sign a book. She then gave the docket to a porter, he went off and came back with my crate. Inside the crate there was night goggles, special phones, spear guns and powerful stun guns, mini-cameras and luminous markers (To help find the way in darkness), two pairs of Greenkatz binoculars, hand guns and rolls of tape.

Fortunately when we returned to my villa, the girls had gone out shopping, so I got the crate opened up, and let Rob and Julian check out the items inside. I managed to get ammo from a dealer giving over the odds, so the weapons could be loaded up. This gear meant we could travel down the tunnel safely, that was my move, making sure we were safe once we go in there. One other item I had got, was a spring loaded metal tape, this can be fired down the tunnel ahead of us, and let us know that the road is clear ahead.

I packed away all the gear in the garage and locked the door. Rob went home, so Julian and I sat at the pool with a drink. We could hear the car pulling up in the driveway the girls are back. I switched on the TV and we sat back enjoying the cool evening breeze.

"Stick on the News Eddie," said Julian as he sipped his drink.

"I hate the News, all trouble every time you look at it."

"I have to agree with you."

I switched channels and got onto an old cartoon character called The RoadRunner. It had Julian laughing his head off.

"You see I told you, skip the News, you'll be a lot happier."

We both stripped off and went into the pool.

Aah it was lovely and cool swimming slowly along, there was a nice breeze blowing and it was very pleasant.

Our silence was disturbed with the two girls bombing us, as they jumped in. It was now dark and the floodlights came on lighting up the whole garden, the little pup stood by watching me as I got out and grabbed a towel, it came and sat at my feet. I looked down at him and said, "We need a good name for you."

I called to the others to give me a name.

So far nothing was forthcoming, so I thought about it then decided I would call my new pup…I know my last dog was named Robbie, and I toyed with the idea. Then Rob came back, he had gone to collect two different sizes of oxygen tanks. The girls had all their shopping on the kitchen table as I walked in with the pup at my feet. I said in German, "Wieveil macht die rechnung."

"Oh stop messing," said Gloria. "What did you just say?"

"I just asked you how much the bill was?"

Julian and I joined Rob at his Landrover, in the back of it he had all the oxygen stacked up.

"That was quick Rob, how did it go?"

"No problem Eddie, we can get whatever we need, I got the smaller ones, easier to handle in water, we can if we have to, use the larger bottles in the tunnel."

Julian chipped in, "We must be careful entering this tunnel, a check on whether there is any gas must be made before we go in there."

Rob said, "I have all that stuff."

I butted in, "In my box I have a new gadget that rolls out and does all that, checks for all gases and even if the tunnel is blocked."

"How far does this thing run?" asked Julian.

"I believe it is about eighteen meters, if there are no other obstructions in its way."

"If there is a U-boat out in the sea near the Villa Winter, it must be two thousand meters from that Villa, that's a long, long way," said Rob.

"I know that Rob, that's nothing to the tunnelling the Nazi's have done in Europe, miles and miles of them. Now what about those oxygen tanks, you say you have different sizes."

"That's right Eddie, we have smaller ones for when we get into the tunnels, then larger ones for the sea search."

"How long will they last Rob?"

"The small ones about twenty to thirty minutes, the large ones forty to sixty minutes. Remember to time from the moment we enter the tunnels or the water. Julian, you can keep 'tabs' on the time for us, you know what it can be like entering a place like this, excitement takes over at what's coming up."

"OK, we go down there in an hour make sure you have all the gear we need Julian, once we are inside the tunnel, you keep in touch with us, these radio's work anywhere, so they should be no problem as we move deeper into the tunnel. Take warm jackets, it gets cold down there after a bit of time."

Well we checked out our own gear and just after sunset we headed down the coast towards Cofete. There was a full moon up as we reached the Villa on foot. Rob and I got inside the small trap door, as Julian eyed up everything as we moved forward to the hidden room, we wasted no time in getting down the stairway and into the cave below. You could feel the cold hitting your body as we reached the bottom of the stairway and stood there in the cave. The roof of the cave was quite high, about seven feet or so, it was dry so that was a good thing. Julian had looked into the rock cupboard, he had found three hidden sockets we all got a bit excited about that, because there was that generator sitting there just wanting us to plug it in. We already knew there was lights all lined across the cave and going in to the airtight doors, if we got these lights working it would make a great deal of difference to the time we would have down in this cold dark place.

Rob was working on the airtight door, it creaked then gave out a low squeal as Rob stepped back and pulled the door open. Julian had been at the generator and would you believe it, the lights flickered and came on even in the tunnel. Inside the tunnel was dry and it had been well cut out, there was no strapping on the roof or sides, just solid rock.

"OK," I said, "Check your watches, right Rob, we will carry one each of the small bottles of oxygen just in case, but before we move any further inside, let me send out my probe. It should tell me on this hand-held monitor if there is any gases further down the tunnel."

In went the probe it reached twenty-five meters, looking at the small monitor I held in my hand I could see there were no gases so Rob and I moved slowly along the tunnel. It sloped away from us going downhill but very slightly, in the centre were two parallel slots running right down the centre.

"What are they?" asked Rob.

"Well they look like little railway lines, probably for hutches, you know, what they put coal in after they mined it."

"I'd better reel in the probe." We stopped only having gone about ten yards as we were taking it very slowly. The probe back in its holder, we moved on.

The lights flickered and then went out, we had walked now for twenty minutes, mind you we were walking very slowly, so the distance we had covered wasn't much. We moved back along the tunnel much faster even though we now used our torches. Arriving back in the cave, Julian told us we needed fuel for the generator.

We all felt sick at the thought of us all forgetting such an important thing. One very good thing, we now knew there was indeed, two tunnels. This would be needed to circulate the air, like they do in a coalmine. We now had to cart more fuel all the way over the mountain, along the coastline and over all the rocks until finally we get it inside the Villa. We could have gone on, but we put safety first, and so we moved back to the Landrover.

I was hoping we could get to the end of the tunnel we were in, it was a long, long tunnel and we hoped that there may be a connecting tunnel joining the two in places.

Back at my place, we sat down at the pool and went over a list of everything we would take with us, on our next journey down to Villa Winter.

The next night we struggled with the large oxygen bottles, moving across all that terrain was exceedingly difficult. We had to stop many times. We took ages getting all our supplies into the hidden room.

We talked over everything, Julian then said,

"These tunnels, they must be over a mile long Eddie?"

"You're right there Julian, could be even more, that's why we need that oxygen, if we get trapped by a fall from the roof, there would be no air flow, it wouldn't take long for us to succumb to lack of oxygen."

Rob asked me, "Eddie, what is it you really expect to find at the end of those tunnels?"

"Well Rob, I hope its not just some hidden pathway from the sea up to that Villa. What I really hope for, is that missing U-boat is lying out there, loaded with tons of gold and we can enter it from the tunnels."

"You have checked out all these things about U-boats Eddie, so you seem certain there's one lying down there in the sea," said Julian.

"Well let's face it, look what we have found already, what about that gold? I'm sure my hunch is right Julian, even if I am wrong we still have made a small fortune already."

"That's true Eddie," said Rob. "Counting the lot damn near half a million, no one would grumble about that amount, now would they?"

"I suppose you're right Rob, but if that U-boat is there, oh boy that would be really something."

Rob went home and Julian and I with our wives sat down to a meal. Julian and I sat with our wives eating, most of our thoughts were elsewhere. It was so unfortunate that we ran out of fuel, but the next time we went to the Villa, we would be well prepared.

Julian's wife Gloria, asked, "Well what are you men looking for that is so important you can't tell us?"

I looked over the table at Julian and nodded for him to answer. Now, I had no idea what Julian was going to say, so I sat there full of anticipation, waiting and waiting. Julian glanced across at me, I nodded for him to go ahead and say something.

"Well," began Julian, "Eddie and I have always thought of growing nice fresh vegetables and oysters, so the reason we are out at night is looking for the right area to start farming oysters."

I couldn't help but smile, but I was dying to burst into laughter as Gloria quickly said, "Now who do you think you're kidding mister Channer?"

"It's true love, really!"

"Well once you find what it is you three are looking for, you will let us know."

"Whatever happens we shall let you both know."

I butted in, "Fancy a swim Julian."

"Yeh why not."

The swimming takes your mind off what we are almost fully involved in. Sometimes you cannot get to sleep but think on this 'Job' all the bloody time.

You know, too much thinking over a subject just is not good for the brain, it can affect the nerves, then in turn affect the brain, but let's not talk about such things, let's get back on the 'Job'.

Later that evening we slipped away to meet up with Rob, he had got more supplies of oxygen, now we had to get back down to the Villa Winter. We had to get closer to the Villa due to the amount of oxygen bottles we had to carry, so this time we took the direct route to the Villa, then drove down onto the beach. Our plan was to drive along to the nearest point to the Villa and carry the bottles over the rocks. But we were in for a big surprise, as we drove into view of Villa Winter there were people setting up a camp, and looked like floodlights being erected.

"Who the hell are they?" said Rob.

There were six people in all, two men and four women, as we drew closer Julian called out to them.

"Hello there, hope we can pass by, going fishing further up the coast."

One of the women answered saying, "Oh you are fine, we are just setting up a dig, we are archaeologists."

"Well have a nice dig, good evening to you all," they all waved as we moved on further along the coast.

Once we got out of sight, we unloaded all the bottles, then Rob drove the Landrover well out of sight further up the beach. When he rejoined us, all we could talk about was the 'diggers' the archaeologists.

"That Villa's been there for over seventy years, why should they be doing a 'dig' now," said Rob, as we all struggled up the incline towards the Villa with the oxygen.

We had several visits to get all the oxygen up and inside the small trap door, the last two items were the fuel for the generator.

We got everything inside the hidden room, then went back to take a look outside at what the 'diggers' were now up to. They were putting up tents and folding tables, the site they were in was to the south of the Villa and just three hundred yards nearer the sea than the Villa, so they were pretty close. We went back inside and moved down to the cave and the two doors. Rob filled up the small generator with fuel, then opened the airtight door and entered the tunnel. I sent off my little gadget to check for gas and it was OK for us to move on down the tunnel. Walking in the tunnel was slow and exciting, because we didn't know what was ahead of us, good or bad, of course we came prepared with my box of tricks.

While we headed into the tunnel Julian stayed at the entrance looking after the small generator, we were in contact with our radiophones, Rob and I walked slowly along the tunnel. We were hoping to find a door joining up the two tunnels at least that's what we hoped for.

We could see ahead of us due to the small lights above our heads…thanks to that generator. I sent out the sensitive-tape roll that would give us a reading on whether there was any gas further down the tunnel, so far there had been none. It was still creepy, with many dark shadows all down the walls of the tunnel. It was getting very cold and we stopped to put on the warm jackets we had brought with us. It was minus nine degrees and dropping. We were in this tunnel and it was like going down hill. Checking our watches, we had been down there for over half an hour, and still the end wasn't in sight. Some broken shovels and picks lay along the side of the tunnel and the rails were broken and some were missing. Some alcoves gave us hope that there was a connection between the two tunnels, but that's all they were.

Then Rob shouted, "Look up ahead, that black area looks like a road through."

We moved faster and when we reached that area it was indeed a doorway through to the other tunnel. Rob went to open it I stopped him.

"Don't open it Rob, we could be hit with gas, we are OK in this one because we've had it opened up for some time, this has allowed fresh air inside."

"At least we do know there is a connection between the two tunnels."

"What next Eddie?"

"How long have we been in here?"

"Just over forty minutes."

"What? As much as that, you sure Rob?"

"Of course I'm sure, that last time I looked it was about half an hour."

"Wonder just how far have we travelled."

"That gadget you use, you've had it spinned out many times, can you remember how many?"

"Yeh, it can reach about a hundred and eighty metres, I put it out eight times."

"OK Eddie, so that's eight times a hundred and eighty, my God, that's 1440 metres."

"That's a long, long way Rob, but this measurement is in yards, over thirteen hundred yards, there's 1760 yards in a mile, so we have walked in all that time three parts of a mile, we could have three times that to walk yet Rob."

"We better get moving faster. Give Julian a call, let him know how far we've gone, better keep checking for gas."

Most of the gadgets I got in, didn't have names, they were all state of the art, brand new and straight out of the private companies dealing in new technology, don't ask me how these radiophones work because I haven't a clue. They work underground just as well. I called Julian and explained all to him and how we were going to move faster, to hopefully get to the other end of this tunnel. All was going well back where he was, he told me that old generator is going great guns. He also said that there was noise of heavy machinery outside. So he had a look and saw that two bulldozers were moving earth and rocks, there was floodlights erected all over the site.

Rob and I pushed on, this time moving much faster, I never gave it much thought that it would take so long to get to the end of the tunnels. Of course I wasn't thinking on just how far out at sea the U-boats might be.

We stopped to look at a cutting that went into the rock about ten feet. It had two hutches, lamps, picks and shovels also had a door at the end of it, an airtight one. We took a good look at the door and it was obvious it was the second connection to the other tunnel. The small, narrow gauge rails now ran unbroken and had done since we left the first door leading through to the other tunnel. I checked my watch and saw we were now in the tunnel, one hour and ten minutes, yet still we had not reached the end. We decided to mark out how far we had gone, leaving marks on the tunnel walls.

We walked quickly back to meet up with Julian, he was now concerned about all the noise going on up near the Villa.

As we came into the cave, Julian switched off the generator, then said, "Did you find the end of the tunnels?"
I answered, "Unfortunately no, it must be a long way out there. What about the noise you mentioned?"

"They're out digging up on the far side of the Villa, two bulldozers and loads of workers all over the place, we'll be lucky to get out of here unseen."

In the short time we had been underground, this team of diggers had a whole camp set up with floodlights. What really troubled us was the guards, there now was two security guards doing a perimeter patrol. We managed to slip out using the shadows and quickly made it back to Rob's Landrover. We came in past these archaeologists, so now we had to take the same route back out along the beach. No one even noticed us, we were out of any direct light coming from the floodlights.

As we drove back to Caleta de Fuste, Julian, who was with me on the last mission The Treasure in Libya, made his thoughts known.

"Eddie, I don't like this business with those people down there at the Villa, you don't think your man is on to us?"

"What man?" asked Rob.

I quickly answered him. "We had trouble two years ago, with a man who steals artefacts and he will kill to get them, his name is Eric

Von Ludendorff a German Billionaire. This man has his own Army, and they are the best. Ex German Special Forces. We must be on our toes from now on. This man has choppers, speedboats, and even submarines. If he is behind this 'DIG' then we must change our routine, maybe even get out near the villa fishing and actually catch some fish. We can then offer some to the archaeologists, but at the same time we fish, we can dive and search the bottom of the ocean, of course first we must get to the end of those tunnels, then we will do all that."

I continued...."I will show you what weapons I have managed to get, they are safely in the garage at my villa."

Arriving back at my villa, we went straight to the garage, I took out the wooden box, opened the padlock and said, "Take your pick." Inside were several types of weapons. Rob picked out a Mph5 automatic sub machinegun, so too did Julian. There were some hand guns too, some explosives and grenades, H.E and smoke. Once Rob had looked them over he said,
"Are we going to war?" We all laughed; Rob knew the weapons as he had used them like we have Julian and I. He worked away cocking the weapon and removing the Mag, of course I hide all the Ammo until we felt we needed it.

I had managed to get more gadgets that night, goggles to let us see our way in the dark. The explosives were c4 and easy to handle. I had a safe, a small one tucked away well out of sight, so I showed Rob and Julian how to open it, should anything happen to me. Inside were all the Mags full of Ammo for every weapon we now had.

"What's on tomorrow then Eddie?" asked Rob.

"We go down fishing and maybe do some diving."

"I'm not diving," said Julian.

"You don't have to Julian, Rob and I will do it."

"Anyway Eddie, looks like we have to return to England, I have Lawyers wanting me to sign some papers."

Rob looked over at me saying, "WELL I'm game for fishing are you?"

"Yeh, sure I am Rob, can you get the boat?"

"No problem Eddie, just a phone call books it, he's my cousin."

"I wish I was coming with you, now I'll miss out on everything."

"No you won't, we can use the time you're away to throw off Von Ludendorff's men."

"You mean you'll wait until I get this business done?"

"That's what Eddie said Julian, there's no real rush about this, we tread softly, get the job done with hopefully the least bit of trouble."

I had to quickly put away my box of tricks, as our wives came into the garage.

It was just after nine a.m. and they came in to tell us they were off shopping. I thought then, with Julian returning to the U.K. why not go out tonight and have a few drinks…and that's what we did, after a good sleep.

The two girls left and Rob went too, so Julian and I had a swim ooh, it was lovely. We sat about, this was now eighteen hundred hours, we had a couple of drinks by the pool, while I lit up my favourite cigar, and this one was laced with rum. I used to smoke cigarettes but they stink out all your clothes and kill your lungs, so I gave them up a few years back. Julian never smoked although he has, when we were drinking together asked me for a cigar…and he smoked it. My advice to smokers, if you can stop them do it, when you get older that's when the shit kicks in and your lungs can't get enough oxygen into your system.

The girls, well I call them the girls, however, they are much older, but it's nice to say it, well they had just returned from their shopping expedition, now it was our turn to go out.

Just after 9.30 p.m. we walked down to Rob's Bar, it was a lovely evening with a fresh breeze blowing that kept us cool. There's something about this Island that makes you feel free and fresh, maybe it's that cool breeze that comes rolling in from the sea.

We were walking downhill past the Police station and down to where the road forks off left and right. A children's playground was over on our right and a restaurant I use sometimes on the left. We went in there and ordered up beers, we sat down, there were a lot of people in the place, including two Germans just across from us, they looked like the two Rob had told me about. Julian and I both understood German, so we could hear what they said, it was just normal chat really. They fitted the description of the two men all right.

I had forgotten my lighter, so I turned to the younger German and asked for a light. I don't think they expected anyone to speak to them in German.

"Entschudigen sie bitte, stort essiewennich rauche."

"Bitte schon," said the older man. I then asked for a light. "Konnen sie mir bitte feuer geben."

The younger man lit my cigar, I thanked him and sat back to enjoy.

A little later the two men got up to leave, that's when we heard the headwaiter saying their names. I turned to face Julian and said, "Did you hear that?"

"Yes I heard it, Von Heisenberg, wasn't he, or a man with that name, help to produce the Atomic Bomb?"

"Yeh, I think you're right Julian, might be a relation."

We then headed down to Rob's bar, the two Germans walking just ahead of us. They went into Rob's bar, we followed and just sat down. Rob was in the bar and brought us over two beers.

"I'll be back over once I get these customers served."

"Just a minute Rob, those two over there, are they the same men you told me about?"

"Yeh, that's them, come in now and again, they're OK I'm sure." As we sat there drinking Julian said, "If that crazy bastard Von Ludendorff comes into all this, we couldn't cope with it all."

"We could get some of the men who helped with the Treasure and the Snatch Mission in Libya."

"Yeh I suppose we could do that, if they are available. I can check them out when I get back home."

Rob came over to join us at the table, he sat down and said,

"You two enjoying yourselves, I see you're taking an interest in the two Germans."

"So you think they are OK?"

"Eddie, they are just like you, me and Julian. They have a clothes shop selling mens ware. Whether they know anything about the gold if it's down there, is anyone's guess."

"You sound as if you think there's nothing down there – no gold, is that what you really think Rob?"

"Well let's face it Eddie, gold down there…over seventy years, and with those deep sea treasure hunters everywhere, I doubt it."

"Rob, those treasure hunters have never been near that area, it's too shallow and they go by archives accounts of vessel sunk, that U-boat, there's no one living that was ever part of it, so I know it's there, because one U-boat is missing, that's it."

"Don't get me wrong Eddie, I'm all for this search and I hope we find the gold."

Julian added, "I'll put it this way Rob, I've known Eddie for years we both served in 22, and I wouldn't be coming back here, if I wasn't sure he had done his homework."

"Don't get me wrong Julian, I back Eddie, he has been right so far, let's wait and see what we find."

I butted in, "Rob, you and I will do some fishing, and just maybe get back into the tunnels, we must find out for sure if Von Ludendorff is behind the 'Dig' down at the Villa Winter."

Rob went off to help serve at the bar, and I walked over to make an order.

"Two double brandies please," the girl looked at me, smiled then got the drinks, I thanked her and went back to our table and gave Julian a glass of brandy then sat down.

"Here, try that."

Julian looked at it and said, "What's that?"

"That is a brandy, get it over your neck."

Julian took a sip, then another, looked at me and smiled. "I could get to like this."

The bar was full and some sporty types were up dancing, and there were some people up singing there was a good lively bunch all sitting together.

When you are enjoying yourself, time really seems to fly in, it was now after midnight and the whole place was swinging.

After a couple more brandies, Julian was up dancing, then as he returned to our table, he asked for a cigar, lit it and sat back like an old hand at it.

Next morning we suffered from all the drink, a quick swim in the pool and then breakfast, then I drove Julian and Gloria to the airport, my wife was with us. All hugs and kisses, a firm handshake and they were off back to the U.K.

Now things were left to just two of us, we planned to fish and as near the Villa Winter as possible. To throw anyone off our trail, we would get all the gear needed for fishing off the boat Rob borrowed from his cousin.

Rob and I went back down to the Villa Winter, this time on a boat, we had all the fishing gear with us, some food and drinks, this was a way of throwing off the interest in us from the Germans and Von Ludendorff.

It was a lovely morning and we got down there pretty early, we anchored about a mile out from the Villa, giving us a very good view of the Villa and all the digging that was going on. While we fished a helicopter landed at the site. One man got out of it he walked over to the head archaeologist and they talked, he was soon off again in the helicopter.

Rob was watching it all through binoculars.

"Well Rob, is it Von Ludendorff?"

"Looks like it Eddie, big, tall man with red hair, smartly dressed had a smoke in a holder, looked a bit odd really."

"That's him OK, we better watch ourselves, he's a bad piece of work."

Rob shouted… "Hey you've caught something."

I raced over, grabbed my rod and sure enough I had a big fish on the end of it. That chopper swooped over us, just as I was taking the fish out of the water. I didn't even look up at it.

I had caught my first big fish, a few minutes later, Rob got another big one. We both were enjoying ourselves, after getting nine fish we stopped for a break and a bite to eat. We ate a few sandwiches and had coffee from a flask, then I lit up a cigar and sat back soaking up the sun.

Over at the Villa Winter archaeologists and moved much closer to the Villa and we could see that there now was at least two men on a patrol around the perimeter of the whole area including the Villa itself.

"Now that is going to make it very difficult for us to gain entrance."

"Yeh so I see Rob, there are two men constantly moving in a circle around the whole area. We can slip inside as they reach the far side of the villa, I don't think it will be a problem…unless they split up."

Rob moved the boat in towards the shoreline, so we could offer some fish to the archaeologists. To our surprise there was a small jetty built, it wasn't there two days ago. Rob docked and we took the fish up across the rocks towards the older man and the two girls.

He came walking towards us, as one of the guards tried to stop us.

"Let them through," said the Professor.

The Professor was very warm and welcoming, I put the bag of fish on the table as he called the girls over and then introduced them and himself. He was David Johnstone and he was working freelance for a Company based in Germany. The two girls got us tea and cakes, so we dug into them as the Professor continued to tell us more.

They were well kitted out, with four or five computers and

ground penetrating radar. The Company he worked for was based in Hamburg, they were here looking for gold, seemingly a Spanish Galleon sank in the area, but before it went under, they brought all the gold on land and buried it.

Rob then asked, "Who owns this Company you are working for?"

"Well actually he just left about half and hour ago, a lovely man called Eric Von Ludendorff."

Rob's head just looked down into the cup he had been drinking from and he never said a word after that.

The Professor added that there once was a Roman site here, so they hoped to find that too.

We thanked the Professor and the girls and left, once on board the boat, Rob said, "Eddie, we have to work out another way of getting to that U-boat."

"I know Rob, I'm thinking."

"How about diving? We could use this time now to search the seabed, we might get lucky and find it."

"It won't be easy with all those people over there."

"Eddie, they now know we are fishermen."

"I'm worried Rob, Von Ludendorff must know something about that gold and he's using them as a cover for his own men, I'll bet those doing the patrolling are his men."

"Now that doesn't sound good Eddie, if they are as bad as you said they were, we need those weapons."

"Rob, do you think we could dive at night?"

"We could Eddie, but we need strong lighting and that could draw attention to us, but there is something else we could get to help us."

"What's that?"

"A mini Sub, I know where to get it too."

"That would help, but getting gold out from a U-boat and up through water onto a boat needs special lifting gear and we don't have that."

"Let's take one step at a time Eddie, let's find the stuff first, then decide how to move it."

"I've just thought about something, inside the U-boats they have inflatables, most Subs have them."

"Gold is very heavy Eddie, how much weight can be put on these things?"

"I don't know Rob, but they can hold eight to ten men, and I know there are a lot of them on board."

"You know something Eddie, if we found that U-boat while diving, we don't need to ever go back near the Villa."

"How do we get inside the bloody thing?"

"That's easy, find the two hatches, they are near the torpedo bays, should be two they are escape hatches for the crew. You could in fact, enter the U-boat then leave by the other hatchway and re enter on the other one, but you need two at least to do this…..and two men to work it."

We steamed off heading back along the coast, talking all the time about the diving, the mini sub and just finding that U-boat. I could feel excited and so too was Rob, it was the talk that did it all the talk about it got us on a high. As we neared the harbour, Rob said,

"This won't be at all easy Eddie, you're looking for a needle in a haystack, that U-boat will look just like the sea bottom after all these years. We must find an area that it could have been sat into, or depression on the sea floor, I doubt if there is anything along the top of it, probably stripped down before it was scuttled."

"What about those metal detectors…any good?"

"We can try them, if they don't work, I have a very strong, solid magnet we can take down with us, if there is any metal down there it will grab it."

We arrived back at my place, I gave Rob two weapons wrapped up together with ammo, he took an Ingram and loaded it, then stuck it under his jacket as my wife came outside.

Rob handed her some fish. "There's your evening meal."

"Oh fish," she said. "I hate the stuff ahhhh."

"OK love, cook some for me!"

"I'll see you later Eddie, bye June.

As we sat down to eat my wife said, "I miss Julian and Gloria, I wish they would come back for another stay."

"Well I'm sure they will love, in fact I'm sure they will."

"Oh that's wonderful, I'll make sure their room is looking just lovely for them."

"Yes, you do that love."

My thoughts were back with the job at hand, I was sure no one really knew that U-boat was down there. I even knew what type it was. I was grateful that Rob too was familiar with them, this would be a great help once we dived down into the deep sea just off the coast of the Villa Winter.

I would have preferred having Julian with us when we are diving, it could mean one of us dives the other stays on the boat.

My wife was always telling me to take care, and that I was not as young as I would like to think I am. She was right of course, but as I always say, it's all in the brains, if you keep your grey matter fresh and well aired, then you're as good as you feel.

Rob and I took time off from the 'job' at hand, just doing a normal daily routine, but we watched for new faces about the town and noted who, and where they were, and what car they drove in.

We didn't go near the Villa Winter for a whole week then had another days fishing, just passing time until we had Julian back with us.

It wasn't at all long before Julian and Gloria returned to Caleta de Fuste. I picked them up from the airport and this time it was around 1800 hours. We left the girls and headed down to Rob's Bar. Not having seen Rob for a few days, he was delighted to see us both. He had just arrived at the Bar himself and was getting ready for the holidaymakers. When we started drinking it wasn't long before the 'Job' came into the conversation.

It was still pretty warm, even though it was now after nine o'clock or if you like 2100 hours.

Many things we talked about were only partly said, as we didn't want anyone to pick up on what we were talking about. That all stopped as the singing started and the Bar filled up.

Julian asked about the fish we caught and the archaeologists. Once he knew who was involved he was cursing.

Julian looked at Rob, who was putting drinks down on our table. "I can tell you this, most people know what a bastard is, well this guy is a pure bastard, he even kills his own men, we don't want him anywhere near us. When you went fishing did you actually see him?"

"We saw him all right, but not for long, he dropped in, spoke to the Professor and two minutes later he was gone."

"Eddie, he knows something, why else would he be down there at that Villa?"

"There's no question he knows about the gold, but he surely doesn't know where it is. That's why we have kept clear of the Villa. He must think it has been hidden somewhere nearby."

Rob sat with us now and again, as he helped out serving at the Bar, he said, while sitting with us,

"This man, this Von Ludendorff he'll have information coming into him, even from people living here on the Island."

"I think that must be the case Rob, you're right, he's going on what people here have told him. Our biggest problem now is getting back into those tunnels, we just have to be certain that U-boat is down in those waters."

Julian then said, "Listen, why go back down there, if this U-boat is hidden, then find it, dive down and search the sea bottom, it can't be very deep, what would you say Rob?"

"That U-boat could be lying in water no deeper than fifty feet, with the diving gear we have we could start a search, what do you think Eddie?"

"Well we must go into all this once we are back at my place, we must go over every step of the way, it's going to be very difficult with all those people on the shore, less than a mile away, they are bound to see us."

"I'd like to see that wallet thing you found Eddie, you said there were letters in German inside."

"Look, I've had enough drink, why don't we go and have a good look at what's inside the wallet, because I didn't look at all the items inside it."

"OK Eddie, by the way, Rob says you have a few weapons at hand, well, I hope we don't ever have to use them."

"Hope not."

We said goodnight to Rob and walked back to my Villa, it was much later than we thought. When we arrived home, the girls were drinking wine. As we walked in we both shouted goodnight, back came a reply, "Come on and join us"…we did.

Hangovers can be a right pain in the arse…and in the head, it was nine o'clock when I stirred, the sun's rays blazing in through the window. I could hear the others getting up, so I quickly dived into the shower, then made a coffee for myself and walked out to the pool, I then sat down and lit a cigar. Just a few minutes later, Julian came out and joined me.

Even with sunglasses on I kept shielding my eyes from the sun, while there was noise coming from the kitchen as the two girls started on breakfast.

As we sat there Julian said, "This is the life, I could retire here."

"I'll be waiting for you at the airport."

We both went in for a swim while our breakfast got cold, when we came out of the pool, the two girls came out in their bikini's, we gave them a wolf whistle and to my surprise Gloria gave the two fingers. Now that's unbecoming of someone of her standing in life she was upper class, and at times showed it. My wife was the same, they were good friends, and stayed together all the time we were away on 'Jobs' with the Regiment. They had their Ladies Club and flower arranging, the Bridge Club, so they had a lot going, but now my wife misses all that. If Julian moves out here, he is well enough off and, like myself, he too, can retire even on his Army Pension.

Julian and I grabbed the cold bacon and eggs, eat the lot then went into the garage to have a better look at the items in the wallet I found in the safe.

I opened the folder, took out the wallet and some letters, then handed them to Julian, he knew German better than I did. He started reading the first letter and looked at me twice as he continued reading, then he said,

"I now believe you are right about that U-boat."

"What do you mean, I know I am right?"

"This letter helps prove that."

"How come?"

"Listen to this." Julian started reading out what was in the letter he picked out first.

"There was three mark V11 U-boats built, all unmarked on standby. They could travel at 36K per mile with a range of 12880 miles they didn't need to surface, because the engines ran on Hydrogen Peroxide fuel, this is dated February 18th 1945."

Julian looked quickly through the other letters, then said, "well it is very clear, going with what is written on these letters, that Top Ranking Officers and families went to Argentina. Some of the German High Command also went south. Two doctors accompanied the Fuhrer and Eva Braun to Argentina. They left Germany later in the year, doubles were used to ensure no one knew that they had left the country. In all over two hundred and sixty Nazi's and families went to Argentina. Going by these letters Hitler and Braun arrived down south on a Sunday, they were then spirited away to some village, not named here. One thing that stands out, these Nazi's may well have put the idea of taking back the Falkland Islands."

"What...are you serious, what does it say in that letter?"

"Take back what is yours, take it by force."

"Bloody hell, I never thought for a second that the Nazi's would have any influence in that War."

"Well this letter indicates that they did."

"Let's see that letter." Julian handed me the letter and I read through it, there was nothing concrete about the Falklands, but it clearly said, take back what is yours, of course that could mean anything.

"Eddie, that U-boat could have sank off shore and divers made sure it was stripped clear outside, those on board were transferred to another U-boat and they sailed on south.

"Well Julian, even if they did get to Argentina, they are all dead by now, but it is certainly interesting, that part about the Falkland Islands. We did find diving gear down there so just maybe what you say could have happened Julian."

"What happens next Eddie, do we go into the Villa or try something else?"

"Rob should be here soon, we ought to discuss it with him, after all, if we dive, he knows the stuff better than I do, so it's all up to him really."

When Rob turned up, about half an hour later, the first thing I asked him was if we can't entered the Villa, what's our chances diving down and searching for the U-boat?"

He replied, "Eddie, let's try and see if we can gain entrance first, if that's a no go, then I can get all the gear we require but we must do it in daylight. At least to get familiar with the dive, and diving down there has its dangers, the currents can pull you out if you're not careful, so I hope if the U-boat is down there, let's hope it's pretty close in to the shoreline."

"I hope not too close," said Julian, I have to stand on the boat fishing, who knows who could be watching?"

I then said, "Just make sure you look the part, maybe you just might catch a fish!"

"Oh, don't worry, I will catch something, that's for sure."

"I bet you will, too, Julian," said Rob.

"OK, what is next, do we try to get inside the Villa? We could get spotted, or do we settle on the diving?"

Rob butted in saying, "Well, I can get a boat, diving gear and anything else we might need along those lines."

Julian then said, "There is no way I am diving, let me make that very clear."

"Don't worry Julian, Rob and I will be doing that. Well if there is an emergency."

"I don't dive Eddie, just like you won't climb mountains anymore."

I left it at that, because I know Julian got a real scare way back while we did a Course with the Royal Marines. His tank malfunctioned and he was lucky to come out of it alive. My thing with climbing was in Africa, I was trapped with nowhere to move up Mount Lilimanjaro, no lifelines nothing, it scared the shit out of me looking down thousands of feet. I had to look away and close my eyes, holding on to what I had, until eventually help came. I swore then no more climbing for me, terra firma thank you very much."

"Right, so it's agreed we will not go near the Villa Winter and concentrate on finding the U-boat by diving down and searching the seabed."

"When will we go Eddie?"

"Tomorrow morning early."

"Right, I'd better arrange for the boat and diving gear to be delivered to the harbour down there. You two call into my Bar later and we'll have a few drinks."

Off went Rob, with that distinct swagger of his.

To kill time I took Julian around the town of Caleta de Fuste, showing him some of the hotels and apartments that were for use whenever he wanted a holiday, and my wife and I was not on the Island. The Harbour was small with a few boats anchored there, just off to our right is the manmade sandy beach, it's well done. There is a round Castle, which the resort is named after, further down the coast is the Golf Club. On a Saturday there is an open air market, and there are so many things on offer, you can knock down the prices even in some shops.

There is a large complex with several swimming pools in its grounds because the seafront is covered in black rocks, not any sand at all and pretty dangerous to walk over…but interesting to see…it reminds people that these Islands once were live volcano's.

The next morning, the doorbell rang, then I heard hammering on the front door. I got up half-naked, with my pup tripping me up as I half ran to the door.

It was Rob.

"You were to meet me an hour ago at the harbour."

"Just give me a minute…. come in. We had a heavy night if you know what I mean."

As I moved to my room to get dressed, Julian came out already fully dressed, ready to go…. I said, "thanks for giving me a call."

"I thought you were already up."

In the back of Rob's Landrover, I could see small picks and shovel handles poking up, fishing rods, and covered over was the diving gear. The idea was that Julian and whoever wasn't down in the water would be fishing. There would be a lifeline fixed to any diver going down.

After we all got into Rob's car, no one said a word all the way down to the harbour, even once we arrived, we loaded up all the gear and Rob took the boat out. We were heading south from Caleta de Fuste down the coast to Morro Jable, round the foot of the Island then up the coast to the area called Cofete. We gave a wide berth to Villa Winter, we could see all the people working away. The Villa itself had now been cordoned off there were more men patrolling around the perimeter. Rob anchored the boat about a mile off shore, so we got out the fishing rods, making sure anyone watching us saw the rods. Rob, who had done this sort of thing before, was going down first to quickly find the wreck and get back on board.

We threw in our fishing rods as Rob slipped over the side and into the blue water. Surprise, surprise, Julian had caught a fish, we both struggled to hold it, and at the same time I had Rob's lifeline tied to my wrist. Ten minutes later I too, caught a fish, not as big as the one Julian had caught, but still a good size. I felt a tug on the lifeline, then soon after that Rob surfaced he slipped into the boat, which was a small cabin cruiser. He moved quickly into the cabin where we helped him get off the gear.

"Well Rob, any luck, did you see anything at all down there?"

"Nothing Eddie, I feel we need to move north a little maybe two hundred yards or so. Remember, those tunnels were coming at an angle. If we look at the Villa, we have to be on the far side of it that's actually northwest… I need you down there with me Eddie, we'll cover more ground that way."

"Well, take a break and have a look at the two fish we caught."

"What! You actually caught something!"

"Sure we did, and look at the size of the one Julian pulled in."

Rob held the fish then said, "They could feed a whole family of four."

Half an hour later, after having a good look around, to make sure no one was watching us, Rob and I slipped into the sea on the side of the boat away from the shoreline. We dived down forty, fifty feet then spread out about ten feet apart, slowly going over the sea bottom. We both knew if any U-boat was down here it would be covered in coral and weeds. Fish swam past us, some of them very big. Rob came over to me and took out his dagger, indicating for me to take out mine, so we were ready if attacked by any fish.

We were ready to go back up when Rob swam over to me

pointing at a mound in the seabed. We went over to it and checked it out. Before we got the chance, Julian was pulling on our lifeline, we knew something was up so we made out way to the surface as quickly as we could.

We popped our heads out of the water, Julian signalled for us to stay low. There was a Police Patrol boat moving in on the boat. Luckily for us the Patrol boat did a long sweep in towards us, this gave us time to get out of the sea, onto the boat and grab a fishing rod.

The Police boat came along side and Julian held up his large fish, I grabbed another one. "Keep smiling, they'll probably go away," said Rob.

They gave us a wave and we waved back, Rob had said that they patrol the Island day and night, stopping drugs coming in from Africa. We didn't move until they were well away and almost out of sight.

"We may as well have our break now, then we go down again," said Rob. We had tea and sandwiches with chicken and tomatoes, fresh ones.

I asked Rob, "How deep were we?"

"About seventy feet, just over that, so it's not too bad, I'm hoping that mound is the U-boat."

"Do you think you have found it then?" asked Julian.

"Could be, there is metal there, my magnet stuck to something, so we are heading straight to that spot when we go back down."

Over at the Villa Winter the Archaeologists had arrived on the site, a large digger rumbled over the rocks as Security checked out everyone entering the site.

Down we went again, Rob and I, a huge fish just missed me as it shot past me, then a smaller shoal of fish swam by. Rob swam towards the mound on the seabed, I followed close behind him. Rob used the magnet and then his small hand pick, I helped remove lumps of coral as Rob pointed to an area where I had just lifted a large piece of coral from. There, in full view was a door, an airtight hatch door, Rob stuck up his thumb, I did too. There was a clear outline of a hatch and it would need cleaning up if we had any chance of getting it open.

Rob signalled for us to go up, so up we went.

Back on board I was quick to point out that there should be another hatchway, they are the escape route from the torpedo room I am almost certain about that. I have drawings of this type of U-boat. I'm sure there are four of these hatchways.

"You're right Eddie, there should be four hatchways, we can find it tomorrow."

"What do you mean tomorrow, what's wrong with right now?"

"We have dived enough for one day Eddie, there's no point in pushing our luck. At least we have found the U-boat, now we want all the materials that will help us get those doors opened up."

"They're hatchways Eddie."

"I know that Rob, it just seems easier saying doors."

"Right you two," said Julian, "Let's sort out all these fish."

While we were diving Julian had caught many fish, enough to fill up a large pail.

"Hey Julian, you did very well catching all those," said Rob.

"I had more, threw in the small ones, I just threw them back into the sea."

When we arrived back at my villa, Julian called out to the two girls, they were having a swim in the pool.

"Got some fish for supper, really good ones," they just waved and my wife shouted, "don't take them inside, leave them out here until we cook them."

I left the fish in a bag, while Julian fetched another one from the kitchen. I tied up two plastic bags and left the fish out on the porch.

I looked out the drawings I had of the U-boat and we sat down with a drink and looked at it.

Rob had gone home and had made sure the boat was berthed safely he would be calling up soon. So Julian and I studied this U-boat a formidable war machine. Julian and I sat drinking, as we waited for Rob. While looking at the drawing, Julian said,

"I didn't think these submarines or as the Germans call them, U-boats, were so big. Mind you, there doesn't seem to be too much space to move about in."

"That's right Julian, there was very little space." I pointed out that there was in fact, four escape compartments and not two as I first thought.

Rob had just joined us, so I let him have a good look at the drawings, it was in detail showing the full length of the U-boat. After having a good look at the U-boat Rob said,

"Those escape compartments may be just what we need. If they still work we can use them to bring up the gold, it needs you and me again Eddie."

"Explain yourself Rob," said Julian.

"Well you can use those escape compartments to get out AND into that U-boat. Some of the crew's bunks are right below them near the torpedo bay and tubes. If we get the generator going we're home and dry. There is the danger that the torpedoes could be damaged, we must check them before we do anything else.

"We'll do that Rob, but I feel I'd better copy this drawing, so we have one each, and keep it with you all the time we go down there."

"And another thing, take those weapons with you, and we might need some explosives, you know, just in case."

"Just in case what Rob?" asked Julian.

"Just in case those hatches don't open."

"You can use explosives on those, you'll let everyone know we are down there."

"On second thoughts maybe that's not a good idea."

"Thoughts hatches will open, they have been covered in coral that helps to protect it."

Julian asked, "Where will the gold be stored?"

I looked at Rob, then answered Julian,

"Well they may well have used the areas where ballast is placed along the bottom of the U-boat. That would be amidships, front and rear, normally there are four areas. I'm hoping we can get the generator working, then we have lights, because no lights makes the search much more difficult."

"Eddie, you and I need to study the layout so we know where to go, even in the dark with torches."

"Or just in the dark, if the batteries go."

"How about getting a camera," said Julian. "I could be watching you two as you move about down there, radio contact as well."

I looked at Rob waiting to hear what he might have to say. Rob thought for a moment then said,

"That is a great idea Julian, not only can you see us, but if we have a probe, we can see even in the dark or areas we cannot see into."

I then asked, "Where are we going to get something like that?"

All was quiet, none of us knew where we could get this type of camera.

"Look up the Internet Eddie, must be something there."

If I did find a place we now had the finances to buy the damn thing…I got on the Internet and saw a firm in England, Surrey, that dealt in these sort of things. Looking at it, there was a helluva lot of equipment to carry. Well I ordered it there and then. It would take four to five days to reach us. Julian and Rob were having a look at the equipment there was, as I said, a lot of it, some of it heavy. Thank goodness it didn't have to be carried up to the Villa that would have been impossible.

"OK, now that's been sorted out, what next?" asked Rob.

"Well we keep fishing and looking for the rest of those escape compartments, open one, see if we can find and clear the others. Because that's the way in and out of that U-boat with whatever gold we find down there."

"If we find this gold, how do we stand by the Law?" asked Rob.

Julian answered, "Maritime Law states, the country of origin owns the gold, but we get salvage rights, that can be considerable. Depends on how much we find."

"Well, with what I have read in the Archives, there is still over two hundred tons of gold missing."

"Are you sure Eddie," asked Julian.

"Of course I am, why do you think we are doing this?"

As we looked over the drawings, the two girls walked past us stirring the pup… "Robbie," I called him as he was running around the girls. He came straight back to me and sat down at my feet.

"You know, I remember you doing that back in England with your other Robbie, I was real sorry when I heard what happened to him Eddie."

"Me too Julian… me too."

"I was unsighted when it happened, bloody fool, said he thought it was a rabbit, I heard the shot and ran like hell. When I saw old Robbie lying there I knew he was dead, as I lifted him up I couldn't see for tears."

Julian quickly cheered me up saying, "Well look at that lovely pup at your feet, you'll soon have him well trained, he comes to you on command already."

"Collies are like that, they know who their Master is."

We could hear someone shouting out, "Fish is ready!"

We walked into the kitchen and I said, "What did you put on the fish?"

"Oh don't worry Eddie, it's as you like it, and your favourite wine is there too."

"Thank you my love." A kiss on the cheek and I sat down with young Robbie at my feet.

All four of us sat down, with two bottles of white and red wine sitting in the centre of the table.

Gloria said, "Who wants white wine?"

June said, "Me thanks."

I poured out the red for Julian and I, we both knocked it back quickly so I refilled the glasses, this time right to the top. Large bowls of carrots, turnip, potatoes, and sauces filled up the table.

The fish was just lovely and I took my fill before heading out to sit by the pool and light a cigar, because June did not allow me to smoke inside… and anyway I wouldn't do that. Julian joined me by the pool and little Robbie came too, he sat looking up at me, while I made sure the fish I had was bone free. I sat it at my feet, he looked up at me, then I said, "Take it." It was gone in a flash.

As we sat quietly by the pool, the sea breeze cooled the now evening air. Julian said, "Eddie, this U-boat, or more to the point… this gold, where did it come from?"

"The Nazi's looted all the Banks across Europe, tons of the stuff, that's history, some people thought it was buried in the Bavarian Mountains, but what went there was peanuts. A huge amount was being moved by U-boat to Argentina, that U-boat was the one taking the gold down there, unfortunately it was attacked by British Warships and limped its way to the staging post to Argentina… Fuerteventura. We now know it is down there, all we have to do is get inside it and find the gold."

"How are we going to get it up out of there?"

"There should be floats, pretty large ones, we can use them to get the gold up."

"If, as you say, there are tons of the stuff, how can all that weight be lifted up onto the boat, that's providing you get those hatches opened. Is there no other way Eddie?"

"There might be Julian, the torpedoes, they used to use them to send up bits and pieces through the tubes to make it look like the U-boat had been 'Hit'. We could use them."

"What about the bridge, surely you can get in there?"

"Julian, there is nothing been left, the bridge, the machine gun position, they are gone. The U-boat was stripped bare on top, that's why it was so hard to find."

"They must have sealed it from inside."

"That's what they have done Julian, then used the escape compartments to get out, or maybe they went out from the bottom into those tunnels."

"Why don't we get into those tunnels and see for ourselves, why not now Eddie, tonight?"

"Are you sure about that."

"Look, I may not like diving, but I am not afraid to get down into those tunnels and go right to the end of them."

"OK, let's do it, we better tell Rob."

Once I told Rob he was all for it, so at 2300 hours we made our way back down to Villa Winter. This time we had to move quietly with cunning and stealth. There was no moon, but as soon as we came into view of the Villa, it was lit up like a fairground. This wasn't going to be easy, with two men patrolling around the Villa, floodlights lighting up the whole Villa and other people working in the large open tents, some sorted out rocks others worked on computers.

We sat well in the shadows, watching the two men on patrol.

Now one of us had to get in there and get that hidden trapdoor open and ready for the other two. Rob would go in. We were a fair distance away from the Villa, we watched through binoculars the movement of the two men on patrol. They met at the far side of the Villa where the track came right up to the entrance.

Julian and I counted every step they took…several times and each time we came to the same number. We could only watch the man nearest to us and he took one hundred and forty seven steps, so we had on the safe side, a minute and a half to get from where we were, in to the trapdoor. Watching for Rob's signal one quick flash of his torch, and we were on the move.

As you look in from the sea, we were coming from the left close to the mountains, moving as fast as we could over the rough terrain. Julian tripped up and I helped him up, we ran on and just made it by seconds, right into the shadows of the Villa and tower where Rob waited for us.

Rob let us into the secret passageway, then he stood guard while we went down to the cave and tunnels.

Rob quickly moved away from the hidden trapdoor and took up position in the tower, from there he could see all around the Villa, he was well hidden in the shadows. He made one radio call to make sure we were OK.

In the tunnel Julian answered his call.

"We are fine Rob, Eddie is sending his probe down the tunnel to check for gas, call you if we need you…over."

The probe I sent out ran for over twenty minutes with two breaks as it stopped due to obstructions, as I checked the readout it showed the temperature very low at 23 degrees.

The actual distance the probe had travelled was not clear, simply because it stopped and maybe travelled along a joining tunnel, the gas shown was very low, so it was safe for us to proceed. We put on the warm jackets we had left here before, then started walking.

Dark and damp, cold and wet as we moved quite fast down the tunnel. The ground sloping away from us as it ran downhill. There was two joining tunnels, it became slippery and we fell several times, then it was bone dry and we came to an area that opened up. Once into this area we saw the other door, it looked like it had just been put there, Julian got it open, there was a sudden rush of air, as the air now circled around the tunnels.

Julian walked into the other tunnel where he found tools inside a metal container, there was a step ladder and torches inside. Julian brought out two of the torches, they were much better than the ones we had. As we shone the torches about, both beams came to rest in the same place, up on the roof of the cave at the end of the tunnels.

There, right in the middle of the roof of the cave was a hatchway door. We looked at each other, and suddenly Julian ran into the other tunnel and brought out the ladder.

"Do you want to go first or will I?" asked Julian.

"Go ahead Julian, but open that hatch slowly, we don't want to be flooded out."

I checked out the drawing I had of the U-boat, making sure I had the bearings right once we entered.

"Julian."

"What Eddie?"

"Here, tie this rope onto your belt."

Julian stopped trying to open up the hatch, tied on the rope then continued turning the wheel on the hatchway. A loud click, then two small turns and it opened. I shone the torch onto the drawing then climbed inside.

"I think we are midship, near where the main periscope comes down, the main control room is off to the left, just go slowly Julian, we have to find where the diesel generator is, it may still work."

Even with the help of torches it was very difficult to move, there was little or no space as we picked out way through the tubes and piping. We passed a row of hammocks as we moved through to the engine room, further on we eventually found the large generator, and it had eleven dials, big ones, and nine smaller ones.

While I held both torches, Julian got to work on the generator. He was talking about bleeding and how to fire it up, then all of a sudden the lights came on.

"That's just what we need Julian, take a look at the panel there it gives all the details needed to keep that running."

"Yes, I know that Eddie, now let's move forward and find those escape compartments."

We moved much faster now, passing the moving past the hammocks and the main periscope, we came to the radio room. We went inside, it looked like it had just been left yesterday. The radio room had two small filing cabinets, a desk, two radio's and locked in a small cupboard was one big surprise. Julian lifted out an Enigma machine, there was three and all the codebooks were there.

"This U-boat must have been very important to have these on board," said Julian.

"How does it work Julian?"

"Well messages are sent with code one, then they are typed out into the first machine then the second one and then you have the message sent, pretty ingenuous piece of work Eddie, wouldn't you say."

"Absolutely Julian."

"We better move on and find those compartments."

"You go ahead Julian, it's straight all the way then at the torpedo room we need to go up through a hatch, they should be just above the bunk-beds in that area."

"I don't see any gold Eddie."

"Of course you won't see any, it will be right at the base of the U-boat, probably replacing the ballast. So it could be well spread out from the front to the rear, but we only need to check out one area, if we find any gold, then it's here."

Up through one door then another until we reached the forward sleeping quarters, there were eighteen bunks all folded up neat and tidy, they still had blankets in them.

A hatchway, just before we came to all the bunk beds, was they way had towards the escape compartments.

I kept looking back to make sure Julian was right behind me, he was and was asking all sorts of questions that I couldn't answer. At last we came to the compartments all four of them.

"Do you know how these work Eddie?"

"No, but Rob does, let's go and find the gold."

"So where do we go?"

"Follow me Julian and stay close."

I retraced our route and arrived back at the Radio room, from there I went down into an area where ballast would be, there was strong metal brides that supported the outer frame of the U-boat and thick metal girders and pipes everywhere. Julian stopped me, he moved over piping and took out his torch to see what lay on the floor. His head turned towards me very quickly,

"There's something down there."

"Can you see what it is?"

"No Eddie, it's covered over give me your hand."

I held Julian's hand so he could reach over all the pipes, he pulled away the cover to reveal wooden boxes. They were tied together in threes by metal strips. I pulled Julian back up and we looked around for anything metal to get a box opened up. I found a large spanner and we went back to the spot, one smash with the spanner split open the box and out fell bars of gold, we stood there with our mouths open. The next words that were spoken came from Julian as he said, "Oh boy, hum, hum look at those!"

I grabbed two bars and said, "Here, stick one of these in your pocket. When I say so bring them out in front of Rob…now let's get to hell out of here."

We moved back to the tunnel after switching off the generator, I filled up the diesel tank because we would need it running again. Down through the bottom hatch and I made sure it was fully closed. We raced along the tunnel, once inside the cave under the Villa I made a quiet call on the radio to Rob.

"We've been in and now we are coming out, let's know when to come out…over."

"All those floodlights are blazing and I was getting worried about you two…stand by…the two guards are this side of the Villa, have you any good news for me?…over."

"Check out those guards…we don't want to be caught at this stage of the mission…over."

"Stand by…stand by… Ok go, go, go."

Out we came with Julian closing the trapdoor and double checking it was secure, then off we ran across the rocks and dusty brown sand between the rocks. We reached the shadows inside thirty-four seconds and once clear started walking to the area where the vehicle was left.

When we were almost at the vehicle, the unthinkable happened. One of Von Ludendorff's men approached us as we moved to the vehicle. He pointed a gun at me and asked in German, "What are you doing here?"

I answered back in English, "We always come here fishing."

He looked us over then said, this time in English. "So you can speak German," I nodded a yes. He reached for his pocket and pulled out a camera. That's when Rob clobbered him. We jumped into the vehicle and moved away as fast as we could.

"That's something we didn't need, they'll soon be on to us."

"They might be Julian, just depends on what that guy says about us, all I said was we were fishermen, anyway we shall stay alert. The good thing now is this, we don't have to go back in there. It will all be from the boat from now on."

Rob was driving and he had asked several times about if we had found anything, meaning of course, the gold. Being well away now from Cofete I asked Rob to stop, he pulled in and stopped, that's when Julian and I took out the gold bars and dropped them into his lap.

"Oh my God, you've found it! I just can't believe it, you were right all along Eddie, how much are they worth?"

"I haven't a clue Rob, they are worth a lot of money and there's a lot more where they came from."

"Unbelievable Eddie, unbelievable!"

"I would have to agree with that, now let's get back home."

Rob pulled back onto the road and we headed back to Caleta de Fuste and over the hill to my villa, with a good night's work done.

"So how much is down there Eddie?"

"Well it's difficult to give a figure, but I'd say there must be at least two hundred tons"…

"What?" shouted Julian. "I couldn't put a price on that."

Rob said, "It's a helluva lot of gold, how do we get it up? One thing's certain, we can't bring it up those tunnels."

"Well Rob, we saw the four escape compartments, we can use them to get inside the U-boat, there's an option on how we get it out, use the compartments or the torpedo tubes."

"That small boat could hold half of half that weight."

"There is the floats, we can use them but they might be unstable, we can try them out."

Julian suggested we use nets to catch the floats as they are ejected from the tubes. I thought it a good idea but then Rob butted in saying it wouldn't work, they would be seen easily.

I then said, "But how do we move all that weight without being seen?" Silence can be golden sometimes, but not in times like this. No one said a word, then Julian said, "Why don't we get a small submarine?"

"Spot on Julian," said Rob. "I know where to get one."

I then said, "You do... Where?"

"From the same man who owns the boat we are using."

"How big is it?"

"Eddie, this thing can take ten people, now that's a lot of weight, well isn't it?"

"Could it take two more people?" asked Julian.

Rob answered, "Why two more?"

"Well, with the average holidaymaker weighing in at eleven stone we could lift or pull one ton at a time on those floats."

I then said, "Now we are getting somewhere, when can you book this mini-Sub Rob?"

"Just say the word Eddie, we can have it for a few days if need be."

"Wait for a couple of days until this gear I ordered arrives from the U.K. then we are in business."

Things seemed to be coming together, but we needed to get down to that U-boat and enter through the escape compartments. So that was our next move. We just had to get into that U-boat because the tunnels were out of our plans now…we would have to ways of getting the gold up, through the compartments or by using the torpedo tubes."

"I suppose we ought to use the time waiting for that gear, to look for a place where we can launch the mini-Sub, then get into the water and deal with those hatches down there," said Julian.

"Tomorrow we will go fishing along the coast way past the Villa Winter. See if we can find a place to put the Mini-Sub into the water. If we can't find a suitable area, then someone has to steer it down the coast to the U-boat."

Back at my Villa, Julian and I hid the gold bars from out wives. We went into the garage and put the bars into a small safe I had under a workbench.

"Come, let's sit by the pool. I'll open a couple of bottles of wine, take a seat you two."

We three sat drinking while the 'girls' were busy flower arranging, something they loved doing back in the U.K. while Julian and I were on a 'Job'. We sat in the shade, the sun was burning up the paving stones around the pool, and young Robbie sat under my chair in the shade. The large parasol kept us cool, of course I did have a huge fan that we could use if it got unbearably hot, it was only good if you were in the shade, but it did cool you down.

Eventually we all went into the pool for a swim it was warm. Rob joked about getting a bucket full of ice to dump in it, to cool it down.

Rob, Julian and myself challenged each other to see who could swim the furthest under water. Rob was younger than us, so he did have the advantage, we all managed two lengths of the pool, however, Rob went further almost three, which was pretty good. When we sat down Rob asked me,

"How much gold is down there Eddie?"

"All I can say is this, the gold is all in boxes, stacked three high…

how much there is we won't know until we check out the whole U-boat, we must weigh one of those boxes, then count how many are there. Rob, what if we use the tubes, how do we go about that?"

"Well Eddie, the tubes should be covered with sand, this means less force when they are released. What we need is for one of us to be outside with a large net, if we use the tubes and those floats, the gold can easily be removed this way. We need strong toe-lines attached to the nets, these can then be attached to the mini-Sub and towed away."

"That sounds OK, but we need a backup plan, I suppose that would have to be the boat."

"Why don't we get on with the Job, we don't need all that fancy stuff you ordered," said Rob.

"I think you're right Rob, we could get on with getting those escape hatches opened, so what are you suggesting?"

"Let's get down there and open those bloody things, that gear you ordered from the U.K. can wait, it'll come whether you're here or down in the sea."

"Our best time is to going down to those escape compartments is during daylight," said Rob, then he continued, "Julian can do the fishing while you and I Eddie, take turns going down."

"You do know we have to be more than just cautious," said Julian. "We have to think the way we were trained in the Army, to leave no clues, not even a shit. That means for a start we can't drive down to the harbour, that means leaving a vehicle with Eric Von Ludendorff's men snooping around it would let them know we are out at sea."

We were working out exactly what our next move would be, it was obvious we couldn't bring anything up those tunnels, so now it was all or nothing. Everything now rested on us being able to get the gold out through the escape compartments or the torpedo tubes. To be honest, I wasn't keen on any of them.

We used a truck to get the gear down to the harbour during the night, loading all the gear we would require. Luckily, there was no one about. We quietly slipped out of the harbour and sailed down the coast around the tail of the Island and up past the Villa Winter. It was pitch black, no moon and no lights anywhere, even at the Villa.

"That's odd," said Julian. "There's no lights on, those people digging must be finished."

We moved more to the northwest about a mile out from the Villa, Julian stood watch as Rob and I geared up to dive.

All we had to do was clear all four escape hatches and hope we could get them open. We swam slowly along the bottom to where Rob had found the hatch. We measured off the distance and soon found the other three hatches. Now we worked to get then cleared of coral and anything else stuck to them. It was hard work chiselling away all the coral. We had to go back up, as the oxygen was low, at least we had now found all four hatches. Back on board Julian asked if we had been successful, I said yes. Rob knew more about diving and about submarines than Julian and I, so I looked to him from quidence.

We sat taking some coffee, and a bite to eat, as Rob explained what was needed next.

"When we go back down, we need to get the two hatches with the bar handles, they open the hatches, there should be two, this is the two we can enter…if we get them open. Once inside, we pull a lever this is done after you close the hatch, it will then fill up, we will be in our diving gear so we are safe enough, once the chamber is full pull the lever down and it will empty the chamber into the U-boat. Once we get the generator going that won't happen again, the water will be dumped back into the sea. So we can come and go through these compartments, this helps a great deal, because we have a search to find where all the gold lies, then I have to check out the torpedo tubes, make sure they still work."

Break over, down we went again, this time we checked the two other escape compartments, we had them working. It was a tight squeeze down here, not much room to move anywhere, there were valves all over the place, and we would often hit ourselves off them…

bloody sore sometimes. We went forward to the torpedo bays and Rob looked over the firing mechanism.

"Well Rob, what do you think, are they OK?"

"Look OK Eddie, but we need the generator running then I will try them."

We moved aft and past the radio room, into the engine room and Rob got to work straight away, within a couple of minutes he had the place lit up and the generator pumping away. We went back to the torpedo room and I watched as Rob worked away at the wheels and levers, he watched the dials, all the time I could hear the rush of something but wasn't sure what it was.

There was a swoooosssh, a thump and Rob turned to me and said, "They work Eddie, they're still working after all these years that's unbelievable."

"Right, where's all this gold?"

"I'd say midship or slightly off midship, right down at the very bottom."

We scrambled over pipes and other structures just down below where the radio room is, and I was surprised it wasn't as cold as I thought it might be. We poked about looking in every dark corner, then I decided to go to where I found the boxes. On closer inspection, we could see that all the boxes were in fact, bounded together in groups of three, this was probably to stop them moving about.

As we stood there looking at the boxes of gold I asked, "Are you sure Rob we can safely go out of those torpedo tubes?"

"It can be done, but we can use them to get the gold out of here, our main way out is through those escape compartments, how much gold is here Eddie?"

"We won't know until we count every box."

"Look, there's where you must have got the two bars from, it's broken open."

"That's it Rob, let's see just how many are in a box."

NAZI GOLD

I pulled the top off the box and counted sixteen bars of gold.

"How much does that lot weigh?" asked Rob.

"There's a weighing thing in that radio room, get it Rob."

Rob returned and I weighed the bar, then three more just to make sure they all weighed the same, they did.

"Come on Rob, we better split up and make a count, don't miss any."

"How far will I go Eddie, what do you think?"

"You know these Subs better than me don't go any further than the engine room, get right down to the bottom, it should be all neatly stacked in those boxes."

Rob walked off and I got in behind all the pipes and structure to get at the row of boxes, some were three high others were four, five and six high, all well strapped together, from below the radio room and filling all this section. I made sure of my count as I did it four times, in total there was 268 boxes and that's a hellva weight to move. I moved aft to check with Rob, I found him kneeling down and with paper and pen in his hand he turned to face me and said, "Almost done."

"That's it, I counted 240 boxes, how about you?"

"I got 268 boxes, so there is a total of 543 boxes with sixteen bars in each, that is a lot of gold."

"Yeh and we have to lift the bloody lot of it, how much Eddie?"

"I've no idea Rob, but I would say around 200 to 250 million."

"My God Eddie, all that much!"

"Yes Rob, all that much, and there could be more in the places we haven't looked at yet."

"Eddie it will take us ages to move all this stuff."

"Yeh I know, that's what I've been thinking about, how to move it, we've to lift every single box over loads of obstructions, and they don't us much if we drop a box. Well Rob, we know we need to get them all into the torpedo bay, and all those floats too, it could take days to get it done."

"We've no choice Eddie, we can't ask Julian down to help, we need him up top. We must weigh those bars and get the total so we can split the loads once we start blasting it out of those torpedo tubes."

"Just how many floats do we have?"

"I'm not sure Eddie, but more than enough, one of those can float a large gun."

"Come on, let's get out of here, we better switch off the generator, then get back on that boat."

So far all went well, now we put back on the diving gear as Rob prepared the escape compartments. I got in and he did too, we came out and surfaced with Julian looking at the wrong area. It was still and calm, the moon lit up the sea with a long stretch of light shining across the water. Julian helped us out of the sea and had warm coffee ready for us. The two of us sat there drinking the coffee, knowing full well that Julian was dying to know what we had found.

"Well, are you not going to tell me what you found?"

"'Course we are Julian," said Rob. "We found a whole lot of gold in neat boxes, 543 of them."

"What? Aah come on, how much did you really find?"

"He just told you Julian, that's what's down there."

"But Eddie, that's a gold mine you found."

"I know Julian, and we are all rich," said Rob as he mouthed more coffee.

"How are you going to get all that up here?"

"We will use floats and the torpedo tubes, Rob will be in charge of that."

"It will take days to move all those boxes," said Julian.

"Eddie, you're good with figures, how long will it take you and me to move them?"

"Ok, now let's see, we take a box each from the two stacks, say it takes five minutes to get them to the torpedo bay. We have 543 boxes…oh my, it will take 45,46 hours to move it all. No wait, that's wrong, we move two at a time in five minutes, so I reckon it will take us over twenty hours to get it all up to the torpedo bays, and that's without a break."

Julian then said, "Is there no other way to move the gold?"

Rob said, "Yeh, you could blow the fuckin' thing out of the water."

"Look," said Julian, "I'm trying to be serious here, is there anything else that can be done? The two of you will be knackered in no time at all, you're lifting heavy boxes."

"Julian, Rob and I will have to man handle them, it's a tough task but we have no choices."

Rob started the engine and we headed back to Caleta de Fuste tired but happy that we had finally found the gold. But it was far from over, we had a stiff job on our hands, and we left ourselves vulnerable to any attack by Von Ludendorff's men, we all knew they were snooping around, but as yet no one had come near us. Now we had the gold things might change for the worst.

We were pretty sure no one followed us, we made a point of doubling back on route, waiting and then going on, so we were certain no one saw us at the site.

The truck we came in was left at the garage, belonging to a friend of Rob's. Julian and I walked it back to my villa where we expected to be met by our wives. It was just after 8.30 a.m. and there was no one at home.

"The car is in the garage Eddie," said Julian as he ran around the back to check the pool area.

As I met Julian inside having checked all the rooms, he said, "I don't like this Eddie, there is something wrong here."

"They've been taken Julian, kidnapped."

We re-checked every room, then went outside and went around the villa even looked in the cars, my wife's and mine…

"Will I call the Police?" asked Julian as Rob came up the driveway.

"No wait, I'll contact the men I know in the Police force, they will get things moving."

"I'll kill the bastards if they harm my wife," shouted Julian. "Is this the work of thugs?"

Rob answered him, "There's no lowlife here on this Island Julian, this must be the work of Von Ludendorff."

It wasn't long after Rob called his Police friends, they arrived and asked loads of questions. While they were in the villa with us the phone rang, I quickly picked it up. I said 'hello', then listened to a voice demanding we hand over the gold, what I was being told over the phone I relayed to the others.

They want the gold. I said then

they gold was sold…for how much?

I said 200,000, where did you get this gold?

"Hooked it in our fishing nets about two miles out from the harbour."

"Are you sure it was two miles from the harbour?"

"Yes, I am sure."

"I will contact you later."

"Yeh, hold on, where's our wives?"

The man hung up.

It was the next morning I was told to go up to Corralejo, then take the ferry to Lanzarote. "I will be in touch," then he added, "I see you have the Police involved that won't help you," he finished by saying, "that gold you sold belongs to the German Federal Banks." The phone went dead.

The others could hear the conversation, so I didn't need to repeat it.

With so much money involved the Bank needed three days before they could give me the 200,000.

Another phone call, this time my wife spoke to me, all they were allowed to say was that they were OK.

I explained we had to wait three days because the Bank needed time for that amount to be delivered.

"Mister Blake, I will see you on Friday."

"I'll be there."

While we waited the Police had traced a letter that had been sent to an address in Lanzarote from a Marketing Firm in Esseh Germany. It tied in with those archaeologists down at the Villa Winter, they were now closing in on the Kidnappers. We still had to take all that money to Lanzarote, and I can tell you this much, if any of us, meaning Rob, Julian and myself got whoever was doing this…we would kill them.

This man, Eric Von Ludendorff was like a fox, Police have been trying to capture him for years, the Police here had already found out that three ships left Germany and one of them docked in the harbour in Lanzarote. It had come from the northern town of Bremerhaven, another ship came from Hamburg.

The Police were certain Von Ludendorff was on one of these ships. One of the ships was registered to Essen Marketing, Police felt sure this was in fact, Von Ludendorff's ship. They searched it as the three of us arrived on the Ferry. We were not allowed on to the ship, but we were having none of that, once the Police cleared off, we slipped on board. It was a lovely ship with ten cabins, when checking the cabins Rob found a message written on a mirror in one of the toilets. It read, Taken to old town at 600 hours.

I was driving my own car and I knew where the old town was, in fact, I once had a villa up the hill from it. We went there by taxi because my car would be well known by now. Just before the old town we turned up the hill to our right, there were rows of villas with a central pool area.

But it was Julian who drew our attention to a much larger villa way over on our right. It was painted white with large iron gates at the front entrance they were painted black. High walls surrounded the villa. We watched as a Landrover raced up the hill and as the gates opened up it went inside. We could see who was in the vehicle, it certainly wasn't Von Ludendorff.

We approached the villa form the left side, there was no windows facing us, so we managed to crawl along where pipes had been laid down. A garbage truck was coming up the tarmac road towards the front gates. We jumped on this and got inside then dived into an open door, inside was the waste bins. We hid at the back as the man came in to empty all the bins, three times he came in and out, then he closed the door behind him. We dived outside, we could see an archway and part of a swimming pool, there were some trees and bushes, and some white doves flew around the tower at the rear. Up on a veranda two armed guards walked out of a doorway, this drew our attention up to this veranda. A noise coming from the front, had us looking towards the gate, it was opening, in came a Police car. The Officer came out and walked towards a man, who held out his hand, they shook hands.

"They look real friendly," said Rob.

"They do don't they, that's another thing we have to be aware of… bent cops."

"We can't do much here with those armed guards, but we can get out of here quickly in that Police car," said Julian.

We all ran for the car, got in and rolled the car through the open gates and on down the hill. I was driving the Police car and stopped it just before we reached the hotel at the corner of the main seafront, we all jumped out and grabbed a taxi, our next stop was the harbour. I wanted to check out the ship anchored there.

As we got out of the taxi, Julian said, "Why haven't they phoned us, if they are watching us they can see you are carrying the money, why haven't they phoned?"

"Come on, let's get onto that ship." As I turned to look at Julian and Rob, it didn't look as if there was anyone on board. We had no trouble getting on board, we checked each cabin and then went into a well furnished lounge. Rob eyed the drinks bar saying what would you like, so we sat there drinking then my phone rang, I put it on loud so the other two could hear what was being said.

"Is that Mister Blake?"

"Yes, this is Blake here."

"Do you have the money mister Blake?"

"Yes I have it here."

"Where are you?"

"On your ship and if our wives are not here in half an hour, we will blow this ship to hell."

The phone went dead.

"Eddie, we can't play about with these people, they have our wives."

"I know that Julian…I know that, we need to let them know we won't be pushed around."

"I still say that was a bad move you made."

"We shall see Julian, we shall see."

I went down to the engine room and came back up with a drum, it looked like fuel, and that's what I hoped they would think it was.

"What's in that?" asked Julian.

"Oil I think, it's only a bluff," Rob then said, "I hope it works, these guys have machine guns."

As Rob said that I pulled out my gun, which I had hidden. I lifted up my sweater and they both saw it. Then Rob showed me his. We then looked at Julian, he didn't move, when he did he turned around to show his handgun stuck in to the back of his trousers.

"Well at least we have something to fight back with," said Rob.

"Well, we better spread out," said Julian. "Rob, you and I will stay inside the bridge, Eddie, you stay out in the open, make sure they see that drum."

We waited for a call, it didn't come instead a Landrover and truck came slowly along the quay and stopped about fifty yards away. The man in the Landrover came out and walked towards me. When he was close enough I made sure he saw me looking down at the drum, supposed to be full of petrol. The German walked to within twenty feet away, I then said, "Where are the girls?"

The German said, "Do you have the money?"

I dropped the bag in front of me all the time watching him and the truck. Two men came from the back of the truck holding onto our wives.

Rob and Julian showed themselves, as the man moved forward to check the bag with the money in it. He waved the other two to come forward with our wives. The man quickly picked up the bag and they left. There were tears and hugs and a few questions that went unanswered. The joy at having our wives back put us in a party mood, so when we got back to my villa it was party time, we invited loads of people and as for the gold, it was staying where it was for at least a few days.

I waited two days before I told Julian and Rob that we still had most of the money, I had replaced most of the money with carefully cut paper. I knew I was taking a chance, but I had always planned to meet in the open, so whoever came for the money would not hang around, a quick look was enough, that's how it was.

Well we left the gold and just went about our every day business, Julian and Gloria returned to the U.K. Rob got on with looking after his businesses and I, well I tried something I have always wanted to do...grow my own vegetables. I was quite serious about this, because I was fed up buying the stuff and two days later it had gone off. I had cleared a plot I bought and worked on it getting the ground prepared for seeding, it took me several days working in the early morning and sometimes when the sun had gone down, and odd times Rob would come up and see me. We met often over the next few weeks, sometimes going fishing but very seldom did we talk about the gold.

Three weeks had past since Julian and Gloria had gone home, Rob and I would make sure all our gear was safely secured in a lockup near his home. Mostly everything we needed to get the gold up was stored away all but the mini Sub, we had to rent it. We knew only too well that Von Ludendorff's men would be keeping watch over what we did. So far there was no one who knew where the gold was, on one except the three of us. This find was fantastic once it became public well anything could happen. We still had to bring it up and if we are seen anywhere near that Villa, it was certain we would be in trouble with Von Ludendorff's men. Rob and I when we got together talked about how we could get the job done without being seen. We were up at my vegetable garden when we talked this over.

We came up with all kinds of ways to get the gold out, the best was the little mini Sub, it had lights so we could work at night. We could approach the mini Sub from some distance away, so therefore cutting down any chances that we could be seen. Rob and I planned every move, even though Julian wasn't with us of course we would Julian.

"How do we get the mini Sub down to the area Rob?"

"Stick it on a trailer and cover it over, we can take a wide berth and move north then cut across the country to the other seaboard."

"Is there a way down to the sea from that far north?"

"Sure Eddie, there are several areas that will give us access to the sea, it's a case of picking the right spot."

"Where would you pick Rob?"

"Well, if we move down the seaboard to Ajuy, it gets tougher travelling south, roads are scarce and tracks are bumpy and in places dangerous. But we could still use them, I'll get a detailed map this should help us decide which route to take."

"Julian and I will have to do that, if you take the boat down to the area."

"I don't know about that Eddie, it would give us away, any boat in that area and Von Ludendorff would have his men surround the whole area."

"Are you suggesting we just use the mini Sub?"

"Yes, why not, we can get the job done without anyone seeing us do it."

"Well you do have a point there Rob, but where do we take the gold? There's over two tons of the stuff."

"That is a problem, we need a truck to transport that weight, and there's no way we can get a truck anywhere near the beach. We will need more help Eddie. If we get the gold out, there are these caves, they're under the sea about a mile and a half further along the seaboard, we could use them, the thing is, I don't know how deep they go."

"I can get more men from the U.K. over here at short notice, let's see how things go. These caves they just might come in handy of we get spotted we can lower the gold down into the caves that gives us time to get help down here."

"That's what we will do Eddie, it would stop Von Ludendorff getting his hands on the gold."

"Once all this comes out and the world hears about it, those in Europe will be after this gold, we didn't look at the markings properly but they're definitely Swiss gold in that box we opened."

"Are you sure about that Eddie?"

"Yeh, of course I'm sure. Tell you something Rob, it's going to take some moving getting that gold out of there."

"Don't talk about it too much, it puts you right off. We don't have 200 tons, I thought you said 200 million, that's more like it."

"To tell you the truth Rob, I don't know how much is down there, all I know is it's bloody heavy, and there could be more still to be found. We've only checked the central area, more could lie forward and aft."

Over the next few days, Rob and I got everything prepared for the lift, we even went down through the mountains to find the safest and easiest way to the shore line. When all that was done we just went about our own business, Rob at his Bar and me at my garden 'patch'.

One night I had just finished working in the garden and had jumped into my vehicle, then the phone rang in my pocket. I rumbled about to get it out. It was Rob.

"Hi Eddie, there's someone here in the bar wanting to talk to you."

"Who is it Rob?"

"I'm not sure, but one thing is certain, they are German."

"Is it Von Ludendorff?"

"I'm not sure Eddie, I didn't get a good look at him, but it could be him, fair hair."

"That's him all right, I'll be down shortly Rob."

I called into the Villa and told my wife where I was going, then drove down the hill to Rob's Bar. As I walked in, Rob nodded his head towards the corner of the Bar, two men sat with drinks on the table in front of them. One of these men was indeed, Eric Von Ludendorff. Rob handed me a beer at the bar and I walked over towards the two Germans.

"Aah, good evening Mister Blake," said Von Ludendorff.

I just looked at him and the other men whom I had never seen before.

"Have a seat Mister Blake." I sat down and waited to hear what he had to say.

"I think you know why I am here…I want you to take me to the area where you found those gold bars."

He knows everything I thought to myself. I glanced over at Rob, he had been keeping an eye on things ever since I joined the two Germans. I said I needed Rob with me he was the boatman, the two Germans got to their feet and Von Ludendorff said,

"Very well, shall see you at the harbour at seven o'clock tomorrow morning…thank you for your co-operation."

They both left the Bar and I went over to tell Rob.

"Bloody hell Eddie, you might have told me, I don't know if the boat is free or where it might be."

"Find out Rob, we need it."

"What do you mean WE need it."

"Well I did say I need you as you are the boatman."

"Oh thanks a million Eddie, here I am swanning off with some German nutcase and you didn't even ask me."

"Rob, I need you, you're part of the team now."

" I did my team work in the Falklands, this in a new game."

"You're not pulling out…are you?"

"I'll have to think about this."

"I'll go on my way then."

"No wait Eddie, I don't like letting you down, especially with that lot, but are you sure about this? What happens after we take them out to sea, then what?"

"We'll be OK Rob, trust me."

"OK then, I'll see you in the morning."

I was up early and fed the pup, had some breakfast and then I heard the blast of the horn, it was Rob he had arrived to pick me up. As I got into Rob's car, he said,

"It's rough isn't it, anyway I feel the same, serve you right for going onto that brandy last night."

"You talk to the German I don't feel like it."

"No Eddie, you talk to him." Rob turned on the radio and the noise was terrible.

"Put that bloody radio off."

A cherry-faced German greeted us at the harbour.

"Good morning gentlemen, shall we proceed."

Rob jumped into the boat and I followed with the two Germans coming on as slow as they could. The sea was lovely and blue, the sun blasting down on us, you could feel the rays penetrating your skin. We set sail down the coast, round the bottom of the Island then up past Cofete. The two Germans stood back in the rear of the boat, as I tried to point my hand, indicating to Rob to go further out to sea. We now had Villa Winter in view, the Germans started talking for the first time since we left the harbour. The words Villa Winter seemed just the same in German as it did in English that's what they talked about. Of course I could understand every word as I speak German. So I was in a good position to know what their plans were, once I showed them the area we were suppose to have found the gold bars. "Right Rob, stop the engine."

I turned to the Germans and said, "Here we are, this is the spot we got those bars."

Von Ludendorff then said, "How are you so sure it was here."

I thought for a few seconds and said what just happened to come into my head. "Because we were almost central to the Villa over there, that's why, this is the area."

He then asked, "What side of the boat did you have your nets?"

Rob quickly said, "Over there," pointing to the portside.

Von Ludendorff then took photographs of the shoreline. Rob tried to be helpful by asking him if he wanted the boat moved to another spot.

Von Ludendorff bluntly said, "No thanks, we can go back now."

Rob turned the boat around and headed back to Caleta de Fuste. Von Ludendorff thanked us both and just left, once we arrived back at the harbour.

A couple of days later a letter arrived from none other than Herr Eric Von Ludendorff, obviously he knew of my exploits in the past, he was asking me to join him in finding lost gold. I just couldn't believe it. It was now pretty obvious he had no idea where the gold was. He even sent a cheque to cover all our expenses.

I was on to Rob like a shot.

"Eddie, is this wise helping this nutcase, we could well be going into a trap."

"I doubt that Rob, he needs us, he needs you because you know this Island, he needs me because he knows I am good at finding things like that treasure in Libya, or the Ark of the Covenant in the Yemen. He knows I found these things, so nothing is going to happen to us, we just play along with his game. He wants us to go to Lanzarote to talk about all this."

"What exactly does he want us to do?"

"I don't know Rob, said he would call me again."

No sooner had I talked with Rob, when the land phone rang. I picked it up…it was Von Ludendorff, he wanted us to go to Lanzarote in the morning, he was quite clear that he wanted our help in finding lost gold.

I got in touch with Rob and told him to collect me.

It was quiet on the Ferry across to Lanzarote, there wasn't many people about, mind you, it was early morning. We drove down towards the old town and then up the hill, the black gates of the Villa stood out like a sore thumb.

Moving up the tarmac road, I could see we were being watched all the time, at least three men were watching us through binoculars the shine gave them away.

The Villa grounds were far bigger than I thought they were. Inside, it had lovely lawns and a swimming pool, lots of flowering bushes and hanging baskets of flowers everywhere.

Von Ludendorff greeted us warmly enough, leading the way into a beautiful lounge. As we sat down a manservant put down a tray then poured us out coffee. Once settled down he came out with one hell of a surprise.

"I want you to come to Hamburg with me. There are things you have to see, before you start helping me find this gold."

Rob looked at me, just as I looked over at him, we couldn't think of what to say. I was amazed at the antiques all over the place. Two large Ming Vases sat on a display unit with golden dolphins on each side of them. Paintings decked the walls, this was the most expensive lounge I have ever sat in, and even the seats were specially made.

"You may take all the time you need to decide, there is no hurry once you agree, then we shall fly to Hamburg. I have a ship there with all the underwater equipment that is necessary to search the sea bottom."

"Well, we do need time to talk this over with our families."

"Of course Mister Blake, I do understand, take all the time you need. Here is my card, phone that number when you have decided."

I took the card and stuck it into my pocket, all the time watched by Rob.

We got into Rob's car and looked back as Von Ludendorff waved to us, then something caught my eye, it was a collie pup.

"Do you see that Rob."

"What?"

"That pup, it's just like mine."

"It is too, you don't think he's done the dirty on you?"

"Naw, how could he, Robbie was at home when I left, I fed him."

My mind was racing so I phoned home. My wife answered the phone and I explained everything, she soon told me my pup was out on the lawn running around. I said, OK honey, see you soon.

"Everything OK Eddie?" asked Rob.

"Yeh, all is well thank God, but it makes me think, the couple we got Robbie from, well where he came from, they were English or so I was told. Now just maybe that's where Von Ludendorff got to know about me on this Island."

Rob was going on about getting someone new on the job, I told him that is out of the question. He was talking about getting out the gold while we are with Von Ludendorff…

"What can we do Eddie, that gold is just sitting there, can't we do something about it? How much do we have in the kitty?"

"300,000 Euros around that amount…why?"

"Let's get that mini Sub and get down there and move all that gold."

"There's just two of us Rob, how can we possibly manage it?"

"We can do it Eddie, first of all we collect all the boxes, take them to the torpedo bay, load them into the floats and tie them up well, then release the power in the tubes and send the gold out. One of us will be waiting with nets on the mini Sub to catch them, and tie them onto the mini Sub until we have the lot up and out. We can pull them underwater and I know some caves along the coast, there under water, we can drop the lot into these caves where they should be safe…what do you think Eddie?"

"Do you think we can do it Rob?"

"Of course we can Eddie, just tell your man we need a few days that will get the job done."

"Wait a minute Rob, how do we secure that mini Sub under water?"

"Easy Eddie, we tie it to the U-boat."

I sat back and thought about it, it seemed straightforward and a pretty good idea. We went over everything we could think about on the way back from Lanzarote.

There was no question about it, what we had to do was very, very dangerous. Going in and out of that escape compartments, even moving all that gold was hard work. We had to do it otherwise it would fall into the hands of Von Ludendorff.

The sweat was running off my head as we came off the Ferry. Rob was full of beans and I could smell it, he had eaten handfuls of nuts at Von Ludendorff's Villa, he kept saying sorry, I said just stick your arse out the door.

He then said, "I would if I could but I can't."

"These caves you talked about, where exactly are they from where the U-boat lies?"

"Maybe just over a mile away, there are three caves, a small one and two large ones, they go down deep, I don't know just how far."

"How much weight will this mini Sub be able to pull?"

"Well Eddie, it holds eight to ten people so I would say it can pull at least a ton. How much gold have we?"

"I'll have to work all that out using the bars I have."

"Well we found so far 508 boxes plus the ones already that is 8128 bars. Each bar is about a pound and three quarters so that's 14224 pounds we have down there, over six plus three quarter tons of the stuff…this means we have at least two trips to make Rob."

"Ok Eddie, that's OK we can do that."

"If we start this we just have to finish it Rob, there's no going back."

"I know that Eddie, once we get all the gold out of there, we can't get back inside, those tubes will fill up."

"Where's the mini Sub?"

"Oh don't worry about that we can pick it up and move under cover of darkness way north of Villa Winter."

"Right, so that's agreed on. I better give Von Ludendorff a call. Tell him we will be with him in two days, that's enough time."

Rob nodded in agreement.

I made the call and Von Ludendorff was very pleased, so were we and we got to work quickly. As soon as we arrived back it was as quick as we could to get things moving. Rob got the mini Sub wrapped up and tied down onto a truck, while I loaded all the diving gear and a couple of weapons. The diving gear was a full set and we had gloves to wear when moving the boxes of gold.

We would enter the U-boat through the escape compartments, then get to work moving all the gold, when that was done Rob would set up the Torpedo tubes and place the floats into position to be loaded. We didn't know yet how many boxes would go inside the tubes, we just had to load them up and see. I never make a list, just in case it may fall into the wrong hands this time I made one, so that Rob could check out anything I may have forgotten…would you believe it, two things I didn't list, a map and torches.

A Covert night mission was about to begin, with a loaded truck and driver (Rob) waiting for me right outside my villa. With a long and dangerous journey ahead of us, we set off.

We were heading over to the West Coast and almost straight across the Island from Caleta de Fuste to an area just south of Ajuy. Rob picked the route because he was sure no one would see us, well he was right on that, this place was like the moon, as we bumped our way along a rough track that just seemed to be getting rougher. I kept looking at the map, then at Rob. This was the roughest track I have ever had to gone down.

"Rob, are you sure you know where you're going?"

"Relax Eddie, it gets rougher but at least we will never be seen, not far now to the shoreline."

Rob's Landrover was pulling the trailer with the mini Sub. As we moved over the ridge he braked and we started to slide, even using the brakes on and off, the Landrover and trailer picked up speed as Rob tried to stop it using the brakes. The tossing around helped reduce the speed of descent and Rob pulled hard on the steering wheel to try and jack-knife the two vehicles, it worked as we came to a stop. But when we got out to look we stood there horrified, we had stopped just short of a 300-foot drop straight down.

Rob lined up the Landrover and moved off very slowly indeed, we could see the sea as the light from the moon shone across the waves. As Rob moved the vehicle in a zigzag fashion down over rocks I held on tightly, with each bump I was ready to jump, then that lovely feeling as we reached the sandy shore. Once we got onto safe ground, I had a look at the map. We were at least four miles away from the U-boat, with a huge sandy beach lit up by the full moon.

"Are we here?" I asked as I handed Rob the map.

"Yes that's near enough, we are actually there," he pointed out the area on the map.

"Let's get this mini Sub down there," said Rob pointing at the waves rolling in over the sandy beach.

The mini Sub was on wheels but we found it hard to move, so Rob used the Landrover to push it while I guided it, once we had it clearly floating I anchored it, then we made sure the Landrover was out of sight.

We fully checked the mini Sub and looked around to make sure that there was no one around, even fishermen, there wasn't a soul anywhere to be seen. Rob powered up the mini Sub and off we went, we stayed on the surface until we came into view of Villa Winter, then Rob took her down, it was pitch black until he switched on the headlights then we could see very well.

"Those lights Rob, won't they be seen from the shoreline?"

"No Eddie, there's never anyone down here, but I will dim them once we get nearer the U-boat."

I was amazed by the amount of fish in these waters some very small, like the size of a pinkie, others huge like long giant eels, even sharks, now that's one big fish we had to watch out for.

While Rob steered the mini Sub, I was busy getting all the diving gear laid out ready to put on. The mini Sub closed in on the U-boat and I checked out how deep we actually were we were just over fifty feet deep. Rob brought the Mini Sub right up close while I stood fully dressed in diving gear ready to get out and tie the mini Sub to the U-boat. But first he had to take it up because there were no way out of it without flooding and sinking it.

We both watched as the small mini Sub surfaced. We didn't think about what was now a big problem, after bringing up the small mini Sub we now couldn't get it to go back under.

"Eddie we are fucked up, how the hell are we going to get the gold moved now?"

"I'm thinking Rob…I'm thinking, the motor is sealed up, right?"

"Yeh it is, why?"

"Well, let's sink the bloody thing, it can still function, it can still pull those floats…right?"

"Sure it can, sure it can, let's sink it."

"No wait Rob, we'll need all the oxygen, we only have a couple of bottles here."

"Eddie, can you change over bottles down there?"

"Never tried it Rob, why do you ask?"

"Because you have to change once you're getting low, I'll show you what to do."

As the mini Sub went lower down, I could see the shapes of both torpedo tube exits. We fixed two lines to the U-boat very firmly, then went along the U-boat to find the escape hatches. We missed them at first that's how well they were covered over by coral. We cleared both hatches then we had to get inside the U-boat this was dangerous.

Rob kept talking to me through our radio system, it was clear and stayed that way as I got inside the compartment Rob closed it down. I opened the valve to fill up the chamber, once filled I opened another valve and the water drained away. To open the chamber's compartment I had to draw a lever across the bottom and the hatch lid opened up. The same procedure went on again as Rob joined me.

Two main things had to be done now, all the floats stacked in the same area that we were in had to be carried down to the torpedo bay. These were bulky and it was awkward carrying them, we took three each down, then the heavy stuff began, moving the boxes of gold. We had to lift every single box up another level and then walk, in some cases, the whole length of the U-boat with them. Rob got the generator working that gave us lights to move around quicker, it also gave power for the torpedo tubes to work. Netting would be used to parcel up the gold inside the floats, once we got things going.

When we moved the last two floats, we noticed water dripping from the escape compartments. Rob tried to get one opened but it was stuck fast, he tried the other one, it too, was stuck. By now we were out of the diving gear having left it down at the torpedo bay.

I then said to Rob, "If those escape hatches are stuck, how are we going to get out of here?"

"The same way we get the gold out."

"You mean in the torpedo tubes."

"Yes, once the gold is out we go out the same way. We have to split the weight up so we can get all the gold out in four loads two from each tube. Now it's important that I check the fuel down in the generator just before we put out the last load. I don't want that generator running on too long after we have left the U-boat, if it runs too long it could cause bubbles to form on the surface."

"OK then Rob, let's get this gold moved, we should start at the furthest point."

We had to go way past the engine room, then down to the lowest level handing up box after box. It was back breaking work, and we were knackered after moving about thirty boxes, with cuts and bruises to our hands and arms, we took a break. We sat there looking at each other, then we laughed.

"You must be thinking like me Rob."

"I am Eddie, we are two crazy men. Look at us, cut to bits for what?"

I pointed at the boxes of gold. "For that there Rob…gold."

"We'll take days to get this out Eddie."

"How many have we moved so far?"

"Thirty seven and there is still over 470 still to move."

"There's more on this side of the U-boat, so it will take less time to move it."

"Well that lot took over an hour Eddie, so work that out with all those boxes that are still to be moved."

"Rob, shove thoughts like that out of your mind, they are very negative, think of what you are going to do with all the money you will get."

"Now that did cheer me up."

"You see, positive thinking wins through Rob…always."

"Come on then, let's get back at it."

"I've just worked it out, it has taken us one hour and seventeen minutes to move thirty seven boxes. It doesn't sound a lot, but it has taken us two minutes per box or just above that."

"Fifteen hours, that's how long it will take to get all those boxes up and out of here."

"It will be daylight Eddie, in less than that time."

"I know Rob, we might get away with it, if we just work away until midday."

"Wait a minute, what about those metal railings, they use them to move heavy equipment, why don't we use them? Tie the boxes on and pull them along."

We had some boxes lying so we made a sort of hammock and stuck two boxes into it, then just pulled them along the metal railing, it worked, soon we had enough boxes to fill up both tubes. We had lots more to get but Rob was keen to get this lot of boxes fired out, we made sure every box was secured inside the floats and netting as we slid them in three at a time until the tubes were full.

Rob then set the firing and off went the loads of gold, we looked at each other, and we then said almost at the same time, "Wonder how far they will travel?"

I said, "downwards I hope."

After a hard day's work all night we finally got all the gold out of the U-boat. It was outside but as yet we didn't know where it had landed. Now it was our turn to use the tubes. Rob reduced the power, checked what fuel was left in the generator, then I got into the tube first with all my diving gear on. Rob set the timer and slammed the tube shut behind him.

"Hold tight to your body Eddie, and tie your legs together."

I did that, we waited then wooooosssssh, I couldn't see for bubbles and the pressure made us tumble over and over, but we were now out safely.

We checked what oxygen we had left, then started looking about the seabed for the gold. The mini Sub had been moved with the blast of the gold coming out, now we were on the far side of it coming back around into view of the U-boat. There it all was four piles of gold, mind you, you wouldn't think so, as they were totally covered over by the floats and netting. All we had to do now was tie all the loads onto the mini Sub and move it.

We swam around the mini Sub and got to work fast fixing the towlines to the rear of the mini Sub. Once all four were tied down and secured, Rob fired up the engines.

I went around the floats getting enough air into them so that the loads lifted off the seabed, once this was done, I joined Rob. As we moved away slowly from the U-boat we heard the generator stop.

"Did you hear that Eddie?"

"Yes I heard it Rob, now let's get to those underwater caves."

We had made good time, as dawn was breaking, it seemed a long time before Rob cut the engines.

"We are right above those caves Eddie," now we have to use the spare rope and tie up those nets before we drop them into what looked like a black hole in the seabed.

We both swam out and around the loads, Rob waited on me as I released the air from the floats, I signalled to him to cut the ties and the rope to release one of the loads. It fell away as I watched it disappear into the abyss, with all four loads gone, we headed back to where the Landrover had been left.

It was daylight and we did better getting the mini Sub back onto the trailer, and off we went feeling tired but contented. With everything in order, we headed back the way we came, going north then cutting across the centre of the Island to Pajara on to Antigua then down into Caleta de Fuste and home. Rob took the mini Sub back and made sure we could get it again.

While Rob and I were messing about with the fishing and the gold, my wife had gone over to the U.K. to stay with Gloria and Julian. She was due back, Julian was coming with her, and this kind of messed things up for Rob and I, because Von Ludendorff wanted us over to Lanzarote that morning at 7.30 hours.

I ended up phoning my wife and explaining what was going on, she would let Julian know. As yet I felt sure we were going to Hamburg, this was soon explained to me on the phone by Von Ludendorff. It became clear that he intended sailing his ship all the way from Hamburg to the Islands. That meant we were stuck with him.

Rob was concerned about the time we would be gone, I was concerned with other things, like what happens when he finds there's no gold to be found.

I was back in my villa, washed and shaved, had a good sleep and was now sitting near the pool. I had Robbie at my side with a cold beer sitting on the table, it was just after 1600 hours and still very warm, when I heard the front door bell ringing. I got up with Robbie following me around the side of the villa to the driveway. I saw a man standing at the front door. I had a good look around before I let him see me, I then said,

"Can I help you."

"Are you Edward Blake?"

"Yes, that's me."

"I am sorry for disturbing you, this business Mister Blake is very delicate, I would rather keep it close to our chests."

"Come on it, I'm around here at the pool, would you like a cold drink?"

"Oh no thanks Mister Blake."

Young Robbie was running around the pool and enjoying himself as the man introduced himself.

"I am Erwin Heisenberg, I have been sent here to ask for your help in finding our lost gold."

My ears pricked up at the name gold. The man went on to say that a Consortium of Bankers wants me to find their gold.

Now I'm sitting there wondering is this guy for real, does he really work for the Bankers, or Herr Von Ludendorff.

Here was a man coming out of the blue, wanting me to help him find gold. Rob and I were off in the morning to Hamburg. What was I to say to this man? He was speaking to me but I didn't hear a word.

"Mister Blake, did you hear what I said?"

"Oh sorry.... yes I did hear what you said, just how much are your Bankers prepared to pay?"

"They will pay you on delivery of their gold 5 million Euros."

I was stuck in a corner not knowing what to say, I just said, "I'm off on holiday tomorrow for about three weeks."

"That is fine Mister Blake, so you can help us?"

"Yes, why not."

Erwin Heisenberg stood up and held out his hand. I shook it as he said, "I have your numbers so I will be in touch…and thank you Mister Blake."

I walked the man out to the driveway and watched as he walked downhill about a hundred yards, then got into a taxi. I called Rob and told him what had happened, he was more concerned with us going to Hamburg.

"Are you playing one side against the other Eddie?"

"It's a thought Rob, but no, there's too much involved in all this."

"Just how much do we have down there Eddie?"

"It's hard to say Rob, we had more boxes than we thought was in that U-boat. That gold was pure, that means it was 24 carat, you see some gold have alloys mixed into it, that's why you get as low as 6, 9 carat. But that stuff down there that's the real McCoy 24 carat."

"I thought when gold was in bars it was one hundred per cent."

"Not always Rob, some does get mixed with alloys, and used as payments in some Arab States and in Asia. We have over, I'd say, 200 million in gold, that can shoot up on the markets. But I could be way off Rob, gold is the commodity and it goes up and up."

"Who was this guy, was he German or what?"

"He was Swiss, works for a Banking Consortium."

"Some of that gold had German Bunk Eidg, that's the German Federal Bank."

"That's right Rob, but on the other side it is Switz gold probably from other European Countries."

"I'd better tell Julian, he is arriving as we leave tomorrow morning."

I told Julian the man's name who visited me and all the details about him, and how Von Ludendorff knew about this rival group who were the rightful owners. He had them shadowed everywhere they went, so I felt we better play this by ear. With this guy paying me a visit, I just had to mention this to Herr Eric Von Ludendorff when we met up.

I was really glad I talked to Julian it put him in the picture, and my wife, my last words were, I'd be in touch.

I had been told that the Bankers had a ship docked in the harbour at Marseille, it was on standby and would set sail once the word got back that I was helping them. They had heard about the gold we cashed in, and the story was how we caught the gold in our fishing nets, news does travel no matter where you are in the world.

Rob was saying we better watch ourselves, as this man is a danger to his own men. He was absolutely right. Von Ludendorff had in the past killed some of his own men, so he was capable of doing the same to us.

I made sure we had knives and guns hidden on our person, I won't tell you where, but it's uncomfortable.

When we arrived in Hamburg, we got first class treatment, a couple of guys took our bags, then we were walked out to a waiting limo, driven to the Hotel and there was complimentary drinks left for us both…by the bottle.

We had separate rooms and Rob came knocking at my door. I opened the door and he just barged in looking around, all he said was, "You got it as well," meaning the drink, chocolates, cigarettes and my favourite cigars, the ones laced with either Rum, Brandy, Wine or Whisky.

I opened a bottle of red wine, and sat down at the table. I filled up two glasses and said, "Sit your arse down there and enjoy these moments."

At last I had Rob relaxed and he was on about us helping Von Ludendorff. I put my finger across my lips, indicating to him to watch what he said. He understood. I wrote down what I wanted to say to him, because I was sure the rooms had been 'bugged'. I wrote…As soon as we can, we will join the Switz Bankers as soon as we get the chance.

Rob quickly said, "We got everything laid on for us, that's just great Eddie."

"That's what I like, people who look after you when you help them."

I reminded Rob by writing more notes, pushing them across the table. "Always, they are listening to us from now on, even in any room, and always on this ship we shall be on."

Rob stuck up his thumb.

Well we had a quiet night, in the morning we had to meet with Von Ludendorff after breakfast, he would then explain what would take place. It was already obvious to us that we would be going on his ship and sailing to the Islands.

We both felt 'heavy' after all the drink, as we approached the dining area Rob stopped, he was looking at a morning paper. I couldn't believe it. Von Ludendorff had sent his men to sink the Bankers ship, there was a gunfight and several on both sides got killed, they failed to sink the ship. Von Ludendorff didn't show up, instead one of his men came into the dining area, saw us and came over to tell us to be ready to move in ten minutes. We had barely started breakfast, but didn't feel like it anyway.

Rob kept looking at me, but was saying nothing.

"What's on your mind Rob?"

"Eddie, we ought to get to hell out of this shit, or we might end up like those Bankers…dead."

"Calm down Rob, we are in no danger, well at least not yet, we wait our chance, but let's play along until we are back at the Island."

"I still say we should get out of this."

"Rob we can't, well not right now, they are all around us, we can't try anything…or we are dead. Let's get onto this ship of Von Ludendorff's, then we are fine. At the Island we can make a move then."

We quickly got our gear together, then carried our bags down to the foyer, someone called out my name.

"Mister Blake, follow me please."

We got into the car and off we went, this driver didn't waste much time, he was racing along. When we came to a stop, there right in front of us was the ship. It looked more like a Cruise Ship. We were taken to our cabins and just left to get on with it.

We put what clothes we had into the draws, Rob was trying to open what he thought was a chest of drawers, but it was in fact, a drinks bar. It opened right out and I turned to Rob and said, "Now does that make you feel like you're on holiday, or what?"

I saw Rob smile for the first time since we left the Island.

"How do you feel now Rob?"

"Better, much better, let's lay into that lot, it's free isn't it?"

"Yes, it's all free."

The phone in my cabin rang, I picked it up and was told that dinner would be at eight thirty, a steward would guide us to the dining room.

The décor in the cabins was very luxurious, the bed was like something out of a Stately home, real windows with curtains hanging to the floor and gold covered taps in the toilet. The paintings on the walls, they were real oils. Plush carpets decked the floors and neatly stacked towels on a rack in the shower room.

Rob sat back as I opened a door out onto a balcony, when I pulled the curtains over the sun hit the wooden panels that was covering the walls of the cabin.

Well we sat there having a drink, and there was plenty of it.

We were on the move and barely on board, maybe just over half an hour. We went back inside and closed over the doors, we sat back down where we had been sitting.

"We better cut down on the drink, our host may not like the fact we took advantage of his hospitality."

"Yeh, you're right Eddie, let's have another!" Rob laughed as he filled the two glasses with the best brandy.

Suddenly the cabin door opened and in came three of Von Ludendorff's men. Before we knew it they had us handcuffed together.

Rob shouted, "What the hell are you doing?"

Then I said, "Why are you doing this?"

One of the men said, "You will be freed once we are well out to sea."

"What if we need the toilet, will you wipe my ass?"

I got a stern look from all three men as they slammed the door shut.

"Dirty bastard," said Rob. "I knew he couldn't be trusted, I told you so…well, didn't I?"

"Shut up Rob and let's see if we can get these off."

"Are you kidding."

"No, move your arms closer to me."

"What for, you can't get these things opened."

I fumbled about to get into my back pocket, hoping to pull out a multi purpose set of screwdrivers, it was very small in its own leather pocket. I knew that when I opened the cufflinks there wasn't much we could do, still it was a challenge and I did it. I opened the cufflinks.

"How did you do that?"

I put my finger across my lips saying, "shooosh."

One word said it all training.

When we talked we knew Von Ludendorff would be listening, so we talked about fishing, we talked about getting contracts from Hotels and supplying them with fish. Rob played along with what I said, saying how we needed a bigger boat.

Not long after this we were set free, then invited to join Von Ludendorff, he apologised for the handcuffs and now thanked us for joining him in the search for the gold.

We were now well out at sea and had not eaten a thing for over eight hours, but your man laid on a feast for us. As we ate he sat and watched us, holding a notebook in his hands, he would explain what was going to happen in the next few days.

"You now have the freedom of my ship, enjoy your stay, I will see you later for the evening meal."

Back in Fuerteventura June and Julian had arrived back at the villa. Julian was going to Morocco to check on the gold I gave him, I wanted to be certain this gold was indeed Switz, and nothing whatever to do with Germany.

I had told Julian under no circumstances must he let the gold merchant see the stamps on the gold bars.

Morocco, famous for the movie Casablanca, was once a French Colony. Today they speak Arabic and French in certain places. Morocco is situated in the north-west corner of Africa, a ridge of mountains called the Atlas Mountains separate the arid south and the fertile regions to the west and north.

Loads of tourists go there on holiday, the Capitol is called Rabat, that's where Julian was heading for. An old friend of mine was a dealer in gold and, although I trusted him, I felt it better if he just took some scrapings off and tested it. When Julian arrived at the airport, which was about fifty miles from his destination, he took a taxi and watched his back at all times.

An old ploy for thieves was to watch who entered the merchants premises, then robbed them when they came back out. But Julian knew all this and he could handle himself. He rang the doorbell while eyeballing all around himself.

One of my old friend's assistants came to the door, then shortly after my old friend greeted Julian warmly. His name was Mohamid Almona Shafir. He was studying at Leeds University when I was there learning a couple of languages, we spent a lot of time together, so I knew he would look after Julian and that gold.

When the gold was checked out it was indeed 24 carat, Julian thanked Mohamid and was keen to get back to the airport and fly back to the Island, where my wife was waiting for him at the airport.

When they arrived back at the villa, Julian saw a man at the front of the villa, Julian told my wife he would deal with it, so he walked around the side of the villa and spoke to the man. It was Erwin

Heisenberg. Julian knew who he was, as I had already told him he would probably call in.

Erwin explained to Julian about their stolen gold, gold that the Nazi's stole during the War. He went on to say that Von Ludendorff was after this gold and he was a ruthless man. He wanted Julian to contact me, to warn me of the danger. My wife was out of earshot when Julian and Erwin were talking. He confirmed what we already knew, that Von Ludendorff was a thief, a robber of antiquities. He will kill anyone to get what he wants.

My wife June, was video taping as Julian talked to Erwin and the other man with him, they looked comfortable even though my wife had been filming them. This convinced Julian that they were genuine. They asked him to get in touch with me, of course that was difficult, Julian knew he could drop Rob and me right in the shit. Instead, he sent a message and it came through as Rob and I was standing out on the deck of the ship. I quickly looked around to see if anyone was near us, then looked at the message.

It was short and sweet…first chance…get off that ship.

I handed the phone to Rob who just looked up at me and said, "Look out there, there's nothing but miles of ocean."

I nodded my head in a…yes.

I got another message, this time Julian came straight out with it, saying on the message, 'I'm getting some of our men over here, you are in danger'.

Julian was referring to the men who we served with in the Regiment, men who like Julian were with me in the search for the treasure in Libya.

Julian had taken over that side of the business, and help from Erwin Heisenberg speeded things up. His H.Q. had worldwide contacts and these were used to contact the men that would be needed on the Island. My wife June was laying into Julian about why he was getting the men from our Regiment. "What is going on Julian?"

"He and Rob are on a ship that's heading here, but the man who owns it, well, he's a bad one, so I am taking precautions, if there's trouble we will handle it, so don't worry June."

"Don't worry! That's all I've done for years, and your Gloria is the same every time you go off on these 'Jobs' as you always call them."

"They are fine June, they will soon be back here."

Erwin Heisenberg was being handed a drink by Julian and the other man with him. He filled up a glass for June, then sat down as Heisenberg said,

"Tell her the truth."

Julian sat there with a stern face, thinking to himself why couldn't he shut up.

"Well Julian, I'm waiting."

Julian whispered…."Gold."

"What gold? There have been no shipwrecks around these Islands."

"It's not a ship June, it's a U-boat."

"Oh my God, he's not on a U-boat?"

"No, of course not, he is on a ship sailing to the Island."

"So who's on this ship?"

"Well, that is the problem, you see, the man who owns this ship could be a danger to Eddie and Rob, so as a precaution I sent for some of the men."

Hans Junge, the man with Erwin said, "Do you have any plans made?"

"Not yet, I'll wait until the others join me."

Things calmed down, as I made a call to the U.K. for my wife to come out and keep June company. This pleased her, so she went off shopping, while the three of us talked over what needed to be done.

I knew I wasn't doing anything until Sammy, Snowy, Pat Curran and Robert Preston arrived here on the Island.

I knew Eddie had some weapons put away in the garage, I didn't mention this to the two Switz. They left and said they would be in touch.

The men coming over to help, I was looking forward to seeing them again. They were due in at the airport at just after 1900 hours.

It was after 2000 hours when all four men arrived at the airport with a lot of hand shaking and backslapping. I took them back to Eddie's villa, they were all impressed by the size of it. June knew all the men and had some food waiting for them. Once the formalities were over and the men had eaten, we sat down at the pool and I explained what was going on. The senior man in our party was Sammy Brown, an ex Sgt. he asked the most questions, just like this one. "OK boss, what's Eddie up to this time?"

"Eddie played on a hunch that has proved to be true. He has found the lost gold that the Nazi's looted from all over Europe, most of it belonging to the Switz. He and a friend have managed to hide the gold and now they had no option but to help a man called Eric Von Ludendorff, he's bad news and has set his heart on taking this gold. Eddie and his friend Rob, managed to remove all the gold from the sunken U-boat, they cashed in some gold bars. This is how Von Ludendorff found out about it, but Eddie and Rob gave them a story that they pulled up the gold in their fishing nets. Now they have to play along with this. They are now on this man's ship and sailing to this Island. There are weapons in the garage, but we don't want to upset June any more than she is, so we will remove them once we know what Eddie and Rob are going to do."

Snowy then asked, "We have to wait on Eddie and Rob making a move, why don't we make the first move? We know they are heading to this Island, we also know the area this ship is heading for, so why wait? Let's get to that area."

"We can't just go into that area, Von Ludendorff has what's supposed to be, an archaeologist team with guards down there, they will be on to us in seconds."

Snowy said, "Why not covert, get in there at night, find a suitable place to lay up. If we wait on Eddie, we might be too late getting help to him and Rob."

Big Pat Curran butted in saying, "You're our boss, always have been when Eddie is not around, you tell us what you think?"

"We have a problem, you see this ship is big so it can anchor well off shore, which means we would need something to get us on to the ship. Another thing, his men will be well armed, I'm in favour of what Snowy said… if we had the right boats at hand to get us out to that ship."

June came walking out to the pool area, looking not too happy, she gave us a bad look saying, "I want my husband back, go and do something will you."

Sammy, always the joker said, "If it wasn't for us, you would never have met Eddie, do you think this man with a Santa Claus name is going to take him away from us…no way June. When we get going, you'll look back on this and say, 'what was I worried about.'" Those few words from Sammy calmed her down, now it was time to get moving…once June had gone back inside.

Sammy asked me, "Is this guy really that bad?"

"He's bad Sammy, he's real bad, killed his own men when they got things wrong."

Suddenly Julian's phone rang. Looking at the others he said, "It's Eddie!"

I explained to Julian that the ship was huge and had it's own helicopter and submersible. The men were well armed, any attempt to try a forced landing on board the ship would end in failure. They have hidden cameras, floodlights and two powerful guns up front and aft, R.P.G's and grenades smoke gas and H.E. if you make a move Julian, do it at night, we arrive tomorrow afternoon…got to go."

Julian looked at the men with him and said, "Well, you heard what Eddie said, doesn't look good."

The men looked at each other with different expressions on their faces they said nothing. Just then the two Bankers came walking in to join them.

Erwin came with a great deal of information, which we were very grateful for, he not only confirmed what Eddie has told me, but he laid out a drawing of Von Ludendorff's ship. It gave precise details of each deck and cabins, where the guns were, the chopper and submersible. He then said,

"I have men from the P.G.C. who can help us."

Sammy butted in. "Who the hell are the P.G.C.?"

Julian knew whom he was talking about and explained to Sammy and the others who they were. "The P.G.C. is The Parachute Grenadier Company. Eddie and I trained with them some years ago, they are very good soldiers. This is by far the biggest job we have ever done. We must not fail in saving the life of Eddie and his friend. We will go in at night, we must hit them fast and hard, no quarter given study that drawing, know every inch of that ship because we don't get a second chance at this one."

Meanwhile after repairs the Bankers ship had reached the Islands before Von Ludendorff's ship. Erwin joined Julian and his men as they went to the harbour, when they arrived the ship was tied up and in plain view was armed men…the P.G.C. Erwin and his partner walked on board, then Julian led his men up. The man commanding the P.G.C. was a Captain, the same rank as Julian had been in the Regiment. Julian marched on boldly right up to the P.G.C. Captain, gave a half salute and said,

"Julian Channer Captain S.A.S." Those on the ship turned to look at this man who had just announced himself.

The two Captains shook hands and then went on a guided tour of the ship, eventually they were taken to what looked like a small ballroom, it was set up with chairs and a giant screen. In all there was twenty-five men that included Julian and his four men. It looked like we all would work together well, as I noticed that the men I had were mixing with the P.G.C. men.

I kept thinking about Eddie and Rob, at the same time sat

watching the big screen as it was showing Von Ludendorff's ship, it was pretty big, it gave good detail that was invaluable to us all, when we put in an attack.

Once the ship's details were over, on came scenes of Von Ludendorff smiling and holding up what was supposed to be the cup of Jesus, then there were other artefacts shown, but when the talk about the Ark of the Covenant came up, Julian and his men shouted out,

"Lies, bullshit, what a load of crap!"

Julian then said, "Eddie found that in the Yemen, not that bastard."

Von Ludendorff spoke firstly in German then English, he was bragging about what he had, when the treasure caves came on screen he bragged that he had found it.

Sammy and Snowy shouted out, "You fuckin' liar, we found that treasure not you, all you found was empty caves, after we cleared them out. Von Ludendorff went on to say… "And now for that gold." The screen went blank as Julian and his four men got up and were all angry over what Von Ludendorff had said about the treasure found in Libya. They had found it along with Eddie Blake. Now, here they were, ready to do battle to save him from this monster of a man.

When they had calmed down, the P.G.C. Captain showed the ship again, so that all the men would take in what they saw. Now a plan had to be agreed on. But first Erwin had now taken over. Again he said how Von Ludendorff was a ruthless man with no morals at all. He even fakes artefacts to sell on to the rich and famous, making millions from them, but he is never satisfied he always wants more, this is why he is after our gold.

Erwin pulled down a map of the coastline, near the Villa Winter, he was now explaining to the P.G.C. men how Eddie, Rob and Julian had found the gold in a sunken submarine (U-boat). How they worked through dangerous moments to get all the gold out and even hide it, knowing then that Von Ludendorff was after it.

"There is more than two tons of gold. What these men have done is a remarkable achievement. Only Mister Eddie Blake and Rob know where this gold now lies, so we must make sure when this attack goes in, these two men come out first, everything else takes second place, is that understood."

The P.G.C. men called out, 'yes', as Erwin continued.

Back on board Von Ludendorff's ship things were getting worse for Eddie and Rob, they were being searched for their phones, and they had been handcuffed again, they soon found Rob's phone but not Eddie's.

"Where's your phone Eddie?" said Rob.

I looked up, it looked so far out of reach where I had taped my phone onto the cabin light. "It's inside that light."

"Oh Eddie, how the hell can we reach up there?"

The cufflinks were attached to the bed and there was no way we could get to it. Then I had an idea, I noticed that in the cupboard near the cabin door, there was a brush with a handle. Getting over to the cupboard would take some doing.

"Rob, let's try pulling the bed over towards the door."

Slowly we scraped along the floor, but had to stop as we heard someone coming, but it was a false alarm. We pulled and pulled slipping on the floor, it looked like we would never make it. So far we had barely moved, when the cabin door opened and in came Von Ludendorff's men, they searched me and showed us Rob's phone.

Von Ludendorff came in. "Where is your phone Mister Blake?"

"I didn't have one, I didn't bring it with me, no need to."

"Search the whole cabin," shouted Von Ludendorff as he walked out of the door.

We lay there watching as three men searched the cabin. They never came close, until one stood looking at the light cover on the wall, he moved off when one of the others called on him. As soon as they had gone we again tried to move the bed, it wouldn't move. That's when I saw that it was fixed solid to the floor...as we crawled under we saw that there was four screws holding each leg.

"Rob, try and get my belt off."

With us both handcuffed back to back, Rob was in a better position to pull the belt around my waist until one of us could get to the buckle...eventually, after a struggle I got it off. Now I had to unscrew four screws, just getting started was hard enough, slowly the first one started turning as I eased the edge of the buckle into it.

It was sore on the hand turning the screw, Rob took over from me, we managed the first one out, and then we heard someone coming along the passageway, so we stopped. I hid the belt, the three men who had searched the cabin, came in again and started another search. Rob and I watched their every move...then it happened, one of them was taking off the cover on the light where I had taped the phone...it looked like they would now have my phone too. The man pulled away the cover so quickly and didn't notice the phone falling onto the velvet curtain, we expected it to clatter onto the floor, but it didn't, it slid down the velvet curtain and softly landed on the floor. Fifteen minutes later they were gone, but my phone was right there under the curtain, with a bit of luck I could use the belt buckle and hopefully pull the phone towards me.

Before I got the chance to try, the door opened and, we were uncuffed, Rob was taken out of the door and they cuffed me. I moved quickly, and now freer to move I managed to unscrew all the screws, I stuck my back against the bed and lifted it so I could free myself. I grabbed the phone and stuck it into my sock. Now freer I walked to the door and listened, all was quiet, so I tried the door but it was locked, then I tapped out some Morse and waited a few moments, I tapped the code again and again.

I was getting worried about Rob and where they had taken him, then I heard something, it didn't sound like Morse code, I got up against the cabin door and listened. There it was again, someone was tapping out a SOS I did the same...sure enough it came back twice.

So I knew Rob was OK, now I thought what do I do, should I use the phone or what? I went over to the glass doors that led out to the balcony they were not locked. I wasn't sure if I went out there would I be spotted. I had to think and think fast. Looking out all I could see was water, the Atlantic Ocean, at least I knew Rob was fine.

I had to tell Rob to be ready as help was on its way. I tried calling out to Rob.

"Rob, can you hear me?" I tried again, this time I could hear Rob.

"I hear you Eddie, I heard what you said."

"Try and get out of the cabin, I will do the same."

Things changed badly for both of us, they heard us, and we were dragged out of the cabin and beaten up black and blue. When they had stopped, Von Ludendorff walked around us saying,

"Do not play games with me Mister Blake, you take me to this gold and don't lie about it. I know you SAS men are trained to lie, lie to me and you will die." He kicked at Rob, then continued, "you too."

I answered him. "I told you where we found the gold, and I will show you."

"Mister Blake, you talk now, or he dies." Von Ludendorff pointed at Rob, he was bleeding badly from the beating they gave him, so was I.

I shouted as loud as I could, "Shoot him, then you will have to shoot me too. Do that and my men will hunt you down and kill you."

"Aaah talk, you British are getting worse that the Americans," Von Ludendorff signalled to one of his men to shoot Rob.

Out of the darkness I heard two shots, then there was an almighty explosion. We were thrown several yards with the blast, but OK, I grabbed Rob and helped him move clear of the fire that had now started, that's when I saw Sammy and Snowy racing along the same deck we were lying on. As they past us, Sammy said,

"Boss move forward, the men there will get you off this ship." We had just got into a speedboat when a helicopter took off from the rear of the ship. Von Ludendorff had escaped.

Erwin and Hans greeted us both as we were taken to Morro de

el Jable, where Hans, who just happens to be a doctor looked after me and Rob. We had taken a beating from Von Ludendorff's men, but we told him nothing.

He had slipped away from us and there was nothing we could do about it. Back on dry land, while Hans the doctor attended to Rob and I, Sammy and Snowy came over to see us, as did the others, Robert Preston and Big Pat Curran. Sammy, seeing the state we were in, shouted out loud and clear, he cursed Von Ludendorff and said, "He won't escape the next time boss, get us the Barrett guns and Snowy and I will double tap him."

"That's right," said Snowy. "Two taps…two bullets right into his fuckin' brains."

The Doc' was now busy giving Rob and I a few 'jabs of morphine'.

This gold business was far from over, because this man Von Ludendorff never seems to give up, so he'd be back. It seemed a long time before I got back home, my wife hugging me before I got in the front door. Erwin and Hans saw Rob home, as I sat down with my wife looking at the cuts and scars on my face and arms. I was knackered I fell asleep, only to be wakened by my wife when Erwin and Hans returned. They both were keen to learn exactly where Rob and I dropped all the gold. I explained all to them but they didn't seem contented with what I had told them.

"Can you see these caves from the surface?" asked Erwin.

I said, "No you can't, they just look like a dark patch on the seabed."

"Could you see the gold once you had dropped it?"

"We couldn't see a thing, the loads dropped into total darkness and just fell out of sight, what we had hoped for."

"You do know how to find the spot?"

"Of course I do, so does Rob."

"Aaah, good, so once you feel better we can go down there and get our gold."

Julian had arranged camp beds for the men, they would stay in the garage area. June looked after them, getting grub up for all of them. The P.G.C. men were well looked after on the lawn next to the swimming pool. June was used to having parties, so it was no trouble getting warm food ready for them.

I needed a cigar so I walked out to the swimming pool area, and thanked the men of the P.G.C. they all were well behaved and settled down later that night to grab some sleep. During the night, they patrolled around the villa, ensuring no one intruded.

I was grateful we had Hans with us, he saved us a lot of pain, giving Rob and I 'shots' of morphine. He had brought all the drugs and other equipment he might need. He knew how grateful I was, because I must have told him four or five times. Come bedtime, he gave me another 'jab' to help me sleep. Erwin and him stayed with us, as we had three beds in the west wing.

The next morning, Rob called up and we sort of hugged each other, knowing full well how lucky we had been…Rob's ear was covered with a bandage and Hans had stitched up his face…mine too. We both looked like an advert for some horror movie.

Erwin's ship had docked in the harbour, now it was time for all of us to get all our gear ready, we would soon be heading down to where we dumped the gold. On the ship were deep-sea divers, men forward and aft with powerful binoculars, watching for anyone that approached the ship.

My men Julian of course, and Big Pat Curran, Robert Preston, Snowy Rouse and Sammy Brown were all cleaning their weapons that Erwin had supplied, including two Barrett sniper rifles. As we sat there cleaning the weapons, Sammy asked, "Just how much are these Bankers going to pay us…for putting our lives at risk?"

I answered him, "Why don't you ask them?"

Sammy walked over to where Erwin, Hans and the Captain of the P.G.C. were sitting also the Sergeant. Sammy held the automatic weapon he had in the cradle position, leaving the Barrett gun slung over his shoulder. He had a look at those sitting around, then he said as he looked at Erwin,

"How much is in this for us?"

Erwin quickly answered, "You all get one per cent."

Sammy shouted out, "What? One bloody per cent! That won't cover our bills."

"What's your name soldier?"

"I'm not a soldier, I'm a civilian, an ex Sergeant S.A.S. and we don't like being paid short."

"I wouldn't say one hundred thousand sterling is short paid."

"Did you say one hundred thousand in sterling?"

"Yes Sergeant Brown, that's exactly what I said."

"Why didn't you say that in the first place?" Sammy came back over to us.

Big Pat Curran then asked him, "Well, did you find out?"

Sammy kept smiling making us all wait, eventually he just had told us when Erwin joined us and said,

"That is a low estimate of what each man will receive."

I butted in saying, "Never mind what you're getting, we still have to deliver so make yourselves ready, because we haven't seen the last of Von Ludendorff and his men."

Julian called the men over to him as he opened up two wooden crates, he pulled off the covers and inside were powerful rocket launchers. There was a few comments made about them to name a few.

Big Pat said, "If he comes back in that chopper, that baby will bring him back down to earth."

Sammy said, "I'd stick that right up his arse and fire it, after what he did to the boss and Rob."

It was funny really, we all talked about these two special rocket launchers, but no one picked then up, they still sat inside the crates. It was good to see everyone was in good form.

Moral is very important when going into action, no matter where it might be all these men did a great job saving Rob and I.

Some hours later, when the ship arrived at the area where Rob and I dropped the gold, everyone was on full alert, Rob and I had to really study the coastline. You would think it is easy to go back to the exact spot, but it is far from easy. There was no building to work on, nothing but a mountain range. It was a case of slowly moving up the coast, checking the sea floor as we moved. Down went the divers and they couldn't find anything either.

Rob shouted up to the man at the wheel, "Take her in closer to the shoreline."

Rob and I were leaning over the side of the ship looking for the caves. We thought it would be easy to jump on a ship or boat and go straight out to the spot we dropped the gold, even with calm seas it wasn't easy.

Rob and I stood talking with Erwin, he couldn't believe it was taking so long to find where we dropped the gold. Rob looked up at him, as he was bent over the railings looking down into the water. "Have some patience man, we were under stress when we dumped that gold."

Looking down there into the deep, I could see the divers three of them, as I stood up and looked along the coast, I felt we had gone further along than this area we were now in. Rob felt the same. So Erwin called in the divers, moved on about maybe five hundred yards. Erwin stood up on the bridge and shouted to us all, "Stay on alert, this man Von Ludendorff can attack from the air or with submarines."

The ship sailed very slowly along the coast, the ship stopped and the divers went back down to search the bottom, they were in radio contact all the time. They had disappeared when I heard Sammy's voice shouting, "Coming in…coming…".

Sammy was pointing skywards, when the guns opened up firing at a plane that dived on the ship and circled and did another dive, this time a missile was fired.

Sammy shouted at Erwin to get the missile launcher primed up for firing, there was so many men running about, as this plane dived again. One of the older men with the P.G.C. ran up and joined Sammy, he showed him what to do, but by the time he got it ready to fire, the plane was gone.

The plane returned and bullets ripped into the ship and into the water where the divers were, this attack lasted just ten minutes. As Sammy let go with the missile, the plane dived very low then lifted high to clear the mountains. While it flew about, there was concern for the divers, they had already been attacked and one was injured. Big Pat Curran and Robert Preston dived in and helped them get on board.

The plane made a wide sweep and was coming in again from the sea and again bullets were hitting everywhere. Sammy and one of the P.G.C. men manned the launcher and set off a missile. The missile shot past the plane, made a wide sweep and zeroed in on the plane, the plane lifted over the mountain ridge with the missile right on its tail, then there was a bang and a big ball of fire filled the sky.

A big cheer went up, it was short lived, as we all had to help those who were injured. The search had to be stopped, so the men shot could be taken to hospital. As soon as the ship docked Erwin called in a chopper to airlift the men inured straight to the hospital, where the medical teams were waiting for them. All my men followed me, so I was sure Big Pat Curran would be OK, he got hit three times and lost a great deal of blood, we all gave some blood. Then once Big Pat had come around after his operation, we said our goodbyes and headed back to the ship. There was now six of us, Robert Preston, Sammy Brown, Snowy Rouse, Julian Rob, and me then of course, the P.G.C. men. The ship lay tight against the small harbour, with the P.G.C. men patrolling. All of us got busy getting the lifting gear on board, then it had to be fitted up.

"Erwin asked me, "Did you have any trouble Eddie?"

I shook my head and said, "Not much, someone in a truck tried to push us off the road, but the weight we carried sent them flying, better tell your men to be on alert, we may well have company."

Erwin warned the men of the P.G.C. while others bolted up the lifting gear, we helped as best we could, but we were more worried about an attack, so we kept looking around the whole area leading to the harbour. As we watched those fixing up the lifting gear, Erwin went on to tell us about Von Ludendorff.

We, meaning my group of men, moved up to the bridge, as the two engineers worked on securing the lifting gear. That's when Erwin told us about Von Ludendorff.

"He was born into a rich family, his father was big in Industry and back then was a multi-millionaire, they owned an Estate near Iserlohn and his father was keen on gold and skiing. His mother died when he was fourteen years old that's when his father sent him to a private school, which he didn't like. One day while they were out skiing, the father was killed in a skiing accident. Many people thought he was to blame for the accident, but nothing came of it. So at an early age he became very rich and greedy, this led him to want more and more, stealing whatever he wanted, even going into Churches, Cathedrals and Museums. This man is wanted all over Europe and no one seems able to catch him."

"We'll nail the bastard," said Sammy.

Just then a couple of the P.G.C. men carried a crate over to where we were, and set it down. Erwin opened it. He pulled out what looked like a toy gun, there was a round Mag' with what looked like shells that fired from mortar, they were much smaller. Erwin signalled for a wooden crate to be thrown into the sea. Erwin let it drift away, then he took aim, fired and the whole crate was gone, blown to pieces.

Snowy asked, "What is that?"

Sammy butted in saying, "I'll have one those please."

"These will soon replace the R.P.G's, they are effective up to three hundred yards, and you can get one Sammy, in fact there is eight here, so help yourselves."

We all dived in and grabbed one each plus a Mag. the Mags. held twelve shots.

The ship was now well out at sea, and everyone was on alert as we all tried to stay in the shade, the sun was very hot and dried you up quick, so water was needed to hydrate our insides.

We spread out along the ship weapons in hand, just like the P.G.C. men, even Erwin and we were moving very close to the area where the divers would be going down.

The two divers stood by as the lights were checked out, the ones that would be going down with them into the cave. The ship edged in top position and the divers made ready to leave the ship, they both were in radio contact with is on the bridge. The leading diver was named Fred, Frederick Green-Grass, the other one was Peter Mandel both very experienced divers. They both dived to do exploratory work below, because it looked certain that what used to be two caves was now one large one, some of it had fallen in. They were going down to check if the fall had covered over the floats with the gold tied up inside.

My group stood near Erwin as he talked to the diver.

"Fred, what's the situation down there?"

"Very dangerous, sharp rocks sticking out everywhere, must be careful."

"Can you see the floats with the gold in it?"

"No, not yet, they must have moved down deeper when the other cave fell in on it. We are going down deeper now."

We all were too busy with what the diver was saying then all I can remember others just falling to the ground.

Getting no response to his calls, Fred Greengrass and Peter Mandel moved up towards the surface. As they raised their heads out of the water, they heard the plane's engine as it flew out of sight. Fred secured the floodlights to the side of the ship, then the two men climbed on board. They could see that everyone was lying unconscious.

"What's happened to them all?" asked Peter Mandel.

Fred answered him. "They have all been gassed."

"Are they dead?"

Fred and Peter came up on deck slowly looking around, all they could see was men lying flat out all over the ship.

"What's that smell?" asked Peter.

"It's gas," answered Fred, "but we are OK the wind has blown most of it away…I can hear something."

"Look," said Peter, "Choppers coming in, two of them."

"Quickly Peter, grab some weapons and any explosives you can find, I'll do the same, get them into that dinghy…hurry."

The two men took what they could and got into the dinghy, but then Fred ran back to the bridge to grab a pair of binoculars.

"OK, let's get out of here."

"What will happen to them?"

"I don't know Peter, but we can't help them at the moment, we might be able to later, if we can get away unseen."

The two men headed for the shoreline and the nearest place was covered in rocks, hard, black volcanic rocks, but they made it unseen. They pulled the dinghy around the rocks until they could find a spot to drag it clear of the water. Then they collected the weapons and other items they had grabbed as they hurriedly left the ship.

All the time they kept looking around, making sure no one had seen them. Fred, who had a spell with the S.A.S. trained as a vet and learnt his English while staying in Ireland. He was a born leader and Peter knew that and let him make the decisions. Peter had asked him if he had a plan.

"What plan? There's only two of us against God knows how many of them."

"You told me when you were with the S.A.S you could do anything. Well those men need our help."

"Peter, don't you think I know that, do you want us killed, because unless we have a very good plan, we don't move anywhere. If we do, it will be to get help."

The two men watched as the two Choppers dropped men onto

the ship, they saw them rounding up everyone on board, the Germans were throwing cold sea water onto the men to wake them up. Fred had watched the rough treatment the men were receiving as Von Ludendorff was dropped from a Chopper on board. He was shouting at Erwin to get the gold up, or he would kill two men every five minutes.

We could see Erwin looking over at Eddie Blake, Blake's head was telling him not to agree. This went on for more than ten minutes. Von Ludendorff took a weapon from one of his men and shot dead two P.G.C. men.

"Did you see that?" said Fred.

"How can I? You have the binoculars."

"Von Ludendorff just shot two of the P.G.C. men in cold blood."

"WHAT...let's get out of here."

"Relax Peter, we are safe enough, but I don't know about the others on that boat."

Erwin was being pushed around as Von Ludendorff's men pushed him around. Von Ludendorff shouted right into his face, "Get your men moving, get that gold up now."

Again Erwin looked over towards Blake, this time Blake nodded his head indicating for Erwin to go ahead. The men were reluctant to move, but when the guns started to point at them, they moved.

On the ship Sammy Brown played dead so too did Julian, they both had their eyes covered over, but could still see what was going on. They could see Von Ludendorff's men force the P.G.C. men to work on the lifting gear.

"They have the lifting gear ready, but they have no diving gear on our ship, we have that," said Peter. But he had no sooner said it when Fred told him that they had, he could see divers.

"Here, take a look." Fred handed Peter the binoculars.

"They have divers, I can see them, what are we going to do?"

"We have to try and stop them somehow."

"But how, what can we do?"

"Peter shut up and let me think," said Fred as he took the binoculars and took another look at what was going on.

"Hey, there's a load of gold coming up, and those two lying as if they are dead are alive, it's Sammy and Julian, they are pretending to be dead." Sammy had managed to pull in two of the weapons that lay near them, they covered them with their bodies.

Peter kept complaining because they didn't go to help those on the ship, and Fred was forever telling him to shut up. There was a hold-up bringing up the gold, as the straps used, had snapped and a load of gold was in danger of falling right back into the cave.

The two divers lay hidden in the rocks watching what was taking place, no one on board could move as weapons were pointing at them. Sammy's eyes were watching the guards and where their weapons pointed, they didn't point at him or Julian, but they both knew one move from them and others would surely die. So they lay still watching for an opportunity. It was a terrible situation to be in, they felt free to act but couldn't…the situation was real bad most of those on board had been beaten, some worse than others had. Rob, who had taken the worse beating, was being pulled around by two of Von Ludendorff's men.

Erwin too, was being dragged around, his glasses hung broken on his face, and he had lost his left hand it had been cut clean off, the poor man was in agony. On seeing this Edward Blake and his men went berserk, killing two and taking their weapons, just as this happened, Von Ludendorff had ordered two of his men to kill Rob. They didn't get the chance, Sammy and Julian shot them, that's when Von Ludendorff made his get-a-way.

Fred and Peter on the shoreline now dragged the dinghy into the sea and moved out towards the ship, they would pick up those who jumped into the sea. Fred and Peter picked up men took them to shore then went back for more…

When I got back on the shore, I thanked Fred and Peter for what they had done, "You put your lives at stake for us, I thank you most sincerely, now we must save that gold."

"Hey boss, look," said Sammy as he scrambled over the rocks. "The load of gold is still hanging there on the lifting gear, I'm making sure that bastard doesn't get it."

Before anyone could say or do anything Sammy was swimming out towards the ship. We all watched as he neared the ship, he dived under to hide from some of Von Ludendorff's men who had just arrived on the ship. All our eyes were watching for Sammy, he had dived down and as Fred said, "He's been down there over three minutes."

"I said, "He can do a bit more than that, he'll be up soon."

Sure enough Sammy resurfaced and swam strongly towards the shore. He had fixed a (charge) on the support for the lifting gear as he swam, he looked back as it went up in a ball of flames. It was now dark and as we all sat about watching the ship it became obvious that repairs were being done.
I then asked Fred, "Is your diving gear OK?"
"Yes it's fine, we can use it if need be."
"We don't want them repairing that lifting gear."

Some shots were fired and we had to dive for cover. They didn't want us around and we sure as hell didn't want them getting that gold. I called over Robert Preston and Snowy Rouse to keep watch on all movements on board, as they had binoculars. I told those men with weapons to spread out along the rocks.

Snowy called out, "Chopper landing on ship."

I went and joined Snowy. "Is it Von Ludendorff?"

"Yeh looks like it, he's shouting at the men, looks really angry, something's happened, he's raced back to the Chopper it's taking off."

Von Ludendorff had slipped away, just as real help arrived.
A Spanish War ship loomed up out of the darkness. We all cheered. The huge ship just swamped the ship we had been on, that must have scared the shit out of Von Ludendorff's men, they could not be seen. Some of the P.G.C. men were picked up by the Naval Ship.
With all this happening meant that the area would be clear of any

danger, because our next move was to get divers down there and bring up that gold. We had access to all our weapons, and that included the two Barrett sniper guns. Now with the Warship cruising off shore, was no chance that Von Ludendorff or his men would show face.

It took a couple of days to get full repairs done, thanks to the Spanish Navy, with their gear we could lift the gold much more easily, the real work had to be done by the divers. They had to lift many bars that fell away when some boxes split open. It looked like a big job for the divers Fred and Peter, they would have some help from the Navy divers.

There was nothing much we could do, so we left it all to the divers, once all the gold was up we would be informed, in the meantime we made a visit to the hospital to see Big Pat Curran and Erwin.

Most of us were bandages up, with Rob looking the worst, the hospital staff just kept looking at us, as we walked inside. It was so good to see Big Pat, he was up and walking, but pretty shaky.

I whispered in his ear, "Your cut is safe," he tried to hug me but pulled back in pain. He sat down and we talked with him a while, then went in to see Erwin. He sat in a chair next to his bed, when he saw us, his face brightened up.

"Eddie, you're OK, that's great, what about all the others?"

"We lost three men, all mine are OK, and the gold is safe we will go and get it tomorrow. We are all sorry this happened to you."

"Well, it just shows that man is evil, how could he do this to me?"

"Erwin, the man is as you say evil, but we hope we meet up with him, I'm sure Sammy or Snowy could repay him."

"I really hope that will happen Eddie, I hope that will happen."

"So do I Erwin, so do I, you join us once you're feeling better do you understand?"

"Yes Eddie, I should be fine, they've given me pills to take for the pain. You know, I still think my hand is still there."

"Yeh, that will be with you for sometime Erwin, some of the men I served with in Nan felt the same."

Big Pat was being shipped back to the U.K. and we that was left, had arranged a game of gold, because we had a lot of time to kill, the gold would take forty eight hours to get up. I called in at my home, the villa up the hill, my men came with me, Rob had called in to his home, he gave me a call and I talked to him, but as I was about to hang up, I heard like someone was listening in.

I told those men with me, that phone calls were something to be very careful about.

Well we had some R&R at the Golf Club, with a surprise number of us taking part, twenty four in all…in fact, that's what was left out of thirty five of us. There was some good players out there, some of us struggled but got by, Rob, who played a good game, had the best shot of the whole match. He landed in a dried up stream that filled up the small lake, his ball landed right on the pinnacle of dried dirt. He hit a seven iron, and you just wouldn't believe it unless you saw it happen, his ball hit the lake twice and landed right on the green. Well, that got the biggest cheer I have ever heard and Rob won the whole game easily. We were having a few drinks after the game, when one of the P.G.C. men spotted some guy taking an interest in us. He came over to me and said,

"I think we have company Eddie."

Two men had been watching us from a distance away, so I sent Robert and Sammy to check them out. Both were holding a golf club, looking like they meant harm, as soon as the two men saw them they started running, so too did Robert and Sammy, the two men jumped into a car and drove off.

We had a presentation to Rob, he won the 200 Euro for having won the competition. He was in no fit state to win anything, but being the only one who played regularly, it was a cakewalk. Sammy Brown, who didn't really play golf, he won too, because he managed to get four birdies, how he did it is anyone's guess. It was great to see all the men mixing well, they had come through a great deal of danger together…and it wasn't over by any means.

The next day Erwin had joined us, and we gathered off shore from the Spanish Warship, they had divers still working down in the cave. It was tough going for them, we all thought they would have all the gold up by now. We brought along a truck and two other vehicles. Now we had to wait until all the gold was brought up.

Erwin had asked us to help him get it back to Switzerland, I had to ask my men about that. Some did have businesses to run, so it wasn't a case of, Ok we'll go with you, they had to think of how long they would be gone. And another thing, gold is heavy and it can draw the heavies who want it for themselves. Gold is a very dangerous thing to have in large amounts.

I asked my men, and I felt sure I could rely on the men with me, Julian, Robert, Rob, Sammy and Snowy. They made arrangements back in the U.K. with regards to their businesses, and now they would stay with me until we delivered the gold to the Bank in Switzerland.

We all returned to the site and were invited on board the Warship by the Captain, we watched as the loose bars of gold were being uplifted in small bundles. Erwin joined us with his missing hand covered well and there was a leather cover over the stump.

The Captain invited us to eat with him, most of us didn't feel hungry but we sat down at the table. The Captain went on to say that all this business had now drawn International interest.

Sammy asked for more food as the cook put the food on his plate. The cook didn't understand him, Sammy took the big spoon off him and helped himself, he then said in Spanish, "gracias" the cook eyed him and moved on.

Once the cooks had served us all and the door was closed, the Captain asked for quietness as he said,

"We have assisted you in getting this gold, now you will load it onto your vehicles and you will be used as bait to catch this Von Ludendorff. You will proceed to the Assay Offices in Corrolejo, it is hoped this man will try to take the gold from you. We will make an announcement that this is being done, so you Mister Blake, and all the men will be armed, you will be now take an Oath so you become Spanish Police Deputies. This allows you all to have the weapons, however there are very strict rules of engagement, you cannot kill anyone, you may aim to wound below the waistline, nothing more, is that understood."

The Captain repeated what he had just said. We all answered, yes.

We finished eating and went up topside, where we could see a metal platform lying on the seabed with gold bars on it. The divers, including Fred and Peter were hard at work bringing up bars of gold in one's and two's, then lying them onto the metal platform. We all could see how tough it was, as the divers would stop for a rest each time they came up. On board others watched the sea and sky, there was a panic as a jet came in low and the men manning the missiles moved with it as it swooped low, and flew over the mountain ridge behind the Villa Winter. We all listened to Sammy as he said,

"That man would be crazy to attack a bloody Warship…he could you know, because he is crazy."

"I doubt it Sammy," said Julian. "He isn't that big a fool."

Erwin said, "That's him alright, he's just checking up on our progress, he'll be back at sometime."

The Captain came over to us. "Better get to your vehicles now, the last of the gold is just about to come up. We shall help load it. There is one point, three tons to go on each truck. Move off now."

We were ferried across to where we left the vehicles. We stood by while the sailors loaded up the gold. Sammy and Robert drove the trucks, Julian, Snowy and myself were in the Landrover.

In the trucks there was heavy machine guns and even some rocket launchers. As we moved off, the men from the P.G.C. came behind us, we took the quieter route up the centre of the Island from La Pared, then we would move on to Pajara, where it would get busier or so we hoped. Someone, more likely Von Ludendorff's men tried to run the leading truck off the road, but Sammy who was driving, crashed straight into them and sent them flying. This all took place near Vega de Rio Palmas, we raced on and instead of cutting off and going down past Antigua we moved on through Valle de Santa Ines. Again we were attacked, this time coming under fire from both sides of the road.

We fought our way through all the gunfire and then we saw a Police escort. The officer in charge called out in English, "Follow me."

We followed the police car down past Angel, but something was wrong, instead of going on straight down into Puerto Del Rosario, the police car turned left heading for Tetir. We all knew then what was going on. We were all in radio contact with each other.

Erwin came on the radio. "Eddie, they are taking us the wrong way."

By now we were in an open area with no houses, just sand and rocks, with hills all around us. We were coming under fire from two positions, I called into my radio, "Can anyone see them?"

Back came a reply, it was Snowy, "Those rocks over to our left 300 yards away."

"I see them, does everyone else see a target, if so lay down as much fire power as you can…over."

Erwin's P.G.C. men brought down two of the false policemen, then they ran to take cover behind one of the trucks. We were slowly being surrounded. Like the Indians running around a wagon train, at least eight vehicles were blasting away at us. We returned fire until most of us ran out of ammo, then out of nowhere came an armoured car…this had us stone dead.

I called up Erwin. "Erwin, Eddie here, can you get help sent in we sure need it."

"There's nothing I can do Eddie, use the rockets."

I called an open channel telling those with the R.P.G's to start using them on the armoured car and on anything else they have moving."

You could hear the woooossh as someone fired off a rocket, then another and another. The armoured car was blown to bits but the other vehicles were all still laying fire onto us. With no more ammo, the P.G.C. men were the first to lay down their weapons, then a rocket hit the front truck and we managed to dive underneath it. There was so much dust flying about it was difficult to see, I told my men to play dead, and using the blood of those already dead they rubbed it over their heads and faces.

As we lay there I heard Sammy saying, "that fuckin' bastard has his own Army."

We lay in a way that we could see everything going on around us. Three of us had ammo left, Sammy picked up another Mag' Julian and Robert both had full mag's left. They lay on top of their weapons making sure they couldn't be seen. Sammy, face and hands smeared in blood lay under the truck his eyes watching every movement, then he whispered into the radio set, "Oh no, the dirty bastards are killing those P.G.C. men."

I quickly said, "Sammy, don't you move, do you hear me…don't move a muscle, they are checking around the vehicles, stay still."

Von Ludendorff's men walked slowly around the vehicles and checked each body including us. There was a hairy moment when a weapon was pointed at Snowy who was lying out in the open. Julian slowly moved his weapon from under his body, then moved back to get the weapon into a position to fire it. But thank God, someone shouted at the man pointing the weapon at Snowy, he ran to join the others.

We saw them lift all the gold onto another two trucks and then they drove off.

We seemed to be the only ones left alive, Snowy found Hans Junge, and then we saw Erwin slumped over in the front seat of his vehicle still holding a weapon in his only hand that he had. We stopped to look at the carnage left after the attack.

Sammy shouted, "There are a few rockets left here and some ammo, I'm going to try this engine." The engine started up and we got on board, I found the binoculars under the seat so I scanned way ahead to see if there was any sign of dust being kicked up by the truck carrying the gold. I couldn't see any. I handed the binoculars to Julian, he kept watch while I drove, I took it easy, because I didn't want to suddenly come face to face with those murderers. Julian told me that the dust he saw had now stopped, that meant the trucks had too.

"They can't have gone very far Eddie, maybe into the next valley, but go very slowly, then we will stop and go on foot over that ridge up ahead of us."

I moved slowly towards the ridge ahead of us, it was about a mile away maybe. Pulling up at the base of the ridge, we all got out and walked up the slope towards the summit, it took quite sometime. To our surprise there was no trucks.

"Where are they?" said Robert Preston. "They couldn't just vanish that quick."

Sammy had the binoculars and as he looked we turned to look at him, I said, "Well Sammy anything, anything at all?"

"Well boss, it's kinda odd."

"What's odd?"

"Those trucks did go into that valley, then went back out, there is one thing I'd like to check closer up."

"Check what Sammy?" asked Julian.

"Those tyre tracks, they might tell us something."

Julian looked at me and screwed up his face, in as much as he would say…"what is Sammy talking about?"

Well once we got down there we all looked around and could see nothing…zero. Sammy however, was walking down the centre of the truck tracks, he had walked a good way down them, and then he turned around and started walking back towards us.

When he reached us, I asked, "What are you doing Sammy?"

"Well it's like this boss, a loaded truck going over sand leaves a deeper track than one running empty. Now look at these tracks all the way in, these tracks are deep, but look at them going back out of the valley, they are not deep."

Robert Preston butted in quickly, "They've hidden the gold right here somewhere."

"Now who's a clever boy then Robert!" said Sammy. "Let's find the bloody stuff and get to hell out of here before they come back."

"Robert, go bring the truck here, and watch yourself, hurry up."

I turned to the others and as we looked around for any area that had been dug up, there was none. Then Rob who had moved up to the rock face called back, "Eddie, up here." We all moved to join him as Robert pulled up with the truck.

Rob stood looking at the rock face, he turned to us and said, "Look carefully at the bottom here, see how there is sand balls all along this area here."

"Yes Rob, so what are you telling us?" asked Julian.

"I am telling you someone has covered over this area using water."

Sammy and Rob hit the rock with their weapons, and low and behold, out popped one of the crates, it burst open as the sixteen bars inside fell out.

"Right, let's get moving. Robert, move the truck as close as you can to here, then get this loaded."

I turned to Julian and said, "Oh, I just love it when things come good for us."

"So do I Eddie, so do I," said Julian as he grabbed a box of gold, these boxes or crates seemed heavier, maybe that's because we were under pressure to get it moved.

The Gold had been neatly stacked and the way they had it covered was pretty good camouflage, although it wouldn't last too long, so that meant they'd be back soon to pick it up. It took us ages to load all the gold, then it dawned on us we were miles from anywhere.

Julian then said, "Eddie, what are we to do with all this? We need to hide it somewhere."

"I think you're right Julian, but where?"

Sammy butted in, "I know boss!"

"OK Sammy, let's hear what you have to say."

NAZI GOLD

"Well there's over four tons of gold there, we are just minutes away from those burnt out vehicles, why not bury the lot there? They won't think of looking there for it, they'll think we got away with it."

"Sammy, if you had brains you would be dangerous."

"Yeh boss, I am dangerous, you know I am."

"Great stuff Sammy, let's do it."

We managed to get all the gold onto the truck, so I told Robert to drive, I knew he would be more careful than Sammy... The heat from the blazing sun was dehydrating us and with more heavy work, more so. At the burnt out vehicles we picked the large truck so we could get the lot underneath it, it was a hard slog, with every box getting heavier. We had no water and badly needed some. Sammy walked off and was going around the burnt out vehicles, when he returned he sat down a drum full of water, we laid into it, then I asked him, "Where did you get all that?"

"Out of the radiators boss."

I clapped Sammy on the back. "What would I do without you."

"You see, how many times over the years did I say that to you?"

With the gold hidden under the sand and truck we moved off then stopped, as Robert who was driving shouted, "Hey look, Erwin has moved."

Julian and I jumped off the truck and went over to the vehicle, Erwin was lying in the sand. We lifted him gently and laid him down in the back of the truck, Snowy attended to him he was trained in such matters...Erwin was semi-conscious. Snowy used water to cool him down, giving him sips at a time until he was able to sit up and talk.

We got a chopper up to airlift Erwin out, Rob went with him and that left five of us. We all moved away to higher ground, but the truck was left amongst the ones that were all damaged in the attack, as we got well up the hillside, we had to dive for cover as we heard the engines of another Helicopter coming in. The sweat was running off us, as we scrambled into rocks to hide.

"It's Von Ludendorff back for the gold," said Julian.

As the chopper came to rest, three vehicles arrived, two men got out of one and walked over to the chopper. That's when we got a good look at Herr Eric Von Ludendorff's face. He was a tall man with blonde hair a bit of red in it, he stood above the two men in front of him. There was a heated quarrel, then the unthinkable, Von Ludendorff pulled out a gun and shot the two men.

Sammy said, "Did you see that! My God, the evil bastard how could he do that to his own men?"

"Calm down Sammy…Calm down," said Julian.

Von Ludendorff stood there taking a good look around, we kissed the earth for those moments.

He spotted where the chopper came in for Erwin and of course, Rob too. He must have thought we had taken the gold out by chopper. They stood looking at the spot for some time, then we saw a convoy of vehicles coming up the valley, right towards us. There were three armoured cars and two trucks. They pulled up next to the chopper and Von Ludendorff, a man got out of the leading vehicles, talked with Von Ludendorff as he pointed down the valley, along the route they had just come from.

The chopper took off so we waited until it was well clear, then saw the vehicles leave the valley. Sammy ran down the hill and jumped into the driver's seat, then drove the truck to meet us. I sat beside Sammy holding a map of the Island in my hand, I told Sammy to take a turn once we were out of the valley. It was a wrong turn but it was the right one for us, because the Germans had gone the way we should have gone. I felt we had to get back and pick up Rob, he had contacts and we needed some help to beat off this mad man. Rob still had his radio, so I called him.

"Where are you now?" he asked.

"Coming down the hill towards Caleta de Fuste."

"Where's the gold?"

"Hidden, we need your help, who can you trust here in the Police Force?"

"Why Eddie?"

"Well once we get the gold we need an escort to go to the Government Vaults and put the gold in safe keeping until we fix up a flight to Switzerland."

"You're joking."

"I wish I was Rob, I wish I was. Can you do that?"

"Sure I can Eddie, where will you be?"

"If we don't crash, I'll be at home." Sammy looked around at me after I spoke.

"One more thing Rob, let all the Officials know what is going on, maybe, just maybe that could keep Von Ludendorff away, I'll talk to you later."

Sammy drove the truck straight to my home, the garage door was open and in he went. I had no sooner got out, when my wife June, came storming around the corner from the front door.

"For God's sake Eddie, look at the state you're in, you're not in the Army anymore Eddie, you all look like the 'A' Team, don't dare come inside, get washed by the pool...all of you."

As I turned I said quietly to Julian, "I think you ought to get Gloria back over here."

"Are you serious, she'd kill me seeing me like this."

They all looked like they had been dragged through a shithole. Well, we cleaned up then all the questions started, my wife doing the asking.

"Where have you, and these others been?"

"I know you won't believe this."

"Just try me Eddie, well go on."

"We have been helping the Switz Bankers get their gold back."

"Do you expect me to believe that."

"It's true June, that's what we are doing."

"You mean it's not over yet?"

"No, not quite."

I jumped in as Julian gave me a bad look.

"Listen honey, all we have to do is delivery this gold, that's it."

"Deliver it where?"

"Well we will know that after it is secured in the vaults up in Corralejo."

"If you lot want food you can eat in the garage, I'll make something for you all."

"Thanks honey, I appreciate that."

We were eating when Rob arrived, he walked around the side of the villa to the pool where we all were sitting.

"Well tell me, what happened out there?"

"I don't want to go into a long story, Von Ludendorff shot us up, stole all the gold, but we found it again."

"Where is it?"

"It's hidden under a burnt out truck."

"They'll find that easy Eddie."

"No they won't, they were standing just feet away from it and went their merry way."

"So what now?"

"I was thinking we might need more men, but I feel we can manage, I want you to inform the Police you know you can trust, and the people in the Army. We will need protection, as well as that gold once it goes into those vaults, can you get that done?"

"Yeh sure Eddie, no problem."

"Rob, we need this backup, this man is hell bent on getting his hands on this gold. Who yeh…and get us a big truck, with the tank full, bring here at night."

"What happened to the other Banker?"

"His vehicle was blown to bits, couldn't find his body anywhere."

"Eddie, you look after yourself, I've kinda grown to like you."

"Me too Rob, they'll watch for me, and we'll all be watching out for each other, like we always did."

I patted Rob on the shoulder, "don't worry, I've been in worse situations."

"I know that Eddie, but you were younger then."

Rob went off and I gave a lot of thought to what he said, I knew I was way far from being fit like I used to be, I was at times short of breath, that never happened to me before. When we had to run for cover I was panting like hell.

"Right you lot, go grab some sleep, we move off after 2000 hours. Later the truck will arrive and we want the weapons put on before we do anything else. When we get the gold loaded up I want two up front and three of us in the back. I have grenades, some explosives and the sniper rifles, there is also the machineguns. Sammy, you and Snowy will have the sniper rifles and rocket launchers in the back of the truck with me. Julian, you and Robert will be up front, that's if you don't mind."

"That's OK with me Eddie…. What about Rob?"

"I don't know if he is coming, we also have Erwin to think about, he's the main man here, so I'd say he will be with us all the way."

Sammy butted in saying, "Rob's not the type of man who would let us down, I'd say he will come with us where ever that may lead us."

We all got some 'kip' (sleep), a big fry up, thanks to my love June, who still wasn't happy about all this, but she had to do her bit in all this. The guys all thanked her, and as asked for, the truck arrived dead on time. We got to work welding metal onto the truck to fit the heavy machinegun on. Rob opened up the long toolboxes and, there was more ammo, rockets, grenades and explosives and other bits and pieces. Julian commented on how good a supplier Rob was, I said.

"Well he did serve with 5Para and at one time did supplies for them. Give him time and he will get anything we need."

Rob had another truck delivered as he felt we would need it. The six of us split up between the two vehicles, soon we were ready to go. My wife was there waving to me as we pulled away from the villa.

Sammy and I took the leading truck, with us was Rob. The others followed behind, with Snowy driving and with him was Robert and Julian. We all checked our radios were working, as we moved out of town of Caleta de Fuste, taking the route that would take us, firstly to Antigua then on up the middle of the Island past Tefia on to Tindaya then further on into the wilderness. It took less than an hour to reach the area where we hid all the gold. I pulled up as the other truck pulled behind me, I got out and talked to everyone.

"Right listen, we are not going straight in there, the area could be watched. We shall do the same, find a place that gives us a good panoramic view of that whole valley. Then one truck goes in with four of us in it, while two stays hidden with the other truck. If we get attacked, firepower will be our best defence that's where the second truck comes in with that powerful machinegun, and of course, those rockets. Julian, I will make contact with you if we need your help, we must be extremely careful now, getting caught with the gold we can't make a run for it with all that weight on board. So let's hope we get in and out, hopefully with no one seeing us go in there. Julian, I'll put Snowy with you he'll have the sniper rifle, it may well come in handy. OK, let's find a spot for an OP (Observation Post)."

We moved along slowly, there was no moon to help guide us, and we had no lights on as they would just draw attention to us. We picked an area and drove into a depression just short of the hills behind us, there we sat and watched for any movement across the whole area. I sent out Sammy and Snowy, as trained snipers they would soon know if there were anyone watching this area. They had gone forty minutes then returned giving the all clear.

We soon got moving along the valley to where the gold lay covered up under the burnt out truck. Four of us cleared the sand away, then two jumped onto the truck and started packing the boxes… While we loaded the gold, Snowy and Julian kept watch. When we arrived here it was pitch dark, but now there was a bright moon shining all over the valley. A noise startled us and a call from Julian told us why. There was something coming along the valley towards our area, we all stopped working and ran for our weapons, the four of us spread out away from the burnt out truck, I called Julian…

"Who's coming in Julian?"

"Just a minute Eddie, it looks like a private car, Snowy's looking through his 'scope, he's telling me it looks like a bunch of kids."

We all lay there in the sand watching as this car came right up to us and just flew past, not one of those kids even looked at the burnt out wrecks, they were too busy messing about.

We soon got on with the job at hand, by midnight we were loaded up. That's when Julian and Snowy came to join us with the other truck.

Robert Preston, he was the best driver amongst us all, he took over driving the truck with the gold on board. When we made to move off, the truck stuck fast in the sand, the weight was too much. It was obvious we had to split the weight between to two trucks, this was done as quickly as we could. Maybe this was a good thing splitting the gold up like this. At last we were on the move. Sammy took the lead truck and Robert followed in the other. I was keeping in touch with Sammy over the radio, as we approached a junction.

"Sammy, take to the right…confirm that."

"OK boss, got that."

"We have company," shouted Julian over the radio.

"Where are they Julian?" I asked.

"Look in your mirror, they are right behind us."

We could hear choppers, but couldn't see where they were.

"Follow me," shouted Sammy on his radio. "Building site up ahead, could hide in there…just follow me in."

Sammy led the way and we found ourselves inside a building site. Sammy had smashed through the gates. The area had been fenced off with sheets of wood and wiremesh.

Several villas were inside the site almost finished, there was rows of pipes all stacked up, with other materials covered with large tarpaulins, we used them to cover over the two trucks. Then we went inside one of the villas.

"Sammy, Snowy, get upstairs, keep your eyes open, don't fire unless it is needed."

From where we were standing inside the villa, the trucks just looked like covered over building materials. It was almost dawn and the sun crept over the hills. I kept moving from one window at the front of the villa, to another at the rear. All six of us just had to wait and see if the Germans would enter the site. Rob and Robert had secured the entrance.

Two choppers, small ones flew over the site, they flew past, then came back just as we thought they had moved on. They swung back and to our utter surprise they landed in another part of the building site, they were only eighty yards away from us. If we had time we could have admired the view, it certainly was beautiful, these villas were sited perfectly, but now two intruders spoiled our view. Snowy and Sammy had a fix on the choppers and anyone coming out of them six pairs of eyes were now watching the choppers, weapons up and ready, as two men got out of the choppers. These two were pilots, but they were with Von Ludendorff so they were targets. I called Snowy and Sammy, they already had them in their sights.

"If they see the trucks or any of us, kill them both."

Back came their reply. "OK boss."

Julian was listening into the open airways, he could hear talking it was all in Spanish, but he was sure it was the Police looking for them.

He came over to me and said, "How can we contact the Police without Von Ludendorff hearing our call?"

"Leave it for now Julian, let's see what these two do."

One of the pilots was having a good look around a villa on the far side, he came nearer to where we were and his head and eyes were looking at every thing. This was a very tense moment for us, as one of the pilots had gone to look under the tarpaulins.

He shouted in German, "Rechnen sie es bitte nach."

The German going over a pile of wood to check what was under the tarpaulins, slipped just as Snowy fired, he missed, Sammy got him. The other pilot seeing what had happened ran towards his chopper. Sammy and Snowy were out of sight of the pilot, he ran very fast.

Robert Preston also ran…after him, with me shouting, "Don't let him use the radio Robert." As Robert ran he stuck up his thumb indicating he had heard me. The pilot pulled open the chopper door and had climbed in as Robert shot him twice.

We all raced for the trucks and got on board just as workers gathered at the site entrance. They were shouting at us, thinking we were stealing their supplies and materials. Sammy shut them up, he took out an automatic weapon and fired off a burst, that got them running for cover.

Sammy's voice came over on the radio, "OK boss, where to?"

"Look at the map Sammy and head straight for Corralejo get to route 600."

We soon left the site with the workers still shouting and waving their arms on the air. Now the sun was beginning to heat up the air, as we moved downhill from the centre of the Island to Corralejo.

All went well as we drove into Corralejo, there was for a change, a pleasant surprise. Not only were the Police there, the Army was too. I had never seen so many people. Word got out of how we had found the gold, almost the people from all over the Island had gathered to cheer us in. The Chief of Police and the Army took over, while we watched every box being moved into the vaults.

Then there was a dinner laid on for us. The Mayor was so excited, he couldn't stand still for a moment. The Official invited us all to this function in the hotel ballroom. We walked into this hotel and everybody was looking at us, and I mean everybody, we were filthy, sweaty, covered in sand and with bandaged wounds looking dirty. After a clean up, shower, shave and anything else we had to do, it was back downstairs to the Ballroom. We were met by the Mayor, Army Officers and Police Officers, it looked like all their wives were there too. We all sat together all six of us. There was going to be a speech by the Mayor, then maybe we'd get around to eating, we were all starving.

Up stood the Mayor and he began talking.

"Let me take this opportunity to thank you brave men for what you have gone through, to secure this massive find of gold here, off our Island. You have not only put our Island on the world Media, which I am sure will see benefits later, but you have landed us with a huge windfall. As we can claim a percentage of the gold found in our waters, all of you have been awarded the Freedom of the Island by the Governing Committee. God Bless you all."

Loud hand clapping and cheering went on for too long. Sammy had filled his glass with wine and had been eating the nuts and crisps and olives that lay in the centre of the table, by the time food appeared he had one bottle emptied.

"Oh, that smell!" said Julian, "must be steak, I'll eat all the fat and leave nothing."

"Me too," said Robert Preston.

Vegetable soup was laid down in front of us all, as the chatter of people talking filled the dance floor. Sammy told the waiter to take the soup away and bring him the main course. The waiter gave him a look, then took the soup away.

The Mayor went on to say that Inspectors from Spain and Switzerland would be checking every single bar, before it would be flown to Switzerland. We all looked at each other, stopping eating, as he rattled on and on and on.

Sammy had now finished his meal first, and while he eyed the young ladies, who had just walked into the ballroom, he opened a box of cigars sitting on the table. He took one, lit one, then rolled one over towards me, then Julian. He then ordered more wine sat back and said,

"Now this I like, this is the life, don't you agree boss?"

I picked up the cigar, took a sniff at it and returned it into the box, I pulled out my own pack of cigars and said, "It could get better Sammy, I wouldn't smoke them, you'll get sick."

Sammy looked quickly at the cigar and threw it down on the table.

"Here, try one of these," he stuck it behind his ear.

He stood up as the band started playing and walked over to a young lady and asked her to dance. All the others were still eating.

I asked Rob what he would be doing if Erwin wanted us to accompany the gold to Switzerland. He said, "I suppose that would be OK."

"I can remember Erwin saying something like that, but I'd wait until he confirmed it to us. What about the rest of you?"

Julian said, "It's OK by me."

"Me too," said Snowy and Sammy. Robert stuck up his thumb, so he was in too. I really expected that the gold would have an official escort.

We were glad the Army was outside guarding the vaults and with drink flying around we sat there without a care in the world most of us had been up dancing several times, the party was in full swing. As we sat Julian passed our table giving us a wink of the eye as he moved on.

Preston, I'll give him his full and proper full name, Robert Linton Marsh Preston, it sounds like something out of an old movie. He said,

"What's the first thing you do when you get out of bed?"

Sammy said, "Scratch my arse."

Rob said, "Make a coffee."

"Wrong, all wrong."

Snowy said, "Go on then Robert, I know you're dying to tell us."

"Your feet," said Robert.

"OK, here's one for you," said Sammy. "This man looks into the mirror and says, if that man's father is my father's son, who is he?"

"It's himself, Sammy, I heard that one before," said Rob.

Julian had just joined us after dancing, he heard part of the last teaser.

"Here's one that no one will get right," said Julian, beaming from ear to ear. "We all have blood running through our veins, but can you tell me where it originates from?"

I actually knew that question but I stayed quiet, let the others answer it."

"Well," said Julian, "Does anyone know?"

Julian looked at me and said, "Tell them."

I looked at Sammy, then said, "What covers over most of this planet?"

Sammy answered, "Water."

"Correct Sammy, but it's not just water, it is salty water with any other ingredients within salty water, that's where our blood came from."

"Aah, come on Eddie," said Rob, "That can't be true."

"Oh yes it is, just ask any top Scientist."

Sammy then said, "Who would believe that, but mind you, when you think about it, sea water has everything in it, even gold."

We all gave a laugh at that remark.

The band was playing a Glen Miller number and the floor was full, I think everyone wanted to dance to the great music. We all were up there dancing and really enjoying the whole evening when suddenly the doors burst open, we all turned around quickly to look. The Police and Army personnel were being marched in at gunpoint, we could do nothing, all our weapons lay beneath our table.

I sized up the situation quickly, and had to tell Sammy and Snowy not to make a move, all the others moved away to the side of the dance floor as Von Ludendorff's men came storming in. The Army and Police had been stripped of weapons, and they stood aside too. The women were scared and some men too, and the Mayor was being calmed down by the Chief of Police.

Sammy said, "Let's get these bastards."

"Stay where you are Sammy," I said, as I moved forward to stand in front of my men and some others.

I stood there facing the entrance to the ballroom, then I heard marching, the double doors were held open and in marched these men in black, all armed, they made a corridor right into the ballroom. Then in strolled Von Ludendorff, what a contrast, he was dressed all in white while his men wore all black. He walked in like he was playing a big part in some movie, arrogant, chin up and full of himself.

The Mayor was shit scared as the Chief of Police tried to help him sit down. Von Ludendorff went straight for the Mayor.

"Where is the gold?" as he shouted at him, he hit him across the face with a fancy cane he was carrying.

"Leave him alone." Von Ludendorff turned quickly to face me.

"You again, you are becoming a pest Mister Blake, and most pests are shall we say, taken care of… Now where is the gold?"

"I thought you would already know where it is."

"Mister Blake, don't get smart with me, you have caused me a great deal of trouble and lost. If you do not tell me now, I shall kill one of your men."

"OK, I will show you where it is."

His men surrounded me and marched me out of the ballroom and out of the hotel into the street. As I moved outside, I caught movement in the corner of my eye, I saw Sammy and Snowy running up the rear of the buildings, the others watching from the hotel entrance, but I could see they had their weapons. I knew they would now act as soon as we got clear of all the people.

I knew I was in for something, as they started roughing me up a bit, but I just didn't expect what lay ahead for me. They pushed me to the ground and kicked me, but I was looking for the others, even though I was in pain from the kicking. I saw Sammy and Robert Preston heading way in front of where I was, Julian and Snowy went on the opposite side of the street, and just across from the Vaults where the gold was stored. Unknown to me at the time, Snowy had run back to get the two sniper rifles in their holdalls.

When Snowy returned to meet up with the others, something was wrong. He stayed out of sight and just watched the others who stood there in a tight group, he knew something had stopped them in their tracks. He climbed up onto the roof of a nearby building, took out the binoculars from the sniper holdall and began searching around the whole area slowly. He couldn't see any of Von Ludendorff's men. He used the telescope to see in through the windows nearby, again he couldn't see anyone. He looked for a signal by hand or body movement, but there was none. His eyes searched everywhere but there was nothing for him to go on.

The rest of his buddies were still standing there, in an open area between the buildings, when Snowy looked through the 'scope on his sniper rifle, he saw the weapons lying on the ground. He knew then that they were being held at gunpoint and that Von Ludendorff's men were keeping out of sight.

Snowy saw his buddies turn around to look at something that's when he saw me. I was strapped to a cross and being wheeled into the area where Sammy and the others all stood…with weapons pointing at them from the shadows.

I had blood running down my face because Von Ludendorff had put a crown of thorns around my head, then they switched on the headlights of one of their vehicles right on to me. I tried to lift my head to look at my men but the pain was too strong and my chin slumped onto my chest. Twice Sammy was going to move for his weapon and twice he was stopped by Julian.

This waste piece of ground between the two buildings was now lit up and I was the centrepiece. I could see some movement from the corner of my eye, in walked Von Ludendorff hitting a fancy walking cane off his leg, he swaggered past my men walked up to me hanging from the cross. He stood there with a wicked smile on his face. He turned to my men and said,

"You will stand there and watch him die, that is what happens to foolish people who try to be smart with me."

Von Ludendorff went on and on and on, talking bullshit...

Meanwhile up on the roof, Snowy was wiping sweat away from his eyes. He had Von Ludendorff in his sights several times, but felt if he took him out, his men would surely kill me. So many things were racing through his mind about his buddies, Eddie, his family and all their families... Then there was more movement down below.

Oh my God thought Snowy, oh no; he can't be doing that. Von Ludendorff's men were piling wood and bracken and rags around the feet of his boss...Snowy, on the roof actually spoke out loud, "Oh God, don't let him do this." Snowy kept an eye on Sammy, he knew him very well, he knew that he wouldn't stand by and do nothing about this, even with weapons aimed at him and the others.

Snowy moved to a better spot on the roof, because he didn't have a clear shot from where he was, a tree blocked his view. He kept watching Sammy and his boss Eddie Blake, he had blood pouring down the left hand side of his face onto his neck, his arms were tied firmly and his legs. Von Ludendorff talked mockingly to him as two of his men stood by ready to light the fire around the cross.

As Von Ludendorff moved past Preston to take the torch to light the fire, he pushed him to the ground, Sammy grabbed for a weapon, on the roof Snowy picked off those firing in on his buddies. Sammy and Julian also had handguns strapped to their legs.

Julian raced in with Preston and went about releasing me. Sammy was fighting hand to hand with two of the Germans, he took care of them as others protected Von Ludendorff as he made his getaway.

When they cut me down I felt so tired, they had to carry me back to the hotel. As we entered, a chopper flew over us that was Von Ludendorff making his escape.

I was taken to the same hospital that Big Pat Curran was in, he looked cheery as the others came in with me on a trolley. I looked a mess, needed an x-ray to check my ribs.

I quietly talked to Julian. "Tell the others to say nothing about this to my wife."

"I'll make sure they don't Eddie, we'll hang around and see how you make out, OK."

It makes you feel better with your buddies around, Big Pat was walking with crutches and his head and arm covered with bandages, but he was smiling.

Me, well I had just received a jab and in seconds I was out cold. They knew I was in a lot of pain. What happened after that I would learn later.

Erwin and Curran stood at my bed, but I was sound asleep with the drug they gave me.

I was in hospital for three days, then I went home and I needed to rest on Doctor's orders. My wife was wonderful, she looked after me well. As I felt better, there were questions I wanted to ask Erwin, and find out about the gold.

I wanted to talk to Erwin, the doctor told him no, he said he must rest, even after the third day I still didn't feel too good. If you've ever had your ribs done in, then you'll know what I'm going through. They had bandaged my chest up, but that was after they checked the x-rays, some cases you might need bandaged, but normally you don't.

At last I was allowed home, and as I said, my wife took good care of me. I had visitors, too many really, what I wanted was my men and Erwin here at my home, so I knew what was to be next with this job.

What I learnt from Erwin, was he wanted us to accompany the gold over to Switzerland, he also said that Von Ludendorff had been captured, but escaped again. Erwin had more support waiting for us, they were all Bank staff, some with Military training. I asked him why the Army didn't help. He told me that they were on arranged Winter Warfare training with N.A.T.O. troops. They could help us later.

Asking about the gold and what happened to it, Erwin was quick to say that the gold was still in tact.

Erwin had done a great deal of work over the last few days, he too, had been badly damaged, losing a hand and those top men at his Bank not doing enough to help him. He had to fix up everything, including the aircraft that would fly the gold back to Switzerland.

Meanwhile, Interpol had issued posters that were now posted all over Europe and beyond. They were determined to catch this thief.

I told Erwin that so far, I had Julian and Sammy joining me the next day. Rob and I hoped the others would too. I felt so tired, that was because I had lost a lot of blood, it takes time for your body to sort that out. But I was.

I couldn't believe that the Police had Von Ludendorff, then he managed to escape, I just couldn't believe it when I was told by Erwin.

A couple of days later, I was up and about, feeling so much better. Julian and Sammy had stayed at my villa while I rested, they sat talking with me out at the pool, and it was lovely and warm. I lit the first cigar I have had in many days, just as my wife brought out a tray with coffee and some cakes on it.

Julian asked, "Are you fit enough to make this trip Eddie?"

"Yeh, I think I'll manage, Julian."

Sammy then asked, "Boss, are you sure you can do this? Don't forget Von Ludendorff is still on the loose and you know what he did to you already."

I stayed quiet because I know Sammy, he would come up with one more reason why I shouldn't take this job on, but this was something I wanted to do. I wanted to make sure that bastard Von Ludendorff didn't get his hands on that gold. This man had escaped from Police guards, Army guards and even from a Courthouse. He was a master of disguises, he could walk right past you and you'd never know it was him. At least the gold was safe with Army patrols and armoured cars on guard outside the vaults, and a Colonel Gomez in charge. He checked up on his men all the time, they would jump to attention on his arrival and draw a crowd as he changed over the guards. Any cars, vans, or trucks were stopped and searched, nothing was allowed to move in or around the vaults.

Everything seemed to be centred around me getting fit enough to get that gold to its destination. I was fed up, so I walked down to Rob's bar, he wasn't there, so I asked the girl behind the bar if he was calling in. She said he'd be calling in about half an hour, I took a beer and sat outside it was cooler there, lit a cigar and settled back on the seat.

Rob soon walked in and was surprised to see me. "Eddie, I thought you had to rest."

"I have Rob, I feel OK."

Rob got two beers from the cooler and brought them out, he sat beside me then said, "Well, what's happening now?"

"Well the gold is going to Switzerland and, flying in to Lausanne then on to Zurich, we could have gone straight to Zurich but the weather is too bad to land there, with the aircraft that will be used. I want to know if you'll join me and the others?"

"Who's coming with us Eddie?"

"Well there's you and me, Julian, Sammy, Snowy and Robert Preston, we have to report back up to Corraljjeo. The Army are now guarding the gold."

"Where are the others now?"

"They're all up there waiting for me, they went up there last night, so we will go up in the morning, so make sure you have all the things you'll need, as we will soon fly out after I talk with Erwin."

Big Pat Curran called in to see us, he was on crutches, he was going home but he had news for us. In the absence of Herr Eric Von Ludendorff, he had to attend a Court, as top Judges from Spain, Switzerland and Germany wanted all the evidence they could get, to pass judgement on this evil man and put him away for life...once he was caught.

Big Pat was coming to see us away, as he couldn't fly right away because of his damaged ribs. He stayed at the same hotel as we did, we booked in the next morning.

The whole place was buzzing with Reporters, T.V. crews and of course, the Spanish Army guards. The Officer in charge took this business of guarding the gold very seriously indeed. They had been doing this for many days now, drawing crowds of holidaymakers to watch him change the guard. There was even a Tank and Armoured Cars standing by.

We walked in and booked in at the desk, then went looking for the others. Sammy was sitting at the pool with his feet dangling in the water he was fully clothed. Julian and the others sat at a table nearby. They all got up as we walked out into the sunshine.

"Great to see you're back on your feet Eddie," said Julian as he shook my hand. Robert, Sammy and Snowy all made nice comments as I took a seat with Rob beside me.

"Right boss, what will you have?" asked Sammy standing there with a pair of boots on, a T-shirt and black shorts.

"A nice cold beer Sammy, thank you."

"What about you Rob?"

"Get me the same Sammy…thanks."

After a good few minutes we all got chatting away, it was Snowy that brought it up.

"You know, it's really bothered me about why Von Ludendorff didn't take that gold."

Julian answered. "He probably had nowhere to hide it, over two tons of gold isn't easy to move or hide when you have so many looking for it and of course, him."

We were well aware of the reporters, they were sniffing around us waiting for the right moment to come in and ask us questions. Just then Erwin joined us, sitting two tables away. He almost repeated what Julian had just said about why Von Ludendorff didn't touch the gold, he then added,

"I suppose with the Army here in strength he wouldn't take that chance."

Just then I looked across at Snowy, he had just screwed up his face at that remark from Erwin. It made me think a little. Why would he say that, even we didn't know the Army was here in full strength, so how did he know that? And more to the point, how did Von Ludendorff know? Because the Army came in quietly from the sea, I wondered about Erwin, I hoped we didn't have a spy in our camp. I didn't like to say anything at that moment, but I was going to keep an eye on him just in case.

You can imagine how we all felt having to wait around for a Court hearing, when we really should have been getting that gold moved over to Switzerland.

When Erwin left us, which wasn't a surprise, because he was busy getting the right aircraft for the gold and us, he also said he was getting help from Bank employees, so when he left us it didn't bother me. We sat there having beers as Newspaper reporters tried to question us, they became very annoying and Sammy jumped from his seat and shouted, "Fuck off and leave us alone."

Reporters moved away, but some stayed, so we all moved at the request of the hotel management, we went to a private bar where we enjoyed a few beers.

The Clerk of the Court came to tell us exactly what we had to do, once we took our seats in Court. We would be called to the witness box, myself, Rob and Julian where we would be asked several questions that must be answered honestly.

Come 1600 hours we were asked to go to the Court, where the same Clerk took us to our seats. It was so very quiet, and there is that smell you get in courtrooms, I have no idea what it is but it reminds me of school days, the classes had the same smell.

Rob, Julian and I sat looking around at the reporters behind us a few locals sat at the back of the courtroom, as the Judges entered we stood up on request by the Clerk of the Court.

All three Judges sat down, then we did. Rob, then Julian went up into the witness box, they answered all their questions, and then it was my turn.

The Senior Judge said, "And you are…"

"Edward Blake your Honour."

"Let this Court know fully who we are talking about. The man in question is Herr Eric Von Ludendorff."

"Mister Blake, explain to this Court what this man has done."

"Well your Honour, he beat me badly and tied me to a cross and was about to light a fire around me, but was stopped by the local people running into this waste ground, where my men too, were being held at gunpoint. This man was going to kill me like he did with at least two of his own men."

"You actually saw this?"

"Yes your Honour, and Rob and Julian seated here beside me."

Questions were repeated and after about an hour we got out of there. The Senior Judge had told us that under International Law, we could claim compensation. I told him we would be well enough rewarded when we get paid for finding the gold.

It wasn't long after this that the Spanish Army removed the gold and took it to the airport. We followed in an Armoured car. I was impressed by Colonel Gomez, he was in charge of the Army Unit, he was like a hawk watching everyone, and when he said anything his men jumped to it.

At the airport the gold was taken up the ramp of the huge aircraft, then secured to the floor. At this stage Colonel Gomez never looked at the aircraft or inside it, he and his men watched all around the area, watching for anyone who might try to make an approach.

At least twenty soldiers stood around the aircraft, with their weapons held across their chests, they looked quite formidable.

With gold secured, we were driven out to the huge aircraft the Armoured car pulled up right at the ramp, we got out and slowly walked up the ramp, all of us taking a look back. Then once inside, the pilot came to tell us to sit along the sides, and in front of the gold towards the front of the plane, as a safeguard. If anything happened and the gold got loose we would be in a safe position on the aircraft.

As he turned to go back up into the cabin he said, "There's

drinks…soft drinks up front over there in the corner, coffee too, some grab sealed up and crisps. We will take off in fifteen minutes, keep strapped in until you see the light up at the door I could through change from red to green. One more thing, we shall hit some bad weather over the Bay of Biscay we will be staying to the west of Spain then going in over France, then on to Lausanne."

The pilot walked forward and up a few stairs and out of sight. The gold sat right to our left in the middle of the fuselage, it did look a lot when you see it stacked up. Next to the gold there was smaller crates, that was our weapons which included two Barrett Sniper rifles, one for Snowy the other for Sammy. We all settled down as the huge aircraft rumbled down the runway, it took forever to get off the ground, but finally did. Once in the air I briefed the men…

"OK listen up, I hope you can hear me over the noise of those bloody engines, here goes. You heard the pilot saying we were going to Lausanne, because bad weather wouldn't allow this huge plane to land there. So what we have to do is get transport from there to Zurich, passing through Bern and Lucerne. Now Erwin has been trying to get help from the Switz Army, but can't as they have a Nato winter Cadre to do. Now Erwin has Bank employees coming to help us, they have all had Army experience and there will be two females."

That last bit didn't go down very well with the men.

"Fuck that," said Sammy. "I'm not working with some bloody girl who has just come out of a Bank."

Julian then asked, "Just how many are coming?"

"Ten, eight men and two women, they have all been trained in the Army."

Robert Preston then said, "So have some of the idiots we've seen in our travels."

"They are coming to help us, they can get killed just like any one of us, so let's give them a chance."

Sammy screwed up his face and waved an arm, in as much as to say, they can do what they like.

In a way I did sympathise with Sammy, because we as soldiers didn't like women attached to us in any way. We trained in small, close knit Units and that was it, full stop.

Once they quietened down, Sammy asked if he could take out one of the sniper rifles. I said no, they had been sealed up.

"When we arrive, we can take the sniper rifles but nothing else, as Erwin will have weapons for us when we arrive."

"This is all very well, none of us have ever been in this country we are going to, we could be led into a trap."

"Erwin will be with us Sammy."

"I know that boss, I know that, but he doesn't seem to mix with us does he? We'll need crampons and the correct type of camouflage gear, proper clothing."

"That will be there waiting for us Sammy, so don't worry, we are being looked after."

I went up to see the pilot, we were getting very cold I asked him if he had a blower, one that blows heat. He switched on a blower and the others could feel it. I did too as I returned and sat down. It is in situations like this, you can just fall asleep in very cold conditions and that is the start of Hypothermia, a very dangerous situation to be in.

The cold was worse for us, coming from a warm climate, now the place was heating up.

We were about three hours into the flight, when the navigator walked in and had six trays all piled up, he sat them down saying, "There's some grub, help yourselves," he then just walked away back up the stairs and into the cabin area.

There was a lot of comment about the food on the trays, but I suppose it was better than nothing at all, at least we all eat it and it did fill the gap.

The aircraft was being knocked about as we hit bad weather, we made sure the belts holding us were secure and also those holding the gold in place.

"My God!" shouted Sammy, "Are we in the air or on the ground?"

It was so bad we were going up and down, to left and right, then the pilot came on over the intercom,

"Sorry about this we have hit bad weather so I am taking her up out of it, stay in your seats."

Snowy called out, "Don't worry, have you any parachutes on board?"

I can remember jumping from one of these types of planes with the American Airborne troops, but at least you could see the ground. In this bucket we couldn't see anything, but we, sure as hell could hear plenty as the aircraft pitched and dived all over the place.

This was a long flight and we were all dying to get on our feet and stretch our legs, but it was so bad we had to stay strapped into our seats. It was getting a bit 'hairy' as we felt like we were inside a bucket, and all that stopped us from being thrown about was the belts tied around us. We all sat there tense and concerned, not knowing how the pilot would cope with this very bad weather. A long journey had finally come to an end as we touched down at Lausanne.

Erwin was there to meet us and we went straight to a hanger, where he had the weapons for us. Snowy and Sammy now carried their sniper rifles. We were introduced to the ten Bank workers then handed out these weapons. Erwin did the handing out, we also got loads of full magazines.

The two girls, Anna and Gertrude both had Glock machineguns, they both were stripping them down to clean Anna called me over.

"Look, there's no firing pins."

I turned to Erwin and so did the others.

"Whose side are you on Erwin?" asked Julian.

"I'm on your side, I made a mistake thinking Von Ludendorff would help me, I know he is no good. I was going to tell you. You see, I used the Banks money four million, to invest and get me some money of the interest to pay off my debts, he told me not to worry that he would give it to me once we had the gold. But I swear I am with you all the way. I will get the firing pins."

"You get those pins and I promise you that four million will be easily paid back," I said, as I looked over towards Julian.

"Thanks Eddie, I'll get those firing pins."

Erwin went to one of the vehicles that were parked outside, he soon came back with the pins.

"Right everybody get these fixed into your weapons, and then double check them. Let's get one thing straight, I'm in charge of this little group, you don't do anything without my permission, is that clear?"

My men said nothing, it was the others who responded to what I said. I didn't need to hear it from them. I knew they were with me always.

"That gold out there is going to your main Bank in Zurich, we all have to make sure it gets there, so be on the alert always, because we have one man who wants it badly and he has an Army out there. Now, they can attack our small convoy at any time, so be ready to fight with those weapons you just received. Now let's get out there, the gold will be loaded up by now."

The route we were taking was through New Chatel on to Bern and then Lucerne from there we would move on to Zurich. Snow was falling as we left the airport, this wasn't good at all, the slower we moved the more danger we were in.

It was then that I made sure Erwin stayed within sight of me. The drivers were all Switz, so they knew which way to go the gold truck was in the middle of the convoy. We had two trucks and three long-based vehicles. The latter spread out front and back and centre, all with rocket launchers and 107's they fire 50mm shells. Each truck was armed likewise with access up through the cabin roof if the need arose.

I was very impressed by the winter clothes we had been supplied with, when we all lined up we looked like a real Commando Unit with our weapons slung over our shoulder, even the two girls looked the part. My men had four weapons on them, two that can be seen and two that remains hidden, handguns and knives or daggers are always hidden. In all we had an admirable amount of firepower, which in its self did make us feel good. But the weather didn't, the snow was thick and fast as it came down, not good when travelling along 'B' class roads. I gave the signal to move off. There was four in each vehicle, the driver and three others, in the leading vehicle there was myself, Sammy and Erwin plus the driver. In the second long-base vehicle there was Robert and Rob plus two of the Bankers, one the driver. In the third long-based vehicle there was Snowy, Julian and two Bankers. In both trucks there was four, including the two girls. We moved slowly through the driving snow, even at this pace it was dangerous, it was so difficult to see up ahead, several times we had to stop. No wonder we couldn't fly into Zurich.

The route we took had been picked out by Erwin, after we found out about those firing pins being missing. He took this route because it would be very difficult for any chopper attacking us and any ambush could be cleared quickly with the firepower we now had. As I said, we moved slowly but the worse thing happened as we took a bend in the road, the leading vehicle slipped off the road, there was no one injured. Sammy and I waved down the second truck, we hooked on the metal towrope and in no time at all were back on the road. From now on we had to be very careful, some parts of the road were sheets of ice.

It was getting so bad a man was sent forward to check out the road ahead, he came running back shouting, ambush, ambush. Total panic you might think …but not at all, we were more than ready for Von Ludendorff's men. I didn't even need to fire orders at the two girls, they knew what to do, and did it well. As planned the two trucks holding the gold were parked off the road, the three other vehicles went forward, blasting away with the heavy machineguns. The reason the trucks were parked off the road was we were about to have a break and a bite to eat. We had been travelling for many hours now, and all of us that came from the Island were hungry.

There was a lot of firepower hitting around us, Sammy had made for the trees on our right, to the left was cliffs rising almost straight up, our only way to seek cover was to take to the trees. Thick firtrees run along the right side of the road that's where we ended up. I could see Sammy and Snowy with their sniper rifles and a light machinegun, standing well into the trees, they were waiting on my giving them the order to move. Just then Robert Preston got hit, Rob and I ran to his side, we moved him further into the trees away from direct gunfire. Snowy ran over to join us, we worked on Robert and got out the bullet then patched him up. Once we saw Robert was OK, I told Sammy and Snowy to get those heavy guns. They kept us pinned down, so off they went.

The rest of us were spread out in the trees as Sammy called in.

"Boss, going high." What he meant by that he was climbing the rocks way over on the left of the road, this would get him above the attackers.

The road we were on was winding up hill with bends that took the road out of sight as you moved along, tall, steep cliffs on the left shot straight up with breaks between the mountains. All to the right was where we now were in the firtrees. There was a small stone dike running along the perimeter of this woodland, it acted as cover for us, as we could move along it if we kept our heads down, we had to with all the gunfire coming in on us.

We had rockets blowing up near our position, but no one was hurt, the biggest problem was the snow, we could fix onto the attackers because of all the heavy snow falling. Julian searched through binoculars to see where the attackers position was, in the meantime we sent off a few bursts, then watched as the area the bullets hit sending snow flying into the air.

As we took more shot hitting around us, I shouted for everybody to move back into the trees, as we ran back I heard the loud crack of the Barrett gun. Snowy or Sammy had found a target. Another crack then another crack, then all went quiet. About half an hour past and there was no sign of the two snipers, Sammy and Snowy, then Anna called out, someone's coming down through the trees.

I shouted, "Everyone get down."

Out through the trees came Sammy and Snowy, they had done a very good job, because we were pinned down where we were. As Snowy came in Gertrude gave him a big hug, then Anna grabbed Sammy who gave her a kiss on the cheek then encouraged Sammy to dance through the trees. When all that was done, the two of them went to see how Robert Preston was.

Robert said, "I'm glad you two are back, I missed you."

"Ah, go on with you," said Sammy, "we did it for you, no German was going to take my buddy."

Robert was in pain so Snowy who is well trained in First Aid and Field Surgery, went to his backpack in one of the trucks, he brought back his First Aid kit.

"Right, make a fist Robert." Robert made a fist with his left hand, Snowy put a tourniquet on, then gave Robert a 'shot' of morphine. "There, that should help you cope with the pain."

"Thanks Snowy."

"Anytime mate...anytime!"

I was watching Snowy and Robert as he gave him the morphine, I gave him a smile and the thumbs up, then I shouted, "OK, let's hear it, is everybody here?"

Sammy shouted back, "All here boss, I checked."

"What can we do now?" asked Erwin. "They are up ahead of us so we cannot move anywhere."

"We can still move Erwin, but there's something else we can do if we get overrun."

Julian standing with me said, "Are you talking about the explosive."

"Yes, it might pay off if we fix up both trucks with charges, just enough to destroy the trucks and even blow the gold all over the place, doing that we could save it going into Von Ludendorff's hands."

"Ok Eddie, let's do it."

"The rest of you keep your eyes on that roadway up the hill, don't let anything come down here while we fix up the charges."

With the others all lying under the trees, Julian and I went down to the trucks. In the toolbox was the explosives, what we had to do, was place each charge, four on each truck so that they would blow up together. This meant fusing each lump of the stuff and taking all the wires over the road and into the trees. Julian set up one truck, while I did the other.

Two lots of the explosive went on each side of the trucks all on the main framework below, there was no charges put on the fuel tanks, this wasn't necessary, the purpose of this was to scatter the gold, if it had to be done.

We had to be very careful how we strapped down the explosive, we didn't want it to slip or move, so we wrapped tape all around each charge, then we checked with each other that all charges were in place, before inserting the explosive caps. Then we brought the wires up from where the plungers, all the wires had been taped together now we had to fix them onto the caps, they had a copper ring on them so it was easy fixing them on. We kept talking on our radios that helped to keep us focused on what we were doing, and so far there had been no more trouble, but we knew it was out there, Von Ludendorff doesn't give up that easily.

When Julian and I checked on what we had just done, we moved back up the road to where the others lay hidden.

When that stuff blew up it would make those trucks disappear, that is how strong the explosives were.

As we rejoined the others, the snow had stopped, we could see all the way up the hill to where the road made a turn out of sight. We had to take the chance of moving on. Julian and I went to the trucks and removed the detonators, kept the wires in place them stuck them into a bag, for use later.

We all got into the vehicles and moved on up the hill, but we moved cautiously with the bend in the road up ahead. We reached it and to our surprise there was no Von Ludendorff's men. So we moved faster and were less than a mile from Lucerne when we came under fire. A heavy machine gun was hitting around us, with chips coming off the trees. Sammy grabbed one of the rocket launchers and ran past our vehicle and down into the trees, we couldn't see him, the bullets were to close for comfort so we all jumped to the safety of the trees.

As we lay there under the cover of the trees, Julian mentioned that these attacks didn't come to anything, which could mean they were holding us back, while they prepared the big one. I agreed with that, and so we moved in and attacked the position Von Ludendorff's men held. We had plenty to throw at them, the rockets and R.P.G's and loads of small arms fire, this soon had them running.

I called in Snowy and Sammy who had moved forward from our position.

"Get back down here pronto, we are moving out."

The vehicles moved on then slowed down as Snowy and Sammy came running into view, they jumped on board and we soon picked up speed. We had to fight our way out, as more bullets came ripping in on us. We had no choice but to fight our way clear, if we stayed here none of us would get out alive, we just had to get the gold to Zurich.

Rob, who had been quiet all the time called over on his radio,

"Eddie…Rob here, let's get to hell out of this even if it means going back down this road."

I call Julian and explain our move. Although Julian held rank above me, everyone knew this was my 'show' but I had too much respect for my boss. In the Regiment he was in charge of the Squadron when he was Acting Major. I would take his advice before any other person. We both knew it would be daylight in an hour, this would be when Von Ludendorff would send in his men to take the gold from us.

Snowy was working on Robert's shoulder where he had been

shot, I checked with the others, all seemed well. While Snowy worked on Robert, Rob and Sammy were busy fixing two more heavy machineguns to the long-based vehicles, this gave us more fire power up front, so it would stop anyone rushing in on us.

It was very cold now, there was no snow falling at all, we had to put on the thick Parka jackets and boy, did we need them. The biggest danger in weather like this, is hypothermia. It can take you over quite easily as you dose off, you must keep the body moving, even if it means jumping up and down, moving the arms and legs. I did keep an eye on everyone, especially the two girls and Robert. The girls were hardy and with what I had seen so far, they were good soldiers. They did all the right things just as you are trained in Bootcamp, or basic training Camp. These girls did exceptionally well, this was probably their first time in combat, at its worst. We moved on and managed to fight through two more attacks.

While we were on the move, Julian had mounted an old 3.5 rocket launcher onto his vehicle, they're the type you have to wire up before you can fire them, but they can get the job done. It was clear we would have nothing but trouble all the way to our destination.

As we reached Langenthal, a call came in from Interpol, the Elite Police Force Europe. They had received a message from A.T.C. (Air Traffic Control) that two helicopters had not responded to their call, they warned us to be ready for any helicopter flying near us.

I thanked them and also said that we are ready for them.

I then called in each vehicle and told them to listen for choppers, telling them to watch and listen.

We had a long way to go, I was hoping we would reach Berne, as the crow flies there was roughly over a hundred miles to travel, but this was tough going. We had already covered forty odds, and Berne wasn't too far away, these back roads are dangerous when it snows, so we had to take it easy. Well we pushed on past Berne and still no choppers around, so we felt OK.

A call from Erwin telling me he was still trying to get the Army involved, as he talked the others could hear as we had open lines, so everyone heard any orders I gave, or indeed Julian.

Julian came on saying, "I doubt if any help is going to come our way Eddie."

He just got those words out when we had incoming fire, by now we were near houses with a river on our right, as the gunfire increased, people were looking out of their homes, ten minutes of this and then we heard the sirens, people had called the Police. I told the convoy to stop, then called Sammy and Snowy to join me up front. I wanted them there so I could send them out if things got bad.

We went through a village and the roadway had trees on each side, again we had incoming fire, we in the leading vehicle heard an almighty scream, so we pulled up, and everyone got into a defensive position as I ran back with Sammy towards the trucks.

It was Anna, she had taken wood splinters in her hand as she stepped down from the truck. Sammy saw the splinters and punched her on chin and knocked her out, he quickly took out the splinters and Snowy did the rest, cleaning it up. When she came she said, "Who hit me?"

Sammy said, "I did, it saved you a lot of pain."

"My chin is very sore."

"Oh, don't worry, that will wear off in an hour or so"...

She moved forward towards Sammy and hit him right on the nose.

Sammy then said, "Now that's some way to thank a guy."

"Come on, let's get out of here," shouted Julian. We were still coming under fire, all the others kept returning it, we just kept going and soon we were on the other side of the Sugar See, now Von Ludendorff's men were behind us. We had cleared the built up area and had trees both sides of the road, we had guns firing front and to our rear, it became obvious that those behind us were trying to push us forward into an ambush. So we went in reverse down hill returning fire all the time. Then one of the trucks came off the road we had to stop. Being under fire we couldn't do much about the truck.

It was now daylight and things could be seen clearly. We were in a sticky situation, with Von Ludendorff's men behind us and others racing down the roadway on foot. Sammy moved forward with Snowy, they both had their sniper's rifles with them and rocket launchers. They climbed over the rocks on our left and took up a position high above the attackers. Sammy fired off first bringing down some trees that fell across the roadway.

This stopped them in their tracks. Robert, who had been shot earlier shouted out, "Something's coming down that roadway, it's moving the trees Sammy blow down."

A vehicle had cleared away the blockage further up the hill, and my two snipers were still up in the rocks, as this J.C.B. pushed the trees blocking the road like they were matchsticks. One thing I had to do was take control of this bad situation, so the first thing I did was to tell everyone to watch what ammo they used up. Then I asked Julian to follow me, as I wanted to move up closer to see what we were up against. We both took the binoculars with us and ran up through the trees that's when Sammy called me.

"Stay where you are boss, too many of them, we can hold them down taking out a few, but they will soon know where we are. Better move back with the others…out."

"Hold on Sammy."

"I'm still here boss."

"Those trucks are wired up with H.E., if we get over, run, they go up, have you got that?"

"I've got it, I'll let Snowy know, he moved away from me, I think he's right up there amongst them, I'll get back…over."

As we watched up ahead, Julian and I saw Sammy running up the left-hand side of the road, just as a rocket hit where he was, when the smoke cleared there was no Sammy to be seen.

"I think we lost Sammy, Julian."

"It looks like we have Eddie, give him a call."

I tried making contact with Sammy, there was no response, I tried again and again, still nothing.

Erwin was ready to go out looking for Sammy, but I told him to stay with us, it was safer. Bullets were still flying around us, we returned fire, but had to watch our ammo, it was getting low. We heard the Barrett gun firing twice, we knew that must be Snowy, he was up in the rocks way above Von Ludendorff's men, if any of them move in on him he could pick them off.

I went over to the Bankers, they seemed to be using up a lot of ammo, I had to tell them to keep what they had, until a target came into view. I tried to get Sammy again, but there was nothing. It went through my mind, what or why didn't he call in? I put myself in his situation and then it dawned on me, either he was too close to Von Ludendorff's men or he may have lost his radio. Again we heard a Barrett gun fire twice, this time it seemed nearer us on the same side of the roadway that we were taking cover.

A sniper often moves after a shot, but not always, if he feels secure in his hideaway, then he'd stay there. If however, he were in a built up area, then he would move, because you can be spotted more easily in buildings. Again there was a crack from the sniper rifle, just after that, Snowy called in.

"Boss, I'm coming in down through the trees on your right, there is a lot of them up here, there is no way we can go on...over."

"OK Snowy, come in but take your time make sure you're not followed we'll be watching for you...out."

When I looked around at what men we had left, it wasn't very encouraging. Three dead, one wounded, we had lost three of the Bankers, one missing, so thank God Snowy was coming in.

Snow started falling again. Luckily we were in the trees and this was an advantage to us, we could see anyone approaching. Although it was daytime, this snowfall dulled down everything, it was like the sun was setting and the more snow that fell the darker it became.

In the Regiment we wouldn't hang around, we'd get right in there and attack, but this was different. The Bankers, they were all young and could run like Robert, Rob, Snowy and Sammy, but myself and Julian were too old for this kind of stuff, OK maybe at close quarter battle stuff, but not this.

I walked up the line of those lying down and keeping their heads down. Erwin and Rob stayed close to the two girls, as did the other Bank employees', Julian, Robert and I were first in line, so any attack would come to us first.

There was a wind getting up and blowing away from us, so any movement ahead of us wouldn't be heard. I turned to Robert and said, "How do you feel?"

He lightly touched where he had been shot, then said, "I'm OK boss."

"Good, will you move further forward, we need someone up there just listening, so you can dig in to the 'brush' and just listen. Call in as soon as you get into position."

Robert moved off holding his weapon in one hand keeping well into the tree line, soon he was out of sight. I couldn't stop thinking about Sammy that really hit home. I made another call, but again there was no response, Julian looked at me and his head bowed.

Erwin had taken down all the heavy machine guns and was now busy laying them into position, two on our side of the road and one on the other side, he even split up what ammo was left between them. Talk about Custer's last stand, this was it, at least we did have some cover, and an option, we could use all the ammo we had, then clear out down through the trees as either I or Julian blew up the gold trucks.

I covered my ears to listen as I thought I could hear an engine running, but I was wrong there was no sound. I think everybody was looking up the hill, well it wasn't really a hill more like a gradual slope… Looking for the tracks we had made, they were all

One of the Bankers called out, "There's someone coming."

Just then Robert came running back through the trees, "Get ready they are coming." Robert dived to the ground on his uninjured side, as the Bankers opened up.

"I remind you all go easy on the ammo."

I looked over at Robert and asked, "How many are coming in?"

"Difficult to say boss, twenty anyway." Robert continued, "I'll go forward with the 107."

"I'll come with you," said Rob.

Julian and I went over to check out the charges we had laid on the trucks, they were fine, on our return Snowy came walking down through the trees, we were all delighted to see him.

We heard Rob and Robert let fly with the 107's and this really scattered the on coming attack, we all started firing just short bursts, as Rob and Robert let off the 107's. Von Ludendorff's men retreated…Julian and I clapped Snowy on the shoulder we were so glad to have him back. Snowy saw that Sammy wasn't with us, he asked, "Where is Sammy?"

Julian answered. "Eddie has called him many times but there's been nothing back."

"I was with him when they sent two rockets down at us, I was sure he got clear."

"Well he's not here Snowy and I have called him many times."

Snowy thought for a moment, then said, "He's gone to ground somewhere up there."

"Well let's hope so." Our conversation was soon disturbed by the sound of helicopters.

This was it I thought, as we all began firing our weapons, then rockets were fired from the choppers but they went wide of our position. Two more were fired they went wide too, then the snow stopped we could see the two choppers, Julian shouted out,

"It's him, it's Von Ludendorff"… We could see him grinning at us, he knew he had us beaten.

Rob shouted out, "They're coming round the bend, they're walking down the road towards us."

Rob was right, they were walking down towards us, but they didn't have any weapons in their hands, they were up in the air. Behind them came the Switz Army. The Switz Army turned up just seconds too late, as Julian and I had triggered off the explosions. Well the gold went shooting out everywhere, into the rocks and some dug right into trees.

"Now that's what I would call bad timing Eddie," said Julian as we stood up and walked back to join the others.

I picked out a bar from a tree we walked past, then I said, "Yes Julian you are absolutely spot on."

The chopper still up there swung away to the left, that's when we heard it, we all heard it, the sniper rifle crack. Sammy was alive and had waited his chance to get a shot at Von Ludendorff, the whole place became suddenly quiet, and then we heard the chopper crash and burst into flames.

Out of the falling show came Sammy holding up the Barrett sniper rifle and shouting, "I said I'd get the bastard, I told you all I'd get him." Sammy was still raving on, getting hugs and kisses from the two girls. All of us well, we were so glad to see him. Our faces said it all, Sammy knew how we felt seeing him back amongst us again.

The Colonel in Charge of the Switz Army unit, shouted out, "Who is in charge here."

Julian pointed at me. The Colonel came walking over to me and said,

"OK, where is the gold?"

I spread out my arms and said, "It's lying all around you."

The Officer looked at the rocks, and on the road and trees, he then said,

"What happened here?"

"We blew up the gold to ensure Von Ludendorff didn't get his hands on it, pity you didn't arrive sooner."

As we jumped on board a truck that would take us in to Zurich, we watched as the Army started collecting all the gold bars. There were some tears as we past the dead bodies of the three Bankers being lifted into an ambulance. Even Erwin had tears in his eyes, after all they were his colleagues.

On the truck we all looked a dirty, scruffy motley crowd, as Sammy said, "Once they get that gold stacked up I will kiss it and ask if I can get a bar to keep forever."

"I'm sure they will do that for you Sammy," said Julian.

Sammy looked over at me, I shook my head in a 'yes' fashion then said, "You'll get your gold bar Sammy, I'll make sure you do."

"Thanks boss, I'm going to keep it for my children, they can have it when I'm gone."

"You do know there is certain to be a Court case over this gold, and you Rob, Eddie and I will definitely have to appear."

Anna asked, "Don't you think we should receive an award to for helping you all."

Sammy quickly answered. "Sure you will and you all deserve it, you girls were very brave out there."

Just then Anna took out a small packet of shag to make a roll up, then she took out a small, black square cut off some if it and put it into the roll up…it was marijuana. None of us said anything. "It's OK to take if you know how much. I tried it in Vietnam and had horrible faces rushing at me with or without my eyes open, it was a terrible experience, so I never did what a lot of other guys did. I was straight from that day on. Being behind the 'lines' you needed a clear head."

I saw Anna pass over a joint to Sammy, and I caught that just in time.

"Sammy, don't do that." Sammy looked at me, thought for a moment then handed it back over to Anna.

It took about an hour to get to the hotel we were to stay in. All of us walked in there, mucky and tired, as the other guests gave us some funny looks. It was a different tune later, when we all had washed up and stood smartly dressed down at the bar. As we walked in the other guests applauded is all the way in.

Sammy had ordered six double Scotch, when he got the bill he turned to face us holding it up, "Bloody hell, look at this bill that's almost half a week's wages back home."

"I did tell you Sammy, it might be expensive here," said Julian.

His tune changed when in came the two girls, they looked very, very pretty, in fact stunning.

"What would you like to drink?" Sammy asked them.

Both asked for a beer. I must say this, they both looked really beautiful.

The whole place was lit up like in a carnival, it being near Christmas, with the trees lit up and decorations everywhere, it had a warm feeling about it. Although not like the Island we had come from, this warmth was more to do with feelings of the heart. There was a big dance laid on for us and the others who helped us. We had been handed on arrival, a letter each, with two thousand Euro's in each, and told to clean up and get out and buy some clothes for this dance, because the President and Army Top Brass would all be there.

We got geared up and came back to the Hotel and went to the bar, we sat with the Bankers who had helped us. We were enjoying this moment alone, just talking about the job we had just done, then the names of those who died came up, that was sad, so much so the girls cried, so too did Erwin and he had just walked in and sat down beside us. It's very sad when you lose anyone of your group in combat, it is even worse when you stop to really think about it. You're not just thinking about them, you think about their family, their girlfriends and it does get to you, you have to harden up and shake all these thoughts from you mind, some people can't, it is tough on them. But don't let me kid you, even hardened Veterans can feel it.

All six of us sat together at the same table, the two girls and the others from the Bank were all at the table next to us. Then there was all those invited from the Government and Army.

Julian asked, "Why do we have to hang about here, they're holding a big party, for what?"

I answered Julian, I knew how he felt about all these functions, all bloody talk, and those who lost their lives forgotten by most of them, just talk and loads of fuckin' bullshit…I felt like Julian did, and so too, did all the men with us. We have heard it all before, the only people that really matter are those who have lost dear ones. Medals, I have loads of them, and quite honestly no one gives a shit about them either.

All of us were praised for the dangerous work we had done, and ridding the World of a monster of a man in Von Ludendorff. We couldn't get out of there quick enough, but we were told that we must stay in Zurich until the Court hearing.

We all went to a private bar, and it was there that we heard about this Court business, but only Julian, Rob and I needed to attend, as we found it and we also were needed to I.D Von Ludendorff's body. They had eight bodies in the mortuary, so we had to visit there with these Judges.

We already sat through a lot of talking and the usual bullshit, now we had to do more of it while listening to Judges in a Court of Law. The hearing began.

Snowy, Robert and Erwin of course, stayed with us, as we reported to the Clerk of the Court, he got us seated.

Before any of us were called to the Stand, the Switz and German Lawyers clearly made claim to their part of the gold. The German gold was as I had thought, was heading for Argentina, with millions of Switz gold too. Lawyers looked at figures they had been given on the actual total of gold we had found AND more gold we missed.

As they talked Sammy, Snowy and Robert sat in the row of seats behind us. Sammy said, "You lot miss some, how could you do that?"

The Clerk of the Court stood up and said, "Keep quiet please."

I turned around and gave Sammy the sign, 'Zip it.'

Suddenly my name was called out by one of the Lawyers.

"Mister Edward Blake, will you take the Stand please."

I stood up and slightly turned to look as Julian and Rob, then I walked over to the Stand as the shaft of light from the sun came in and almost blinded me. There was a seat in the Witness Stand, I sat down as the Lawyer said,

"Mister Blake, you were the main reason behind the finding of this gold?"

"Yes, that is true, me and my two companions over there," I raised my hand and pointed to Rob and Julian.

"When you found this gold Mister Blake, what country did you believe it to belong to?"

"Switzerland."

"Why was that?"

"Well, the bars we actually saw when we broke open one of the boxes the bars were marked, I later confirmed that this gold was from Switzerland."

"Tell me Mister Blake, at anytime did you find any gold with German markings on the bars?"

I felt stumped, because we sold those bars and some of it was definitely German. The Lawyer repeated the question. I looked at Rob and Julian, they both indicated with a nod of their heads to go ahead and tell.

"There was bars with German markings on them."

"Mister Blake, thank you very much, stay there please."

Another Lawyer stood up and introduced himself. He was working for the Switz Bankers.

"Mister Blake, you said that there was bars with German marks on them."

"That's correct."

"What about gold bars with Switz markings on them, did you see any of these?"

"Yes I did."

"Can you tell me how many?"

"I'm afraid not, most of the boxes remained sealed, we only opened two or three in all, well, that was until we were attacked by

Von Ludendorff and his men. We blew up the trucks so the bars would be well mixed up."

"So you can confirm that there was indeed not just German gold inside that U-boat but also Switz gold."

"Yes, that is correct."

"Thank you Mister Blake, that will be all."

"Just a moment, I want to ask a question here, after all, we found this gold, you would never have found it but for us, many searches in the Atlantic came up with nothing. We are in fact, entitled to salvage rights, so how much was that gold worth?"

The Courtroom became silent, as we waited to hear just how much we had found. The two Lawyers looked towards the Judge, he nodded a yes, so we waited for the Lawyers or one of them to stand up and tell us how much was there. One of the Lawyers stood up, looked down at his papers in front of him, he then looked over at me, then said,

"The estimate we have at hand, is 800 millions."

Sammy shouted, "Oh boy! Oh boy! How much do we get?"

The Judge told Sammy to be quiet, then said,

"If you will ask the three men who can identify Eric Von Ludendorff to follow us to the mortuary."

Most of my group of men had seen Von Ludendorff, so they all followed the Judge and Lawyers to the nearby mortuary.

When the mortuary door was opened, Sammy just dived in there first, he was keen to see the body of Von Ludendorff. In all there was eight bodies lying out and covered over. The three Banker employees, who died fighting with us, they lay further away being cleaned up.

The Judge and Lawyers stepped aside, as we all took turns to look at each body, we were all spread out looking at different corpses when Sammy way ahead of us, reached the last body.

He shouted out, "HE'S NOT HERE!"

We all couldn't believe it, all of us quickly looked over the bodies again, and there was no Von Ludendorff.

"There's no way he could have survived, I brought down that chopper, the pilot and navigator are here, where is that bastard?"

The Judge and Lawyers looked scared, and I felt naked without a weapon. The Judge said,

"Well there is nothing we can do about this, but I must contact Interpol and they will have men out searching for him."

The Lawyer told us, "Von Ludendorff has lost a great deal trying to steal this gold, he will certainly want his revenge, so warn all your men Mister Blake."

"Don't worry Sir, I will."

Once back in the Courtroom, the Judge thanked us and then went on to say,

"The Bank consortium has put up a reward of twenty million paid to anyone who brings in Von Ludendorff, dead or alive. Mister Blake, I have been instructed to ask you first, if you wish to pursue this dangerous job."

I stood up and said, "Why me? I'm getting too old for jobs like this." I was aware that Snowy and Sammy were looking at me.

"Boss, take the job, we can do the legwork," said Sammy. Sammy was leaning forward quietly talking to me. "Take the job boss, take it."

The Judge then said, "Mister Blake, it is your decision, do you wish to accept?"

"Yeh, we'll take the job Sir."

"You will have help not only Special Forces from Germany and Switzerland also Interpol, they will be able to contact you no matter where you may be. A contract will be written up for you and the men you select to accompany you. There is still Reichbank gold inside that U-boat, however, that will be taken car of."

We sat there and listened as the Judge told us that more gold was used building inside parts of the U-boat. We were told to keep things quiet, no one must know about that or the fact that my team was picked to go after Von Ludendorff.

We could all go home, with a huge check (cheque) and just wait on a call from Interpol that would see us back in action. I was issued with a special radio set, so that Interpol had direct contact with me, once Von Ludendorff was spotted. Rob and I watched as all the others walked out to the plane that would take them back to home and the U.K. We waved them off, then Rob and I walked over to the plane that was taking us back home to Fuerteventura and what I loved, the warm weather.

When I arrived at the villa, there was no one at home. It took me time to realise it was our day for shopping, so my wife was out at the shops. I had been fed on the plane so I didn't need anything. I took young Robbie out to the pool with a cold beer lit a cigar and sat back and relaxed. As I sat there with my feet up on another chair, young Robbie, my lovely collie lay under my legs. When here at the villa, I trained him each morning, he was coming on fine, obeying all my commands, a good sign for such a young dog.

Rob said he'd call up later with his wife, he did, just as my wife pulled up at the front of the villa. There was big hugs and kisses, then we all took in the shopping.

We all ended up at the pool, it felt so good to be back home, and you really appreciate it, once you have roamed about elsewhere. Rob had gone into the kitchen to make his special drink. I let Rob see where the special radio set was that Interpol gave me, so he would know where it was and I also showed him how to operate it, it was easy enough. When he came out with a big jug full to the top, he filled up our glasses. The two women were also in the kitchen making something, I took a swig from the glass and licked my lips.

"Hey, this is good, what's in it?"

"There's Irish whisky, and scotch, black rum and brandy with loads of ice, and coke."

"Well I'll tell you this, by the time that jug is empty you and I will be pissed."

"Eddie, you're spot on, about time we relaxed don't you think."

I was messing about with young Robbie, throwing a ball for him to bring back to me, I slipped and fell into the pool, you know what, he dived in and grabbed me by the shirt, he was pulling me out towards the steps at the far end.

"Now that's what you call a well trained dog," said Rob.

"Just as well, I hit my head and was dazed, I only came round as Robbie pulled me onto the steps."

"What, Eddie, I thought you were messing about."

"No way, he really saved me."

I gave him a big hug and then another and another. As Robbie sat down next to me, Rob filled up the glasses again; I felt a little drunk, happy and contented just being right here at home. I looked over at Rob and he was smiling for no other reason but what we were drinking.

"Do you feel it yet?"

"Feel what, Rob?"

"Do you feel the drink getting at you?"

"Oh definitely, like my grey matter is floating around in my head."

"There's something else going through my head, Sammy was certain he got Von Ludendorff, yet he wasn't amongst those bodies, what do you think Eddie?"

"He obviously jumped clear as the chopper was hit."

"Surely someone would have reported something like that."

"Not really Rob, don't forget the weather at the time, it was snowing for most of the time up there."

"So what happens now?"

"We wait Rob and as soon as Interpol get on his trail, they will contact me."

"Where do you think he might be Eddie?"

"Rob, he could be right on this Island."

"You are joking Eddie."

"No I'm not, he could be here."

"What for…why?"

"You heard what the Judge said in that court, that U-boat, parts of it are made of gold."

"So that's how we couldn't find this other gold, that was all heading to Argentina, probably to start up an new German in that country. When you think about it, there is a great deal of Germans living there even now. That war in the Falkland Islands, could they have instigated that?"

"You know Rob, I don't think anyone has thought much about that side of the war down there."

"Why after all those years that has gone by, does Argentina suddenly cause a war, I believe there is a strong Nazi group still working quietly away down there."

"Well Eddie, they can stay down there, there's only one German that we are interested in…Von Ludendorff."

We were both getting drunk, the drink made up by Rob was very strong, but it was easy to drink with the coke in it…I think we talked about everything…

I could hear Rob's wife calling on him, she was going home, I watched him go. The next thing I can remember was waking up at the pool, where we had been drinking, covered over with a blanket. My wife would probably say, you sat there drinking all night, well you can stay there, then she covered me over.

Dawn was breaking and young Robbie moved that's what woke me up, I looked at my watch, my God! It was six o'clock in the morning! I wrapped the blanket around me, and Robbie jumped onto my lap, eventually I fell asleep again, waking up as my wife sat a tray down on the table next to me.

"I hope you have a hangover, there's some breakfast…now eat it."

Well I must say, I did have a good sleep, mind you, it wasn't cold because young Robbie kept me warm. Around midday Rob called up, he was his usual happy self.

"Did you sleep well Eddie?"

"Sure I did, right here with Robbie."

"What, you mean you haven't moved since I left you last night?"

"That's right, June stuck a blanket over me and left me here."

"Serves you right, for drinking that stuff."

"You made the bloody stuff, I drank it because I didn't want to hurt your feelings."

"My arse inside a bottle, you drank that stuff because you enjoyed it…didn't you?"

"OK Rob I give in, you win, I loved it."

My wife June came walking out to the pool, she had a face on her that would have frightened a bear. Looking at Rob she said,

"Don't you dare make any more of that drink you did last night. He was on Mars, so I left him there. Don't do it, OK."

"I'll leave it for a while June, that's a promise."

Looking at me she said, "And you get inside and wash yourself, that dog has been slavering all over you during the night."

I looked at Rob and said,

"I better have a shower, give me ten minutes and I will be back to join you."

Rob sat at the pool; June made him a coffee while he waited for me. When I did join Rob, the first thing he said was,

"Eddie, surely this man Von Ludendorff wouldn't try anything with all the Army and Police Forces from all over Europe looking for him?"

"He'll try anything if the prize is big enough."

"How big is the prize in that sunken U-boat Eddie?"

"Well going by what that Judge said, there must be at least 400 million."

"Now that is a big prize, so who is watching the wreck?"

"The spy satellites up in space do that job, some of them can read motorway signs, if Von Ludendorff moves anywhere near that U-boat they will be onto me in a flash."

"So what's your next move Eddie?"

"Well, I thought we would live a normal life and go fishing, play some gold, then I plan to do something I have always wanted to do."

"And what's that?"

"Grow veg, all good saleable crops, from carrots, turnips, you name it, I'll do it, and I hope to end up supplying the shops all over the Island. I intend to plant at different times so there will be fresh plants over an extended time, this will go down well with the big supermarkets."

"You do know there are people doing that here already Eddie."

"I know, but they don't stagger their growing period, I will."

"It sounds a good idea Eddie, so when are you starting up?"

"I thought I'd get a crop grown first, see what they are like, if they turn out good, I'll take samples around the biggest supermarkets, then see what happens."

"OK Eddie, so what comes next?"

"Well, I thought we could take a trip down to where Villa Winter is, do some fishing and just enjoy it."

Over the next few days we enjoyed fishing and golf, went down to Villa Winter, there was no one at all working anywhere near the Villa, all the archaeologists had gone. Rob at one visit wanted to dive down to the U-boat, however, I stopped him he didn't mind really.

Those few days were just great for both of us. Rob and I had been with this gold from day one, it was good we had struck together. Now I had to start planting, that took over five days, I had decided to have everything growing under cover, so all the plants were under canopies. I had two helpers, both Majoreros, that's the name given to people who live here, the natives. The older of the two was called Montana, and the young man was Miguel. They were good workers, anything I told them to do even if I wasn't there they did it. I intended to keep these two men in a job, then as things grew bigger, get two more for deliveries. I had everything worked out, so far I was really enjoying it all, the challenge was there, that meant something to me.

I had Rob up seeing me now and again, one of those days I was working at one of my plantations, covering some hessian over plants to protect them from a very warm sun, when the buzzer went. This was Interpol making contact with me. Rob stood next to me as I switched it on, Rob followed me home as I left Montana in charge. Once home I switched on the special radio set they had given me… Von Ludendorff had been seen in the Azores, when I told Rob he asked, "I suppose we will have to be on our guard now?"

The Portuguese are in no doubt it was him, he moored a large ship off the Island. The Spanish are sending in the Army to help keep tourists' away from the area near the Villa Winter, as they don't want to chase Von Ludendorff away. They will allow some tourist with cars in the area, but they will be Police.

"We cannot make any move on him, just the two of us wouldn't stand a chance. But he must now know about the gold that is still down there."

"Eddie, don't worry we don't make any move on that man, he will no doubt be closer come tomorrow we need to arm ourselves."

"I have weapons, but I'd love to see that U-boat, just to see where they used the gold in it's building."

"Are you sure about that Eddie, with Von Ludendorff close by?"

"Aah, it will take him two days to sail from the Azores."

"I suppose you're right Eddie, we could get down there and well clear before he shows up. When will we go?"

"We can go right now, the sooner the better, you get the diving gear and I'll get the weapons ready, don't forget the boat."

"It's still down at the harbour, I'll meet you there OK."

"Ok Rob, talk to you later…bye."

When Rob left, I went into the garage to check out what weapons I had locked away. I got what was needed to protect us, so I headed down to the harbour. Rob wasn't there yet, so I went on board the boat, Rob soon turned up and I could see he had all the diving gear on his trailer. I jumped off the boat and gave him a hand to get all the gear on board.

It takes a great deal of time to sail down to the Villa Winter, but it is safer we had to sail down around the Island then sail up the coast towards the area where the U-boat lay. When we arrived at the area, the Villa seemed to look older there was no one about, so Rob and I dived to the U-boat. Down we went Rob leading the way, a large fish swam past us as we dived, then another one. We were making for the area on the U-boat where we fired the tubes and we got a big surprise. We could actually see the gold shining as the light from the sun hit it... On seeing this we went back up and got on board the boat.

"We need to do something about that Eddie, anyone on a boat out here could easily see that."

"Any suggestions Rob?"

"Well all I can think of, is that barrel of grease, at least it would stick to the metal and it's black."

"OK, let's do it."

"How much oxygen is left Rob?"

I waited while Rob checked his, then mine, we had about just twenty minutes left each.

"That's more than enough Eddie, but we have to move ourselves get down there quicker this time."

We swam fast, this time wasting no time at all getting to where the gold was visible, we covered over the part we had seen and saw other area's, which we smeared with the grease.

Back up we went and as I got out of the water with Rob's help, he quickly handed me a cold beer. I lit up a cigar and we sat enjoying the sun's heat. What a contrast from Switzerland, cold, falling snow and where you could barely see two yards in front of you, to this, a warm sun, crystal clear water and a view that goes on and on without interference.

We took a really good look down into the sea, making sure there was no shines coming from the gold, it looked OK, so Rob and I took out the fishing rods and set about catching some fish. I went off the packeted fish, because you don't know just how long these boxed up fish are sitting in deep freeze. But I love a fresh fish…magic.

I really got to know Rob very well, with us going fishing a lot, and we always caught something. But it was his talk about U.F.O.s that grabbed my attention.

"I'm sure Eddie, you've heard about all the conspiracies, having spent time with the American Army, what do you think about it all?"

"Do you mean the U.F.O.s or the conspiracies?"

"Well what about the U.F.O.s what do you think about them?"

We both sat with our fishing rods in the water the lines with floats on them, so that a movement let us know we had a bite.

"Well Rob these U.F.O.s are real, they are black projects that the U.S.A. work on and develop. These craft can shoot straight up, turn left or right without reducing speed."

"How do you know that Eddie?"

"Because I have seen them."

"But these supersonic speeds would kill any pilot."

"That's true Rob, but they have a system on board that can cancel out gravity."

"Who invented that?"

"It's called back engineering Rob…Alien."

"Ah, come on Eddie, you don't expect me to believe that shit."

"That's exactly what it would do to you if you saw this stuff, it would make you shit yourself. Least said the better."

"You can't be serious Eddie, what's so important you can't even tell me?"

I really gave this some thought before I said anything, I really didn't want to, so I just said, "ALIENS."

"Aah, now you are joking."

"Rob, I haven't told this to anyone else, I have never been more serious in my life before…ALIENS do exist."

Those last few words had Rob sitting there in silence, he just looked at me, after some time he said,

"ARE you telling me, that all these U.F.O.s we are seeing are ALIENS?"

"No for God's sake, what people are seeing is back engineering that came from Alien Craft, also German."

This talk finished the fishing, so we set sail, or were about to when Rob shouted over to me.

"Look over there Eddie."

A large ship was rounding the tip of the Island, so we got the fishing rods back out, put on hats and sunglasses and just sat there pretending to fish. I couldn't believe it, I had caught a fish and I wasn't really holding on to the rod, I soon had to, because it was a big fish. I was struggling to hold on to it, Rob came over and took the rod. He pulled in a Barracuda, the biggest fish I have ever caught...with Rob's help. Rob pulled the fish on board and it really was big easily five feet long. Rob had to kill it with a knife through the head.

I've killed when I had to, but when I saw that fish die it really touched me, such a beautiful creature and now it was dead...but it did mean we had something for dinner.

The ship we had seen had moved on, so we could relax and head back to Caleta de Fuste.

My wife hates fish, so I prepared it myself and eat it by myself out near the pool, she wouldn't let me near the kitchen, I had the barbecue fired up. While I eat up the fish, young Robbie was running around the pool and in and out the bushes. I had fixed up a framework so my wife could grow flowers all different colours, lovely orchids.

I brought out to the pool my briefcase with all bits and pieces I had gathered about the Gold and the U-boats. There was over eleven hundred U-boats built, then there was the one partly built with the gold. This special U-boat must have been under construction long before the end of the war, it would have been nice to find out more about that, anyway, it sailed from out of France through the Straits of Gibraltar and into the Atlantic, where a British warship attacked it.

This meant that Germany knew well before the war ended that they would lose it.

They already had many Germans living in Argentina, so this plan was to shift the Reichmark gold reserves to there, and reunite sometime later. All they needed was this gold, but that didn't happen after being attacked, the U-boat limped its way to the Canary Islands and either sank or was scuttled. Those on board were most likely killed to keep this secret, that's why the U-boat lay in these waters, and those who knew about it, died over the years. Those in Argentina didn't make a move, because they would give themselves away, and didn't want to face a trial in Europe.

Now there was more than just the gold to consider, most countries in Europe has had artefacts stolen by Von Ludendorff, they want them back, this was made clear by the Judges, Von Ludendorff must be taken alive or no one will ever find the treasures he stole.

I now knew who would be with me on this 'job', Julian, Sammy, Snowy and Rob, the five of us. Several weeks had past since the hearing over in Switzerland, there was just one piece of information on Von Ludendorff…he was in the Azores.

This time all the guys were bringing their wives over for a holiday, Julian and his wife were staying with me and June, while Sammy and Snowy and their wives would stay at a nearby Hotel. My wife and I went to the airport to pick them up. There were loads of hugs and kisses, because they all knew each other, it was like a reunion for them. We all went to get them settled in at the hotel, then after we all went to my villa for a laid on dinner, even with waiters, wine and champagne. We had big lights that lit up our whole garden area at night.

All the food had been brought in and cooks and waiters to deal with all my guests needs. All eight of us sat there with a lovely dinner in the cool of the evening. Up above us the stars twinkled across the sky, the moon shone like a welcoming beacon. As the night moved to the witching hour, we all had a good few drinks in us, all except my wife, she doesn't drink. We had a singsong going and points given for the performances. Sammy won hands down. I believe it was almost five o'clock in the morning when we crawled into bed.

I asked for everyone, meaning the men, to join me at the poolside in the late afternoon. I waited at the poolside for the men who would help me get Von Ludendorff. Julian was already here with me, Rob had gone and picked up Snowy and Sammy. They all sat around me at the tables near the pool. I lit a cigar and sat back with a cold beer. On one of the tables was an icebox full of beers. I told the men to help themselves. Then I explained what we had to do.

"Well we all know that Von Ludendorff got away, I now know he is in the Azores, our job is to take him alive."

"There's no way he'd come back here," said Snowy.

"Oh yes there is Snowy, there is! That U-boat down there was partly built with gold!"

No one said anything, so I continued, "The German Judge reckons there is at least 1200 million in gold built into that U-boat and it doesn't all belong to Germany, other nations in Europe are making claims. That is the lure that will have Von Ludendorff coming back to that wreck. Once he knows that gold is down there and he will, because there will be an announcement about it, but not in the normal way. There will be a meeting held in Berlin and this is surely the way to let Von Ludendorff know. If they broadcast it on T.V. we would have thousands of people going down there."

"Let me kill the bastard," said Sammy.

"You can't, he must be taken alive, because they want to know where he had put all the artefacts he had stolen over the years."

"What is happening now Eddie?" asked Julian.

"Well we have to hear what the Judges say tomorrow, then we may know more of what we have to do. There are too many countries involved in this now. Seeming some of the gold belongs to them, not Germany or the Switz."

"Well it seems to me they cannot do a thing without us, we are the only people who know where the U-boat lies. So they need us," said Julian.

"Look boss, what is it they want us to do?" asked Snowy.

"Just stay out of sight until I get the go ahead where Von Ludendorff is hanging out, then we go get him."

"Why us? There's Armies out there, Police Forces, why not use them?" said Sammy.

"Because we know what he looks like, there is no photos or tapes that T.V. crews had, they got stolen so they have nothing to go on… but we have, we have all seen him in the flesh."

Snowy then asked, "Where are the weapons, boss?"

"I have them under lock and key, you'll get them when I get the word from Interpol to go get him."

Sammy then said, "Boss, we have to zero in those weapons, they've been moved around, know what I mean?"

"You can take them up to that valley, where we had the trouble with the gold, there's no one lives anywhere near there, but look out for holidaymakers, you know the 'score'.

Julian, being an ex Captain, was concerned about them firing off these Barrett guns, anyone hearing shots could bring the Police even the Army onto you both."

Snowy then said, "We will be very careful, if people are about then we call it off."

This meeting ended with caution, for Sammy and Snowy. They had to fire off at least fifteen, twenty rounds, aiming at the exact same spot on the target, then moving the sightings on the telescope until the shots grouped together. Once that happened then they had zeroed their eyes in to that weapon. If say, Sammy used Snowy's weapon he would not get the same results, because that weapon was zeroed in to Snowy's eyesight, as any sniper knows, they have their own weapon always. I was trained as a sniper way back, having to negotiate jungle and deserts, the desert one we had officers looking for us using binoculars. I can honestly say I beat everyone, being a country lad helped me, I knew all about movement, shine, shadow and so on.

But there's a lot more to sniping than just hitting a target, so I understood exactly what Snowy and Sammy had to do. They had to zero their weapons, but there wasn't really a suitable place, that's why that valley area would do.

The next morning we all gathered for the meeting, it was held in one of the function rooms. There was loads of Police around all of course armed. At least at this meeting we were all smartly dressed for a change.

Snowy said, as we took our seats, "Where is our stuff?" (Meaning the sniper rifles).

"June has the keys Snowy, if I don't happen to be around when you call up."

"OK boss."

This looked like the gathering of United Nations. There was Lawyers and Judges from six different countries, Holland, Belgium, France, Germany, Austria and Switzerland.

The Judges and Lawyers entered from a doorway at the rear of the room. Once seated, it was a German Judge who opened the meeting. He praised us for finding the gold but never actually mentioned it. He went on to say how everyone's interests would be given total consideration, then in his broken English said,

"Our Consortium will take over this operation."

I stood up and said, "Hold on a minute, don't we have some part to play in this?"

"And you are?" asked the Judge.

"I'm Eddie Blake, I found this gold."

"Yes, so I believe Mister Blake…you and your friends found this…"

This man was reluctant to say gold so I stood up and said it.

"Yes we found this gold."

"I'd rather you didn't say that word."

He was right too, the Spanish local Authority was walking out.

The German Judge said, "Please come back and sit down, I still have something to say in your interest."

The Local Council men and women sat back down to hear that because the gold was found on the Island's territory they would receive a percentage by Law.

That cheered up the locals, but not us.

Julian stood up and said, "Excuse me Sir?"

"Your name please?"

"Julian Channer Sir."

"I'm afraid that we don't seem to be included in getting that gold up, we want to be a part of that."

"Mister Channer, you and the other men seated here are a part of this whole operation. Your job is to get Herr Von Ludendorff alive, so he can stand trial and give us the information we require to return all the artefacts he has stolen."

Julian had just sat down when his phone rang. He listened then shouted out loud, "Get out of here there is a bomb…"

Everyone headed for the nearest door, we all ran out front, then saw a plane dive in towards the hotel, it dropped a bomb and the hotel was flattened. We helped people who had been injured and took them to the ambulances, there were children and old people hurt, some badly…this type of action is unforgivable.

We moved to a makeshift set-up, this bombing changed everything as the Judge said, "Mister Blake, you now have total control over this operation. You will have support from the Spanish Army, the Police and the German Special Forces."

"I'll need some specialist equipment."

"That will be arranged, and I have to say, that bomb was meant for us, not you men, he needs you all to get the gold out of the sea."

The lure to catch Von Ludendorff was simple, talking over the phones would soon get him moving. But it was a different matter for us if we were to get that U-boat up out of the sea. I don't think it has ever been done.

With everything agreed on, we set off by boat down to the U-boat. We would have to wait for a special lifting device to arrive by ship. This thing, so I am told is huge, it would have to be to lift all that weight from the seabed. But first, we and some others would dive down to the U-boat and weld on large rings, these would be used to lift the wreck up. Firstly, small charges of explosives would be placed all around the sub to help free it that's when the lift would begin. This lift would take several hours.

This story about the gold was making more headlines across the world, as a deliberate leak to the Press, intent on snaring Von Ludendorff. There was specialists called in to help with this operation.

Julian had become a dab hand at handling the boat, the three of us meaning Rob, me and Julian set off, with Snowy and Sammy doing their jobs as snipers. They went across country by Landrover, they would stay low and observe anyone going near the area where we worked on the U-boat. From their vantagepoint on the mountain behind the Villa Winter they could see for miles.

The Army patrolled a wide area to stop treasure hunters coming into the area we were working in.

Rob and I managed to get started first, we welded on two of these rings, but when the Americans arrived they said they were no good, not positioned correctly. They sent down divers and repositioned the rings. The German divers and the American divers were always giving out, there was arguments all the time. They never seemed to stop, positioning of these rings was more to do with weight, that's what they argued about, they knew the weight of this type of U-boat, but not the amount of gold laid into its construction. We stayed out of the fight. But it got so bad, we had to step in to stop them fighting. Rob and I stopped two of them, a German and an American. I told them, this is what Von Ludendorff wants you to do, it then makes his job easier...to take the gold away from us all.

This whole Island was buzzing with people and there is no way you can tell friend or foe. As we now had stayed on the boat we watched as the giant floating barge moved slowly into position for the lift. Around us there were some other boats, all part of this group, all had to make sure they anchored well because once the lift started, nothing can move about. It would cause a movement in the sea and this in turn would disturb the lifting, and send the U-boat back down causing a lot of damage, so far they had just got it to move, it was a crucial time in the lift. Suddenly from nowhere, we were attacked by a plane firing twin machineguns, everybody took cover, as the plane made repeated attacks. I called in Snowy and Sammy, to see if they had a shot at it.

Snowy answered, "We're working on it, there's two of them, one coming in now."

"Take them out, we are at a crucial stage of the lift, if they hit the crane platform that U-boat will go down nose first."

"OK boss, we both will aim at this one coming in...over."

We all watched as the attacking plane came in low, it was firing twin guns and then it dropped two bombs, one hit the American's boat, one damaged ours, the plane was now heading towards where Snowy and Sammy lay hidden. Two cracks from the Barrett gun and the plane burst into flames and swung around heading out to sea, where it crashed. The other plane moved away.

The man inside the giant crane shouted, "Can I carry on now?"

The American in charge called back, "Yeh, go ahead, it's OK."

Some forty minutes later we got the first sight of the U-boat as it cleared the water, but then it stopped, it was stuck there was something holding it. Divers went down and sure enough there was something holding it an anchor wedged into the sea floor. Men were running everywhere on board the ships, on our boat we went to look at the damage, it wasn't too bad, we could still sail. The American's boat was starting to sink, so Julian moved along side it to help the men get off...we had to dive for cover as the other plane came in. It blasted away with high calibre machineguns, but no rockets or bombs, and then it flew off.

We rushed to help those who had been injured, some were pretty bad, and one guy had his leg twisted up his back almost. Others had bullet wounds.

I could see Sammy and Snowy driving along the beach in their Landrover. I waved to them to come out to the boats. They both had trained in First Aid and had dealt with bullet wounds before. They came out and did what they could for the injured, as we waited for a helicopter to arrive and evacuate those needing more medical help. One young guy had part of his face blown away, it looked terrible, poor guy.

Sammy took one look at him and shouted up to the sky, "I'll get you, you evil bastard, I'll get you for this."

The others looked on not knowing how to take it all in, they were thinking Sammy was just raving on. A comment by one of the German engineers made me speak up. He spoke in German, but I knew what he had said, so I looked over at him and said, "Habe schmerzen auf dem kopf."

"He doesn't have a pain in his head, but he sure as hell will give Von Ludendorff one."

The German looked at me, then walked away. I know Sammy was just dying to kill Von Ludendorff, but orders are, bring him in alive.

There was something very important to do, stabilise the U-boat and get it moved to the harbour, where engineers can work on it.

Two Spanish warships stood by ready to help in the move to the harbour, this was a specially built harbour, one that could be drained out, once the U-boat was inside it.

There was always one thing or another going wrong, like the thick wire ropes twisting or breaking. The man in charge of the lifting, and the American was shouting to the men to stand well clear, the sheer power of the two warships pulled too quickly, this caused the ropes to twist and break. New lines were attached and after more than two hours, we started to move. It was a long way to go to the dry dock area.

The head ganger as I will call him, was at loggerheads with his German counterpart. They just couldn't agree on anything. We all kept together on Rob's friend's boat, but Julian made sure we were well away from those metal ropes.

The area we were heading to was just short of Morro Jable. Engineers had cut out the drydock at the west of Morro Jable, cutting away rock, roming sand by the tons. We didn't even know about this place until Erwin told us. As we rounded the southern tip of the Island, we were attacked. This time it wasn't aircraft, this time it was a Submarine. Men on the huge lifting barge screamed…Torpedoes. I got the binoculars out, but I didn't need them I could see the two missiles flying under the water, heading for the barge. Thank God the two warships were with us, they blasted the torpedoes, with one racing off to drop depth charges.

It worked the Sub moved on…but for how long?"

We all wondered what else Von Ludendorff would have, one thing was certain, he wanted that gold and no Naval ships or Army was going to stop him. Ruthless and cunning a bit like us really in our heyday. A loudhailer was shouting out, telling all those on other boats to be alert, as more trouble looked certain. Sammy and Snowy had taken up position each side of the bridge, they sat there ready to go into action the minute Von Ludendorff tried anything else. They'd be ready.

Julian was still at the helm, while Rob and I scanned the horizon through binoculars. It was a terrible slow move, like when they move oil rigs. We knew we were vulnerable out in the ocean, so too, did Von Ludendorff.

We moved like a little Armada, with the giant floating crane at U-boat closely escorted by the two Warships, three smaller boats including ours and two high speed boats out on each flank. We were still heading towards the drydock area near Morro Jable then more trouble. A small jet plane attacked with rockets, it sank our boat and we had to scramble onto the nearest boat... It came in again, firing two more rockets, Sammy and Snowy didn't get off a shot, we were being helped on board another boat. Just when we thought we were sitting ducks, two Spanish Airforce jets chased after the plane over the mountains, then just seconds after we heard an explosion, the plane had been brought down. We had boarded the German's boat, the one who did all the talking with the American team leader. He was OK with us, I think the fact that I spoke to him in German, went down well, even though it was a dig at him.

Von Ludendorff was attacking us all the way along the coast, with holidaymakers not knowing what was going on. Some thought we were making a Movie. It made our job worse, with people milling around everywhere as we made an approach towards the drydock area. Police had to move them away, as the giant crane inched nearer the dock.

A delicate manoeuvre was about to begin, as we watched from the dry land. We had been left off by the speedboats. It was then we saw for the first time, about a dozen GSG9 men, the German equivalent to the SAS, come from their hiding place on the German boat. They came at the right time as a much larger attack was coming in, this time from the air and land. Behind us were Von Ludendorff's men all in their grey uniforms and armed to the teeth. We opened up with what we had, then out came the GSG9 men they spread out and soon the attackers took to cover.

Being the oldest Julian, Rob and I moved to what was a safer area, while Sammy and Snowy took to the mountains behind us. Bullets were flying around everywhere, it wasn't a place where you could shoot and scoot. There were too many rocks to get over. Can you imagine trying to run across huge rocks, with someone firing weapons at you. That's why we stayed put. I heard the crack of one of the Barrett guns, the GSG9 noticed this, and they looked to the area where Sammy was. They knew Sammy and Snowy had gone to higher ground, so they kept an eye on them, as we did too.

At times it became a running battle, having to move about as soon as you fire off your weapon. Julian, Rob and I watched as the GSG9 men spread out and took to higher ground. Meanwhile, little could be done with the floating crane and U-boat, for ten maybe fifteen minutes we came under heavy fire. I got down low so I could use the binoculars and check out on Sammy and Snowy. I could see both of them they were about a hundred yards apart, just as I zeroed in on Sammy, he was hit on the shoulder I saw him fall back, then moments past and he was struggling to lift up the Barrett gun.

I radioed Snowy and he went to his aid, so too did two of the GSG9 men. When they reached him, Sammy had managed to get the sniper rifle up into a position where he could fire it. He was hit right on the pivotal bone in his shoulder, there was a lot of blood. Snowy moved quickly to Sammy's side, and he always carried a First Aid pack. He cleaned Sammy up, took out the bullet, while the two men of the GSG9 stood guard. Sammy was all for carrying on, but he was helped out by the two GSG9 men. Snowy stayed up there and took out a couple of Von Ludendorff's men. Sammy, when he arrived off the mountain, came to join us, a Doctor from the warship gave him a painkiller 'shot.' The firefight was still going on, locals and holidaymakers thought we were making a movie, some even came close enough to ask, but once they knew the truth, they soon ran off.

The attack was soon over as the warships pounded the positions of Von Ludendorff's men, they retreated.

We then could relax and watch as the U-boat rested in the drydock and then we all had time to have a look at it. It was a very impressive bit of engineering, a slick piece of work and much longer than we thought it was. This was in fact, a V11 C it had a range of 12600 miles or 20300Km, it had a diesel motor with modified parts throughout, another important factor was it had an air intake allowing it to stay under longer.

This one as Rob and I found out, did not have a number on it, it certainly must have been built after 1943, because some of the technology wasn't available until later.

We had gathered in a large tent that had been erected for us, with a cookhouse area inside, and a sleeping area for the men cutting up the U-boat. We had still to talk with the senior Judge, the German one about getting the proper type drug that Sammy and Snowy can use to bring down Von Ludendorff. Doctors gave their opinion, and then special bullets were made. Something else came to light, there was something else on that U-boat, just as valuable as the gold.

I knew before there was something else on that U-boat, because the senior Judge cut short what he was about to tell me. I pulled him up about it, as we were getting fed up, I told my men I would go and sit with the Judge, because I wanted to talk to him. Of course, my guys wanted to know what about, I told them I'd talk to them later.

I was in no hurry to ask him, as we felt safe enough, with the Spanish Army now in full strength, very impressive with Tanks and armoured cars placed at strategic positions all around us.

The Judge greeted me warmly as I sat down at the table, these long fold up types. He praised what we had done finding the gold, that gave me the opening to ask, "What was it you were going to tell me?"

"Ah…yes, I wondered when you would get around to asking me. There is something else on that U-boat…Diamonds…lots of them."

"What…are you sure about that?"

"Oh yes I am sure, there is 180 millions worth of diamonds hidden somewhere on that U-boat."

"Does anyone else know about this?"

"I doubt it, I found out by accident, I was re-checking old papers when the word 'diamonds' came up. I read on and learnt that they went with the gold."

"We need to stop them cutting up the U-boat, if we don't, those diamonds could be lost forever."

"I shall deal with that, the other thing needed will be given to the men who want them."

"Do you mean the special bullets?"

"Yes I do, one hit with these will make Herr Von Ludendorff very sleepy and he will doze off, then we have him."

"They will be able to use their sniper rifles."

"Oh yes, they can still use them, but there is a maximum of 1000 yards or below, very effective."

"When will you have them?"

"I believe they will be delivered tomorrow."

"That's good news, they have been asking me about them, now what about these diamonds?"

When I returned to my men, I told them the good news about the special bullets, then Julian said, "Eddie, I know you too well, is there something you haven't told us?"

I looked at the others, then around me to see if anyone was within earshot, there wasn't anyone who could hear what I was about to say. Rob, Snowy, Sammy and Julian were all looking straight at me, as I said,

"There is 180 millions in diamonds on that U-boat." I expected a lot of questions, but no, they all sat quietly not a word was said.

"They will be told to stop cutting up the U-boat so we can make a search."

"They could be anywhere?" said Snowy.

"I know that, so start thinking, where would you safely hide as many diamonds as that?"

No one answered me.

We walked down towards the drydock and the U-boat, the whole place was lit up like a fairground. The Officer in Charge of the Army guards, he had seen us before, so he waved us through. We stood there looking at the U-boat and looking at each other.

I turned to Julian and said, "Any ideas?" He shook his head in a

Richard Nisbet

'no' fashion. Now the U-boat looked so much bigger, now that we had to search it. The moon had our shadows stretching out to sea, as we stood there not knowing where to start. Some of the U-boat had already been cut away, enough for us to just walk into it.

"I have thought about this," said Julian. "If you board a U-boat or submarine with diamonds, you would put them under lock and key, so why don't we check the safe, there's one in the radio room."

With the whole bridge and machinegun post gone, we found it easy to get to the radio room, once inside the room, it was all neat and tidy, two small doors covered the safe, now he had to open it.

"Let me try boss, I've always wanted to open a safe."

Sammy got down on his knees and started turning the knob in the middle, he had his ear up close to it. "Keep quiet now, I am listening to the clicks." Some ten minutes later he was still trying to open it, Julian said,

"Step aside Sammy." He stuck on some H.E. and we moved away very smartly. Twelve seconds later there was a Boooommm the door wasn't fully opened but there was enough room to stick a hand in, out came a green velvet holdall in Sammy's hand. He opened it up and laid it out on the radio desk. We all stood there just looking at these beautiful stones. None of us had ever seen anything like them in our life. They sparkled like stars, so magical to look at.

"What did that Judge tell these were worth?" asked Sammy.

"He said, 800 millions."

Sammy picked up one. "Why don't we keep one each? I know someone who would just love having one of them."

I looked at each man, picked up five diamonds and handed them out, they all took a really good look at the diamonds in their hands, me too.

"At a wild guess, I'd say diamonds that size are worth at least 40,000 pounds, sterling. I don't think there is as much as what the Judge said. There's certainly millions, but not 800. Stick those away safely."

My next move was to hand the diamonds to the top Judge, who had to list all items taken from the U-boat. I'm sure they won't miss five lovely diamonds. I could be way out on their price, I was going on the price of a diamond ring a French friend had, way back twenty odd years ago, so these could be worth a lot more.

Rob was holding the wallet full of the gems, as Julian said, "Just hold on a minute Eddie, why don't we hold on to these as a security, until we get paid out for what we have done."

We knew well, that there was no one saw us find the diamonds, so I drove home and stuck them in the safe in my garage, then went back on the site, it was still dark, so no one missed me.

By dawn the cut up gold had mounted up, with a strong guard watching over it, there must have been a few tons of the stuff, cleverly worked into the U-boat. Trucks came in and stood by ready to load up, I could see Snowy and Rob having another look at their diamonds, so I did as well.

We watched as the first truck was loaded up with the chunks of gold, they would go to Lanzarote to a smelting plant, while we hung about waiting on news about Von Ludendorff.

We did know he was last seen near the Islands of the Azores, but he could be anywhere now. He could move around the world, with the transport he had at his disposal. We got attacked, even though he was nowhere near this Island. The Spanish Commanders hit back ferociously, sending out missiles to counter the air attack, then ground troops fought a running battle with Von Ludendorff's men. Sammy, still in pain, had got up into the cabin of one of the trucks, opened the hatch and was now using the sniper rifle. Snowy had raced forward to get onto higher ground, he too was firing his weapon. Sammy downed a chopper with two shots.

From my position I quickly called over the radio the Commander telling him that Sammy had sighted two boats racing out to sea. Shortly afterwards, the Air Force fired off two warning shots, there was a sudden flash of light coming from the larger boat, something had shot straight up into the sky and flew off.

On the radio, Snowy said, "What the hell was that?"

Sammy then said over his radio, "That was one of those U.F.O.'s. and that bastard has escaped us again."

I then asked, "Are you sure it was him?"

"Who else could it be, did the others see it?"

"We all saw it Sammy, it moved very fast indeed, faster than the rockets fired from the Spanish Airforce jet."

Snowy came on, "What was that boss?"

"Probably some new technology, there's a lot of that going on in Canada, the U.S.A. Germany, Japan and China."

Sammy butted in, "That was Alien technology boss, wasn't it?"

Julian was standing beside me, he asked, "Eddie, what in the world was that to move at such a remarkable speed? There's nothing on this planet with that sort of power."

"Well you saw it as I did, it did come from the boat out there, we should be asking, where did it go to?"

"What can possibly travel at that speed?"

"There was some tests done in secret, something to do with Anti Gravity propulsion. Now maybe that's what was on board that U.F.O.?"

"I heard that boss," said Sammy. "I knew it, I knew that is Alien technology."

"Don't be daft Sammy, Aliens, if there are any, they are too far away to be coming here to our earth."

Just then the Commander of the Spanish Army called in. "We have tracked that object, it landed near the Azores. Not certain where, sending in two Aircraft on reconnaissance, will get back to you… over."

"Thank you for that information…out."

My next move was to call in Sammy and Snowy, then we had to join forces with a crack team of GSG9, Germany's Elite Force. Their

Commander was named as Rudi Goering. Like us he went over and over the plan of attack, once we reached the Azores. While they protected us, allowing us a safer passageway to identify Von Ludendorff…This crack team reminded us of our days in uniform. Just looking at them made you wary of them, thank God they were on our side.

We all boarded a Spanish warship just as the sun was setting, the attack was going in under darkness. Conformation was needed long before we came within range of the Islands. The Azores has about a dozen Islands, so it is of the utmost importance to get the Island right…

This archipelago was Portuguese, the main Island was Sao Miguel. A smaller Island south of there called Santa Maria, was where we were now heading for, a call came in, Von Ludendorff was on this Island of Santa Maria. Now all we had to do was get there unseen, find where Von Ludendorff was and then let Sammy and Snowy do the rest. They had two shots each of these special bullets, the drug inside them would knock out Von Ludendorff within a few seconds.

All five of us, myself, Julian, Rob, Snowy and Sammy had been geared up by the GSG9 unit, all geared up for it, we had the heart and mind to do the job, but not the legs. Sammy and Snowy would follow the GSG9 men once on the Island to seek out Von Ludendorff. Rob, Julian and I would I.D. him first, then the two snipers would put him down. But Rudi knew there would be a firefight, as Von Ludendorff's men did all they could to protect the man who paid their wages. This would be very dangerous, so Rudi to us to stay well behind the attacking groups of men, they like us, worked with a four man team, which is the best small unit you have a man covering each point of the compass.

This area some say, was the lost Island of Atlantis, but that has never been proven.

On the warship, Rudi went over the assault plan again, asking his men questions, then they checked their weapons, as Rudi gave Rob

Julian and me a handgun with two full Mag's each. His only words were, "I want these back after we get him…OK."

With those words said, Rudi and sixteen men got into the dingys, we followed well behind them. As we drew close to shore, we saw the lights coming from a villa, which sat on higher ground. The shadows of men patrolling around the villa could be seen. I helped strap up Sammy's arm, he was much better and out of serious pain, he wanted a part in getting Von Ludendorff. Sammy hated him for what he had done to me, this was his moment of glory. Snowy knew that too, he would only use his shots if Sammy missed.

The attack went in and we could hear the exchange and see the flashes from the weapons as they fired. The GSG9 men moved so quickly it was hard to keep track of them. We had to get closer, which we did, all three of us were in contact with Snowy and Sammy, through binoculars we watched every movement looking for Von Ludendorff, Julian and Rob saw him, they put me on to him and then I radioed Sammy and Snowy. We sat waiting with gunfire and bullets flying everywhere. It helped when the moon came out at least we could see where to put our feet, then we saw a track and walked along it keeping our heads down. Rudi's men were being held down by heavy fire, two heavy machineguns were blasting all around them. One group of four men had managed to get behind the villa, then the firing became heavier, and suddenly all was quiet. We sat there and knew full well Von Ludendorff was in that villa, all it needed now was one shot and all this would be over.

We moved closer to the villa, then all hell broke loose, a big firefight was now on, with Rudi's men firing off bursts then moving quickly to a different spot to take cover, this went on for some twenty to thirty minutes.

The shooting stopped. I looked at Rob and Julian, then I said, "Wonder if it's over?"

Rob said, "Give Sammy a call."

I called Sammy and he gave us the great news, his exact words were, "I nailed him boss, he'll be coming out soon."

The dawn was breaking as Rudi's men came walking out of the villa, four of them carrying Von Ludendorff in a makeshift stretcher. He had his hands shackled and his feet, as he passed by he spat at me.

He was ranting on in German as I said, "Go to hell where you belong."

Sammy and Snowy turned up, just as Von Ludendorff went past Julian Rob and me. Sammy punched him in the face, as Von Ludendorff shouted in English, "Coward…coward, let me free I will beat you black and blue."

Sammy shouted, "Go on, let him free so I can kill the bastard."

Rudi walked over to Sammy and said, "Calm down, calm down, he'll get what he's due, don't worry about that. Some of those men he killed were once part of my Unit, that's what money does to some people, turns them bad, just like him."

Rudi looked at Von Ludendorff, stuck up his thumb then turned it downwards, showing his disgust at the man.

We now had to deliver him back to Fuerteventura and there he would face a panel of top Judges from across Europe.

Back on what is my home Island of Fuerteventura, the whole world's Press and T.V. Crews were lined up to get shots of Eric Von Ludendorff, the first time anyone had ever seen him. He was taken from the courtroom on the Island to Germany, where he was put away for life. No one knows where he is serving life, what gaol, or indeed what country.

We all came out of this very well indeed, as for the diamonds well, they were handed in, resulting in more money to split between us.

My wife and I took Julian, Sammy and Snowy to the airport. Once they got their baggage checked in, we sat and had a beer or in my case, coffee along with my wife…the talk came back to the craft Von Ludendorff used, as Sammy said, "What happened to that flying machine?"

"Rudi's men blew it to bits."

"So it wasn't some Alien craft after all."
"Well we will never know about that, will we."
My wife then said, "What's this about Alien's Eddie?"
"Aah it's nothing Honey."
"Eddie, don't you dare get mixed up with Aliens."
Sammy held on to his injured arm, while giving me a long, long look.

Snowy said, "I know when you are hiding something," he paused then said, "You have another job lined up already, haven't you?"

"Wrong, I don't, but I did get a letter from this guy from Norway, that was about a U.F.O."

"Eddie," shouted my wife. "Don't you dare go messing about with Aliens."

"Honey, Aliens are just people from another country, not outer space."

"So you are saying there are no Aliens out there."

"No Honey, I didn't say that."

"Hey, we're off now Eddie," said Julian.

We stood there watching as the three men walked out of sight. As we headed back to the car, my wife asked me,

"Eddie, tell me the truth, have you some other job lined up?"

Watch this SPACE!

THE END

Lightning Source UK Ltd.
Milton Keynes UK
UKOW04f0308071213

222538UK00001B/16/P